He started to rise with his Christmas mug in hand.

"I should go and let you get some sleep."

Paige placed a hand lightly on his forearm. "No. Please stay. Finish your coffee."

Daniel watched her for a moment, as if having a silent debate with himself, then nodded and sat back down. He took a sip from his mug. "Thank you again for a wonderful dinner."

"I'm glad you could be here. It meant a lot to Jason." She glanced at the train set on the coffee table. "I don't think we could have figured out how to put it all together, at least not in the time it took the two of you." She set her mug aside, linked her fingers and looked down at her hands. "Thank you for all the gifts. The ones for me were totally unexpected, unnecessary, but very much appreciated. I...I like to take care of things myself, but without your generosity, I frankly don't know what I would have done."

He started to say something, but she shook her head.

"I don't have the words to adequately thank you for what you've given Jason, and I don't just mean in a material sense." She raised her eyes to his. "You've made Jason very happy and taken his mind off... everything, other than the sheer joy of Christmas."

Dear Reader,

Christmas is magical. It's one of my favorite times of the year. As Christmas approaches, I still feel a bit of that giddy excitement I did as a child. My parents always made Christmas special for me. There were times when they couldn't afford much, but every gathering and every gift was thoughtful and filled with love.

Sadly, I lost my father just before Christmas while I was in university. I chose not to celebrate Christmas the following year, and the holiday had a very different quality for me for a number of years.

But the magic of Christmas prevailed. Although I still have some bittersweet moments, I truly love Christmas. The passage of time helped, of course, but what made the biggest difference was being able to see the wonder of Christmas through the eyes of a child.

If Christmas is a special time of year for you, as it is for me, I hope *A Child's Christmas* enriches your joy. If you find that Christmas has lost a bit of its sparkle, I hope this story will help you recapture its magic.

Thank you for reading *A Child's Christmas*. I would love to hear from you. You can contact me by email at readers@kate-james.com, through my website at www.kate-james.com or by mail at P.O. Box 446, Schomberg, ON, L7B 0H7, Canada.

Merry Christmas, and much love and happiness to you and yours!

Kate

HEARTWARMING

A Child's Christmas

———

Kate James

◆ HARLEQUIN® HEARTWARMING™

Recycling programs
for this product may
not exist in your area.

ISBN-13: 978-0-373-36701-6

A Child's Christmas

H HARLEQUIN®

Printed in U.S.A.

™ www.Harlequin.com

KATE JAMES

spent much of her childhood abroad before attending university in Canada. She built a successful business career, but her passion has always been fiction, both reading and writing it. As a result, she turned her energy to her love of the written word. Kate's goal is to entertain her readers with engaging stories featuring strong, likable characters. She's been honored with numerous awards for her writing. She and her husband, Ken, enjoy traveling and the outdoors with their beloved Labrador retrievers.

To my husband, Ken, who believed in my writing even before there was anything to believe in, for starting me down the path by giving me my first laptop to use solely for writing, for supporting me unfailingly when I was on the precipice of leaping from a rewarding business career into uncharted territory with my writing, and for being by my side every step of the way. Ken...I still choose you!

To our friend Carl Compton. Carl...you know why.

To my editor, the amazing Paula Eykelhof, for believing in me and taking me—a fledgling author—under her wing, for her generosity with her much-in-demand time, limitless knowledge and incredible expertise, and for already having taught me so much.

And to Victoria Curran, for giving me the opportunity to write for Harlequin Heartwarming, and for appealing to my competitive nature to see if I can adopt as many dogs as she can cats!

CHAPTER ONE

IT WAS HER worst nightmare. Her son had less than a year to live, Paige Summerville thought incredulously, then defiantly rejected the very idea.

Standing outside the train terminal, she couldn't help the short, bitter laugh that escaped her lips—then realized she'd let her guard down when she felt Jason tug on her hand.

Paige was immediately contrite and forced a bright smile onto her face. Seeing the worry in her little boy's blue eyes, she bent down and lovingly brushed his ash-blond hair from his forehead.

Knowing the perfect distraction, she suggested, with a cheer she didn't feel, "How about we go to McDonald's for lunch?" His eyes cleared, and a grin spread across his freckled face. "Can we, Mom?"

She zipped up his jacket to shield him from the biting November wind. "We most certainly can!"

After lunch, they walked along Camden Falls' tree-lined Main Street, pausing whenever Jason wanted to examine a brightly colored leaf or greet a passing dog. He clutched her hand tightly as they made their way home, glancing up at her periodically with eyes strikingly similar to her own. Occasionally, she'd lean toward him and whisper something in his ear or simply touch his arm, his shoulder, the top of his head.

Paige couldn't imagine her life without her little boy, but it was a possibility she might have to face.

Jason had a malignant brain tumor.

They'd taken the train that morning to see an oncologist at the Rosenthal Cancer Center in nearby Boston. If he was correct, this could be her son's last year. Paige had to believe they could beat the disease, but she knew the odds were stacked against them. After all, this wasn't their first battle with the devastating disease.

The day had taken its toll on Jason. By the time they reached their small ground-floor apartment, he could barely keep his eyes open. He yawned as Paige tucked him in for a nap. She sat beside him long after he fell asleep, not wanting to leave him, needing always and forever to protect him, wishing

she could smooth the furrows between his brows—a constant sign that he was never fully free from pain.

Yet Jason had an indomitable spirit. He never complained. He was a warm and loving child. Intelligent, even-tempered, so easy to please. Paige was thankful for that, since she didn't have the means to give him much. What Jason lacked in material things, she was determined to make up for with her love.

Hearing the tap on her front door reminded Paige that she was running late. She wouldn't have time to change into something more businesslike for work. Fortunately, she was employed at a call center for a financial collection agency. Since her interactions with people were over the phone, it didn't matter if she wore the jeans she had on, although she preferred not to. She took another moment to tuck the blanket more snugly around her little boy and place a kiss on his brow.

Opening the door, she welcomed her silver-haired neighbor. "Hello, Mrs. Bennett. How's Mr. Bennett's arthritis today?"

"He's doing well. Thank you for asking."

Paige was immensely grateful to Mrs. Bennett for her willingness to take care of Jason while Paige was at work. She felt guilty that Mrs. Bennett wouldn't accept any payment,

but it was also a relief that she didn't have to stretch her limited funds.

Mrs. Bennett glanced around. "Is our little man in his room reading?"

Paige shook her head and opened the hall closet. "He's sleeping. It was a hard day for him." As Paige put on her coat, Mrs. Bennett placed a hand lightly on her arm. Concern infused her voice and clouded her eyes as she asked, "How did it go at the hospital this morning?"

The simple question threatened Paige's self-control. She closed her eyes and inhaled deeply before responding in a shaky voice, "Not well."

Mrs. Bennett tightened her grip on Paige's arm. "What did the oncologist say?"

Paige shook her head. "I have to get to work. I can't go into it now."

Mrs. Bennett pulled Paige into a comforting hug. "Okay, dear. Go to work. When you come home, I'll make us a nice pot of tea and we'll talk."

WHAT WAS IT about the holidays, Daniel Kinsley wondered as he returned to his desk, that seemed to bring out the worst in people?

He was glad he had some time to spare before his next appointment. His meeting with

Gloria Farnsworth had put him in a miserable mood. He dropped heavily into his chair and swung it around to stare out the window. Across the street, a billboard displaying a Norman Rockwell–style scene seemed to mock him. It showed a cheerful, ruddy-faced Santa distributing brightly wrapped gifts to an elegantly dressed and ridiculously happy family. The husband clasped his wife's hand affectionately, and the model-perfect woman stroked the blonde curls of a little girl in a red velvet dress. Daniel snorted. Did anyone really live like that? Not in his experience.

He thought of his own parents and their respectful, polite relationship. When was the last time he'd seen his parents touch? For that matter, his mother's obligatory cheek kisses aside, he couldn't recall his parents ever touching him with affection. They never argued. They never fought. But he also wasn't sure they actually loved each other. A sad statement, especially after forty-three years of marriage.

It didn't help his mood to remember that he'd agreed to spend more than a week with them in Newport over the holidays. He knew there'd be no Christmas cheer in that. At times he questioned why his parents stayed together. Then again, maybe they had it right. No love, no pain. Not wanting to dwell on it, he allowed his thoughts to come full circle to Gloria Farnsworth.

Daniel turned away from the window and looked down at the open Farnsworth case file on his desk. He'd been tempted to tell Gloria to find another lawyer. But would that really have accomplished anything? More than half his cases disgusted him in one way or another. Okay, maybe none quite as much as the Farnsworth case, but if he wanted to extricate himself from cases that he found morally reprehensible, where exactly would he draw the line?

He picked up his pen and twirled it between his fingers.

Gloria Farnsworth was definitely at the extreme end. She'd torn a strip off him when he told her she should be satisfied with the spousal support her husband had agreed to—generous in his estimation—and accept that she was on shaky ground trying to get child support for a nineteen-year-old who wasn't attending school and didn't have a job. Gloria had demanded to know under what conditions she *would* be entitled. And fool that he was, he'd treated her like a rational person and explained some of the circumstances under which case law might entitle her to child support. He never would've imagined that she'd jump on one of the alternatives and willingly label her own son mentally disabled for the sake of gouging more money out of her soon-to-be-ex.

It was repugnant. Daniel knew it wouldn't hold up in court—no expert witness would testify to it—but things probably wouldn't come to that. Having met the husband on a couple of occasions, he sensed that the man cared about his child. Daniel was quite certain he'd settle rather than subject his son to the pain and humiliation of being questioned in court about his mental capacity.

Maybe Daniel should tell Gloria Farnsworth to take a long hike off a short— *Whoa!* She'd really gotten to him. In more polite terms, he would ask her to hire another lawyer. He refused to be party to what essentially amounted to fraud.

He straightened the papers, closed the file folder and tossed his pen on top.

With his parents' loveless marriage, plus the hostile family disputes he witnessed at work, it was hardly surprising that he was still single at thirty-six.

Why couldn't people be civil to one another? As an idealistic law student, he'd chosen family law because he wanted to help people, yet his caseload was dominated by nasty divorce and custody battles. Who was he kidding? He hadn't helped anyone in a long time in any way other than to better their financial circumstances or inflict hardship and pain on their spouses. It was a bitter disappointment to see how people who'd supposedly once loved each other and been committed to each other ended up.

Yes, he told himself again, maybe his parents had it right, after all.

Selena, his executive assistant, interrupted his thoughts, calling to announce his next appointment—probably a good thing, as he was getting more and more depressed. Checking his schedule, he felt his mood lighten. This meeting would be a nice antithesis to his day so far.

He rose as Selena escorted a plainly dressed, middle-aged woman into his office. "Ms. Andrews, I'm Daniel Kinsley." He extended a hand in greeting. "Would you like a coffee? Some water?"

"Call me Laura, please," she said, shaking his hand, "and no. I'm fine, thank you."

Daniel signaled to Selena that she could leave and offered Laura Andrews a seat.

"Thank you for meeting with me," Laura began.

"The pleasure is mine. Your organization has a stellar reputation, and so do you as its executive director."

"All of us at the Wish I May Foundation believe wholeheartedly in what we do, and we work very hard for our program's children and their families. Yet we always have more families in need than we have sponsors, especially at this time of year. I can assure you that if your firm sponsors a child, you won't regret it. All our sponsors tell us how much it means to them to make a difference in a young person's life."

"What's involved in sponsorship?"

"It's straightforward. You'd be given information on a chronically ill child and that child's family and Christmas wish list. You'll find that their wishes, for the most part, are very basic. Winter clothing, books, some small toys." Laura's smile conveyed sadness rather than pleasure. "Basic because these families often endure hardships that extend well beyond the illness of the child. We encourage sponsors to consider doing something extra for the child, if they can." Daniel thought he saw a mischievous glint in her eye. "A trip to Walt Disney World, perhaps, or a PlayStation gaming system."

It didn't take Daniel long to commit his firm.

"All that's left is to decide on the family you'll be sponsoring." Laura reached into her bag and pulled out a folder. Flipping through the papers, she finally drew out two sheets.

"Problem?" Daniel asked when Laura continued to scrutinize the two pages.

"Hmm? No. Not really." She glanced up. "It's just that I know both these families personally, and I'm having a hard time choosing between them." She held out both sheets. "Here. Why don't you decide?"

Daniel read the pages and examined the photographs at the top of each. Choosing between the two children and their families was impossible. Finally, coming to the only decision he could, he set the pages on his desk and looked up at Laura. Her eyes were focused on him, and a small smile played at the corners of her mouth. Her expression made him think that he'd been masterfully manipulated. In this case, he didn't mind. "You're very good at your job," he acknowledged.

She gave a slight nod, and her smile remained in place. "I do my best."

Daniel knew that when he shared the children's stories with his partners, he'd be able to raise the needed money for each of them, including enough for some nice extras. "We'll sponsor them both," he said.

For the first time in months—no, years—
he felt he was doing something worthwhile.
And it had nothing to do with the law.

CHAPTER TWO

IT MIGHT HAVE been a blessing, Paige mused as she unlocked her door that evening. Nearly every call she'd made at work had ended with the recipients arguing that they didn't owe the money. In a few cases, they'd turned their anger on her. Although unpleasant, it kept her mind—at least briefly—off her own troubles. She'd worked late but was grateful for the extra hours. She could barely make ends meet, even without factoring in Jason's medical expenses not covered by her insurance or any indulgences for Christmas.

Despite her worries, she smiled as she entered her living room. Louise Bennett had been true to her word. A teapot covered in a quilted cozy sat on the coffee table. Mrs. Bennett reclined on the sofa, her hands folded tidily on her lap, her head drooping forward in sleep. She snored softly.

Paige nudged her gently. "Mrs. Bennett. I'm home."

Mrs. Bennett's head jerked up, and a hand

flew to her chest. "Oh, my goodness. I must've fallen asleep." She smoothed her short, wavy hair. "Sit down, honey. I've made our tea." She lifted the cozy and tested the temperature of the pot to make sure the tea was still warm.

"I appreciate that, but it's quite late. You should go home."

"Nonsense!" She waved dismissively. "I said we'd talk when you got home, and we will. You shouldn't keep things bottled up inside."

"Mrs. Bennett…"

"We're going to talk," Mrs. Bennett declared emphatically.

Paige realized it would be useless to argue. "All right. Let me check on Jason first."

She opened his bedroom door quietly. In the glow of the nightlight, she could see her little boy snuggled in his blanket. His arms were wrapped around his teddy bear, his eyes closed and his mouth slightly parted. She heard his even breathing. Satisfied that he was sleeping peacefully, she closed his door.

Mrs. Bennett was pouring their tea when Paige rejoined her. "Go ahead, dear. Tell me what happened," she said.

"Oh, Mrs. Bennett. It's awful," Paige began. "Jason's tumor has recurred since his last checkup a year ago. His oncologist, he…he believes Jason has less than a year left. He…" Paige dropped her head into her hands and struggled to hold back the tears. Mrs. Bennett folded Paige in her arms and held her tightly as Paige's body shook in despair.

When the tears changed into dry, hitching gasps, Paige pulled back and wiped her eyes with her fingertips. Accepting the tissue Mrs. Bennett offered, she blew her nose and fought to collect herself. "The doctor…he feels Jason's only chance now is surgery to remove the tumor. But even if I could afford it…" She choked back a sob. "The tumor's too big right now, and the risks are significant. His chances of survival are…low."

Mrs. Bennett's eyes filled with tears, too. "I know it's hard. But think about all the challenges he's already overcome."

Paige raised anguished eyes to Mrs. Bennett's.

"Wasn't Jason just three when he was first diagnosed? And didn't you both get through it, despite his father deserting you?" When Paige was about to interrupt, Mrs. Bennett raised her hand. "I know what you're going to say in his defense. 'It wasn't that simple.' But let's face it. He abandoned you. You and Jason were both strong and determined, and you made it through. Then the tumor came back."

The horrific day when Paige learned the tumor had recurred the first time was indelibly etched in her mind, as today would be. "Yes, it came back five months later."

"And?"

"And…" Paige said in a whisper, "Jason underwent treatment and made it through again."

"Twice you've beaten it. *Twice.* Can't you believe you can beat it again? And this time for good?"

"I'd like to think so, but I don't know." Paige shook her head. "I just don't know."

"What did the doctor say about treatment?"

"Jason has to undergo aggressive treatment again." She tried to stay composed, but the tears welled up in her eyes and spilled down her cheeks. "The oncologist is recommending a new cancer drug that's still in the clinical trial stage. It specifically targets the cancer cells to shrink the tumor so they can do the surgery. With the size of the tumor now, surgery isn't an option. The drugs are going to make Jason very sick, just like the last time. How much can he take?" Paige broke down again.

"There, there," Mrs. Bennett soothed. "As much as he needs to."

"But Christmas… He'll be going through the worst of it at Christmas. And this might be his last…" Her voice trailed off, and she glanced at his bedroom door. "With the limitations on my healthcare plan, I have no idea how I'll handle the medical expenses, let alone give him a special Christmas."

"If you need to work more hours, it's no trouble for me to watch Jason. And what about one of those charities that helps people with sick kids?"

Things might have been tight, but Paige had always managed. She knew there were many needy, deserving people who relied on the generosity of the more fortunate, but she didn't feel comfortable with receiving charity. She thought of her ex-husband, and her resolve grew. It was pride speaking as she said, "Jason is *my* responsibility."

"But there are organizations that help parents make sick kids' Christmas wishes come true. That's all I'm talking about."

Paige relented a little. "Oh, yes, of course. But I've also heard they have long waiting lists. This close to Christmas, they probably have more families than they can handle."

Mrs. Bennett patted Paige's hand. "Leave it with me. Let me look into it for you." Her voice softened. "Dear…?"

When Paige's eyes met hers again, Mrs.

Bennett continued. "Have you told your mother?"

Paige's shoulders sagged. "Oh, good heavens, no."

"Now, Paige. You have to tell her, especially if…" She left the sentence unfinished, but Paige understood. Her parents might have limited time to see Jason.

Paige rubbed her temples. "I don't know. Mom already has so much to cope with. Dad's not doing well. His Alzheimer's is progressing. Mom has her hands full just dealing with day-to-day living."

Mrs. Bennett nodded sadly. "But do you really think your mother would want you to keep this from her?"

"No." Paige exhaled. "No, I don't." She had no siblings, so Jason was their only grandchild. She had to tell them.

All of a sudden, she felt impossibly weary but somewhat steadier. "Thank you for talking this through with me. It's helped a lot. Now we both need to get some sleep."

When Mrs. Bennett rose to clear the tea neither of them had drunk, Paige stopped her. "Please don't worry about that. I'll take care of it." When Mrs. Bennett hesitated, Paige added, "Tomorrow. I'll take care of it tomorrow."

Still, when Paige closed and locked the door

behind her neighbor, she went about the task of clearing up. She was exhausted, but she knew she wouldn't be able to sleep. Even mindless tasks were a distraction, and preferable to lying in bed with sleep eluding her and worries crowding her mind.

OVER THE COURSE of a long, sleepless night, Paige decided that not only did she have to tell her mother, she needed to do it sooner rather than later. If she didn't, her mother—understandably—would never forgive her. She had a right to know. The question was how she should go about it…

Paige tried to be as cheerful as possible as she made Jason breakfast and helped him get ready for school.

As they were saying good-bye on the steps of his school building, Jason looked up at her, his face solemn, and asked, "Are you okay, Mom?"

She was quick to assure him, "Of course, sweetheart."

He studied her carefully, his eyes mature beyond his years, and she wondered if he could sense that she was lying to him for the first time in his life.

"Okay." He scuffed the toe of his sneaker on the concrete step. "It'll be like before, won't it?"

Paige knew he was referring to his treatment. At least in this, she could be honest. "I'm not sure, but I think so." She recognized every expression, every nuance of his face. "Your head hurts, doesn't it, sweetie?"

He nodded. "Yeah, but it's okay, Mom."

"Oh, baby. Come here." She opened her arms. He threw his small body against hers, and she hugged him fiercely.

They held on to each other for a while. Then Paige kissed Jason good-bye and watched him walk up the stairs, open the door and disappear inside the school. Only when he was completely out of sight did her legs buckle. She crumpled to the steps. Burying her face in her hands, she let the sobs burst forth.

PAIGE DIDN'T GO straight home. She couldn't stand the thought of being in the empty apartment. As she was on the evening shift this week, she wasn't due at work until seven. She walked along the town's cobblestone streets. She sat on a bench in the square and watched the coal-black squirrels scurry over the light dusting of snow, foraging for food. Finally, she picked up some groceries and headed home.

After putting the groceries away, she called her parents in Great Barrington, where they'd retired years ago. "Mom, it's me."

"Paige. How are you?"

Paige evaded the question and hoped her mother wouldn't notice. Before she broached the reason for her call, she wanted to see how her mother was holding up. "Is Dad having a good day?"

"He's keeping me on my toes, as usual. Always up to something. He decided he wants to build a bird feeder."

"But Mom—"

"I know what you're thinking. Don't worry. I'm not letting him anywhere near power tools. They're long gone. I bought him a balsa-wood kit that he can assemble. The pieces are pre-cut, and all he needs is children's glue." She chuckled. "You should see him. He's having a grand time! That's what counts."

Paige smiled through her tears. Her mother was sixty-eight now, her father eleven years her senior. Her father was the only man her mother had ever loved. They'd enjoyed a good life, and a long and loving marriage. In two years, they would be celebrating their fiftieth anniversary. But knowing that her strong, intelligent, capable father had been reduced to relying almost entirely on her mother tore Paige apart. She had enormous respect for the way her mother was coping.

"Are you still there, Paige?"

"Yes, Mom." Paige realized she couldn't break the news to her mother over the phone. She'd somehow have to find the time—and the money—to take the train. "Mom, I wanted to let you know I'm coming for a visit. I want to see you and Dad."

Her mother's voice brightened. "That's wonderful! When are you coming?"

Paige felt remorseful hearing her mother sound so happy. Her heart would break when she learned the reason for Paige's impromptu visit. Why hadn't she thought of visiting her parents with Jason weeks ago, when they could've had a happy reunion? Jason loved his grandparents dearly and was so sweet with his Gramps—so patient and kind. "I'm not sure, Mom. I'll have to check my work schedule. I'll call you back and let you know. But it'll be soon."

"That's wonderful," her mother repeated. "Your father will be very happy to see you."

Paige doubted it, since the last couple of times she'd visited, he hadn't remembered her at all.

"We look forward to seeing Jason, too."

Paige paused. She considered taking Jason with her. Under the circumstances, it wasn't a good idea. She anticipated the discussion with her mother would be a difficult one, and she didn't want Jason to see either of them break down. "No, Mom. Jason won't be coming with me." Paige pulled the elastic from her ponytail and shook her hair loose. "Um…he can't miss school right now," she improvised. "And I'm scheduled to work some hours over the next couple of weekends."

She felt relief when she heard someone at her door. It gave her an excuse to end the conversation. "I need to get the door, Mom. I'll call you again soon." They said their goodbyes, and Paige went to open the door.

Chelsea Owens, her upstairs neighbor, stood in the hallway, uncharacteristically subdued, her eyes rimmed in red, her lower lip quivering. "Chelsea, what's—"

Before Paige could finish, she was smothered in a powerful embrace. To her shock, Chelsea started to cry, and Paige stroked her back reassuringly. "Hey, what's up?"

Chelsea pushed away, ran her fingers through her spiky black hair and tried to speak through an attack of hiccups. "Me? What's up with *me*?" She began crying again. "Mrs. Bennett…" She clapped her hand over her mouth. Her eyes were huge. She bent forward to peer at Jason's door. "He's…he's not…"

She pointed repeatedly toward his room.

Understanding, Paige sighed heavily. "No.

He's not home. He's at school. Mrs. Bennett told you."

Chelsea sniffled and swiped the back of her hand under her nose. "I'm *sooooo* sorry. I don't know what to say."

Paige gestured for her to come in and closed the door. Chelsea stepped into the small living room and collapsed on the sofa. "Jason is such a wonderful kid. This is *so* unfair."

Paige dropped down beside her. She'd had the better part of a day to come to terms with it and simply couldn't. "Yeah. It really is."

"Is there anything I can do? Anything at all? Just say the word."

"I appreciate it. All I ask is please don't fall apart in front of Jason. He's already been through this twice. As hard as it was on him, he's coping, thinking he'll be through it again in a few months."

Chelsea flopped back on the sofa and stared up at the ceiling. "Poor kid. I mean, I didn't know you back then, but I can't imagine how he does it. How you *both* do it." She turned to Paige. "And your folks. How did they take it?"

Paige rubbed her forehead where a throb was intensifying. "I haven't told them yet. I was just on the phone with Mom. I was going to tell her, but then she went on about Dad, and I couldn't." She pressed her lips together. "I'm planning to go and see them instead." She leaned forward to fidget with the decorative bowl on the coffee table. "If I can get the time off work. And put aside the train fare. I'm sure Mrs. Bennett won't mind taking care of Jason for a few days." Tears gathered in Paige's eyes, and she reached for the box of tissues on the end table. "I couldn't tell my mother on the phone. It's not as if she can turn to Dad for comfort. I just couldn't do it."

Chelsea straightened. "Wait! I'll drive you."

"I appreciate the offer, but no, I couldn't let you do that."

"Then take my car."

"I can't do that, either. You need it to get to work."

Chelsea shook her head. "Nah. I'll schedule my shifts at the art gallery so they're the same as Joel's. You remember me telling you about Joel? He's the cute events coordinator at work. I'll have him pick me up. That way, I can manage without my car for a few days. You need it—so use it. It'll be cheaper and easier for you." Chelsea smiled. "Besides, that'll give me a chance to spend time with Joel!"

Yes, it would be cheaper. More importantly, Paige could set her own schedule, reduce the travel time and get home to Jason faster. "Really? You don't mind?"

"No, not at all. Honestly, it's the least I can do."

"It's very generous of you, Chels. Thank you."

THE NEXT FEW days passed quickly. Paige arranged for the time off, and she was working double shifts to make up for it. Jason also had a number of doctors' appointments and tests in preparation for the start of his treatments, so he was missing school. Paige set up a journal—as she first had when Jason was three—to track his temperature, blood pressure and general well-being against his treatment schedule. She knew it would get progressively harder for Jason as his treatment cycle progressed, and she wanted to make sure she could accurately discuss his reaction to the drugs with his doctors.

The appointments weren't easy for Jason, but he was very brave. The strain was wearing on Paige, though. She let herself into their apartment after a long day at work, thankful they were on the ground floor of the small three-story walk-up. She was tired and worried.

Mrs. Bennett greeted her excitedly. "Go say

hello to Jason and hurry back, dear. I have good news for you."

Paige thought she could use some good news as she checked on Jason doing his homework. She spent a few minutes chatting with him, then returned to the living room. "I've found an organization that should be able to help," Mrs. Bennett announced.

"Sorry. What?"

"A charitable organization that can help you and Jason."

With so much else on her mind, Paige had forgotten their conversation. Remembering now, she wasn't sure she wanted to pursue it. Not only because she didn't feel comfortable with charity, but because she knew there'd be an application process. It would mean more time and effort for her, with no guarantees. "What organization?"

"The Wish I May Foundation. It's wonderful! They make Christmas dreams come true for sick kids. Their mission is to help families in situations like yours."

Although not convinced, Paige agreed to speak to the organization's executive director.

"Her name is Laura Andrews. What harm is there in talking with her?" Mrs. Bennett asked.

It wasn't at the top of Paige's list of priorities, but since she'd promised Mrs. Bennett that she'd call Laura, she made time for it the next day.

Paige immediately liked Laura. Laura didn't cause her to feel inadequate or as if she was unable to care for her own child. Just the opposite. Laura gave her a sense of pride in what she'd accomplished as a single mother. Laura also shared stories of children who'd overcome equally dire illnesses, leaving Paige with a glimmer of hope.

"All you have to do is send me a picture of Jason and a list of the things he'd like for Christmas. I'll take care of the rest," Laura assured Paige. "But please do it quickly."

Shortly after they hung up, Paige emailed Laura a picture of Jason, with a promise to get his Christmas list to her soon. For the first time since Jason's diagnosis, Paige felt encouraged.

LAURA WAS IMPRESSED by Paige's resilience and commitment to her son. She was deeply touched by the small family's plight. Despite the number of people Laura still had on her waiting list, she couldn't turn Paige down. Ignoring all the obstacles she knew she'd have to overcome, she promised Paige the Foundation would ensure that Jason's Christmas wishes were fulfilled.

It meant that Laura now faced a significant challenge—to find a sponsor for Jason, with other families still needing sponsors. She'd just have to work extra-hard. She sat at her desk, staring at the image of the tousle-haired little boy grinning at her from the computer screen, when her phone rang.

"It's Daniel Kinsley, Laura. How are you?"

"Fine, Daniel." Laura felt a smile spread across her face. *God works in mysterious ways*, she thought, and gave silent thanks.

"We've raised enough money for everything on both kids' lists and then some."

"That's terrific, Daniel! Two very deserving families will be ecstatic."

"It's been my pleasure. It was no trouble shopping for the families."

Laura knew Daniel was a successful lawyer, a managing partner with his firm. She would never have expected him to do the shopping *himself*. Her smile broadened. "The families will be grateful."

"I won't keep you, Laura. I just need to know where I should send the packages."

She gave him the address for the Foundation's warehouse, then tested the waters. "Ah, Daniel? I just received a last-minute request for a brave little boy in dire need. With our program already in full gear for Christmas, I don't have another company to turn to. I realize it's asking a lot, but would your firm be willing to sponsor one more child?"

DANIEL DIDN'T THINK his partners would be enthusiastic about contributing more money. He'd pushed their generosity to the limit with the two families they were sponsoring, especially since he'd made sure they'd gone well above what was requested. No, he couldn't commit his firm to more.

Laura rushed on before he could decline. "How about if I email you Jason's picture and his story? Then decide."

He didn't see how he could refuse without sounding rude. Besides, if he'd learned one thing about Laura during their brief interactions, it was that she wouldn't take no for an answer. In fact, he could hear her nails tapping on the keyboard as they spoke. He remembered their initial meeting, and how she'd good-naturedly maneuvered him into sponsoring two families instead of one. He sighed. She was good at her job, and he couldn't fault her for that. "Okay. Send it to me."

"Thanks again, Daniel. Please don't take too

long to think about it. Time's running out…
especially for Jason."

Daniel opened Laura's email and then the
attachments. Reading Jason's story, he ached
for both the boy and his mother. They lived
in Camden Falls, a town he hadn't heard of.
According to the report, it was just outside
Springfield, Massachusetts, less than an hour
from his office in Hartford. The brief overview told him that the mother was single
and doing her best to take care of her very
sick child. Daniel sat in front of his computer
monitor, staring at the little boy who'd been
through so much in his short life and—miraculously—was still able to grin. Jason's blue
eyes seemed to gaze directly into his.

Daniel wasn't going back to his partners
for more money. But little Jason would have
everything he wanted for Christmas. Daniel
would see to it—*personally.*

CHAPTER THREE

PAIGE WORKED EXTRA hours for a week straight, since she'd traded shifts with a colleague so she could take a few days off to visit her parents. She tried to save her vacation days to accommodate Jason's medical appointments, and she didn't want him to be without her over the weekend, either. She hated to leave him, but things were hard enough for Jason as it was; she didn't want him overhearing their conversations, easily done in her parents' small bungalow.

As they'd agreed, Paige borrowed Chelsea's ancient silver Honda Accord for the drive to Great Barrington. The weather forecast concerned her. An accumulation of wet, heavy snow was expected, but she didn't have much choice. Between her work schedule and Jason's first treatment, these three days were the only real opportunity she had.

Jason was staying with Mrs. Bennett—a great adventure for him. Other than his visits to the hospital, it was the first time he'd be away from home without her. Chelsea had offered to take him to the park, promising they'd make a snowman if there was enough snow. To prove that she was serious, she'd bought carrots, a small bag of coal and even a toy pipe. Mr. Weatherly, their next-door neighbor, also offered to spend some time with him.

Paige drove through a few intense snow squalls, clinging white-knuckled to the steering wheel. She thought about stopping for a coffee but feared the storm would only get worse. She didn't want to risk not being able to get to Great Barrington that afternoon. She drove on and hoped for the best.

Fortunately, the squalls were localized and short. She made it to Great Barrington without incident. She breathed a heavy sigh of relief when she pulled up outside her parents' house.

Her parents adored the little bungalow, with its board-and-batten exterior stained a pale blue-gray and the shutters and trim painted a sunflower yellow. She remembered the excitement in her mother's voice when her parents had first seen the house. Her mother had said it reminded her of a bright summer sky. Even in the dreary twilight, the house glowed with warmth and welcome.

Her mother loved to tend the gardens on either side of the porch steps. In the summer, ever-blooming annuals crowded the small space with a riot of colors. Now the gardens were cut back and neatly edged, laid to rest for the winter. With Christmas fast approaching, the house was decorated for the holidays. As a child, Paige had loved that she was the envy of all her friends at Christmastime because their house was always the brightest and most cheerful in the neighborhood.

Feeling nostalgic, Paige grabbed her overnight bag from the Accord's trunk, stood beside the car and inhaled deeply. From the familiar subtle, smoky scent, she knew her mother had a fire going in the fireplace. She mounted the three short steps to the porch, and the muffled strains of Bing Crosby's "White Christmas" drifted out to her.

The glossy red door, adorned with a wreath of holly, was framed by a garland entwined with twinkling white fairy lights. Pewter-gray urns stood on either side of the door, filled with evergreen boughs, birch branches and twigs laden with red berries.

Despite her father's illness, joy and love emanated from the simple little house.

Paige felt guilty about bringing sadness to her parents' door, especially at this time of year. How was she going to do this? For once, her father's loss of memory might be a blessing, if it spared him the cruelty of the news she had to impart.

Now that she was here, she was terrified of the impact her revelation about Jason's condition would have on her mother, who'd been so eager for Paige to visit. In a few short hours, she'd be breaking her mother's heart.

Paige took another fortifying breath and let herself in. Almost immediately, a sheltie scrambled out of a room on the right, bounded over to Paige and took little leaps all around her in greeting. Paige put her bag next to the front door and bent down to scratch the dog. "Hey, Iris. How're you doing? Have you been a good girl?" Paige was rewarded with an energetic face wash.

The greeting ritual completed, Paige straightened. She brushed some dog hair from her pants, pulled off her boots and simply stood where she was. The combined living/dining area was to her left, the kitchen ahead of her, and a small den and powder room to her right. Pretty Christmas touches were everywhere—the poinsettia on the hall table beside a photograph of her, Jason and her parents, the mistletoe hung from a chandelier, and a plastic snowman they'd had since she was a child, which stood as a friendly sentinel in a corner of the hallway.

From her vantage point, she could see the Christmas tree in the living room with its bright decorations and more flickering lights, a half dozen neatly wrapped packages beneath it. A miniature tree, no more than eight inches high, with a dusting of fake snow, sat on the coffee table beside a dish of sugar cookies.

Although the fireplace was out of Paige's sight, she could hear the logs crackling, smell the rich aroma of applewood and see the dancing reflections of the flames.

Just as she had when Paige was a child, her mother made every occasion special. All of a sudden, Paige had an overwhelming need to be held by her. She took a few steps forward, the dog at her heels. "Mom! I'm here."

Charlotte Brooks emerged from the kitchen, drying her hands on a dish towel. "Hi, honey." Her hair was snow-white, short and stylish. Behind her glasses, her eyes were clear and bright, and the same shade of cornflower blue as her daughter's. Her face was remarkably unlined for a woman approaching seventy. She wasn't as tall as Paige but had a slim, youthful figure. She wore neatly pressed black pants and a pale pink sweater. A white apron was tied around her waist.

Love and admiration swelled in Paige's

chest, as they never failed to do whenever she saw her mother.

They hugged, swaying gently together. "It's so good to see you, Mom." Paige held on, taking strength from her mother.

When they parted, Charlotte grasped Paige's shoulders and stepped back. "Let me have a look at you." After a moment's hesitation, she asked, "What's wrong, honey?"

"We'll talk, Mom. But I'd like to see Dad first."

"He's in the den. Reading, I think."

Charlotte followed Paige into the cozy room. There was a fireplace here, too, faced in green marble, with a small fire sputtering in the hearth. The room, paneled in deep, rich oak, had ample bookshelves. There was an upholstered bench seat in the bay window, with forest-green brocade drapes tied back on either side. A large, overstuffed reclining chair was positioned near the hearth.

Her father sat in the chair, his hands linked across his slightly protruding belly, his head bent forward. His chest rose and fell rhythmically with his breathing. A book was splayed open on his lap. Seeing her father like this, still youthful looking and so peaceful, Paige found it even harder to accept his illness.

Iris bolted past Paige and skidded to a stop

at her father's feet, tail thumping against the side of the chair. Paige followed her in and bent down to run a hand along her back. "Watching over Dad while he sleeps, are you?"

Charlotte had moved over to stand beside her husband. It was never lost on Paige that after nearly five decades of marriage, her parents' love had not only endured but seemed to intensify year after year. With a loving touch, her mother brushed back the still-thick lock of salt-and-pepper hair that had fallen over her father's forehead. When he stirred, she murmured softly, "Stephen, honey, look who's here."

Appearing disoriented, he gazed up at his wife and smiled. "Good morning." Charlotte didn't bother to correct him about the time of day. Rather, she took one of his hands in her own, gesturing with the other. "Stephen, it's Paige."

Stephen turned his bright smile on his daughter, and Paige's heart melted as she crouched down so they were eye to eye. "Hi, Dad."

Confusion flitted across Stephen's face, but his smile didn't waver. "Hello, young lady."

Still uncertain whether he recognized her, Paige reached for his free hand. "How're you feeling?"

"Oh, just fine, thank you." His eyes cleared, and Paige held her breath. "You must be the new nurse."

Charlotte was about to interject, but Paige shook her head. She didn't want to cause discomfort for either of her parents, or further pain for herself. She spoke quietly with her father for a few minutes about generalities, the weather and a TV show he remembered watching. When it was evident that he was struggling to keep his eyelids from drifting shut again, she rose. By the time her mother replaced the book on the end table next to the chair and tucked a light throw around his lap, he was sound asleep.

Paige kissed his forehead and skimmed her hand over his. With a final longing glance at her father, she accompanied her mother out of the room. Iris gamboled after them to the doorway. There she paused, considered and did a quick shuffle. With a small sigh, she returned to the foot of the easy chair to curl up by her master again.

Paige prepared a pot of coffee while her mother set out mugs, plates, napkins and—despite Paige's protests—some homemade biscuits.

With their hands joined across the kitchen table, Paige told her mother everything there was to tell. When they finished the first pot of coffee, Charlotte brewed another. Painful as it was for Paige to share her burden, she did feel slightly better. They sat at the table, eyes brimming with tears.

"Honey, what can I do to help?"

"Just *be* here for me, Mom."

Charlotte squeezed Paige's hands. "Have I ever not been?"

On a long breath, Paige turned her hand over and curled her fingers around her mother's.

"Do you need money?"

Paige heaved a huge sigh. "Of course. But I'll manage."

"How much do you need?"

"Mom, you can't. Where would you get it?"

"Our savings. If need be, we can borrow against the house."

"Mom, no! You need your savings to live on. And how would you repay a loan? You're already stretching your retirement benefits as it is."

Charlotte patted Paige's hand. "Let me worry about that. Jason is our priority." She gave her daughter a firm look. "If you need money, you tell me."

Paige sighed again. "I will, but I can't let

you use your savings or take any equity out of the house."

"What about Mark? Does he know?"

"No." Paige realized her answer sounded abrupt, but given how things had ended with her ex-husband four years ago—over Jason's initial diagnosis–she couldn't help it. "I can't see him offering any assistance."

Charlotte peered at Paige over her glasses. It was the look that had put fear into Paige as a child. "Maybe not. But he *is* Jason's father."

"You remember what happened the first time Jason was ill. Remember, that's why I decided to trade off child support for sole legal custody. I can't risk that again, for either of us."

"But he has a right to know."

"I'll think about it." That was the most Paige was prepared to commit.

THEY HAD A quiet dinner together, and Paige decided to leave early the next morning. She'd originally planned to stay three days but was anxious to get back to Jason. The weather forecast was also calling for inclement weather the next day.

After breakfast, Paige packed her small bag and stowed it in the trunk of the Honda. Her father was back in the den, in his favorite chair, Iris at his feet, when she went to say good-bye.

"Hi, Dad." Paige sank down on one knee in front of her father and rewarded the faithful Iris with a scratch behind her ears.

Her father lowered the paper he'd been reading, then gave her a warm, friendly smile. "Well, hello, young lady."

Paige placed a hand on his knee. "It's me. Paige." She needed to try before she left, just to see if he would remember her at all.

"Paige…" He rolled her name around his tongue. "It's a pretty name, isn't it?"

Paige continued to smile, but she withdrew her hand. "Yes, it is."

"Such a lovely name for a lovely young woman." He looked vague for a moment. "I've always favored it, I think."

Paige felt the sting of tears, lowered her eyelashes and gave her attention to the dog. There was no reason her father should see her pain. When the mist had cleared, she reached into the pocket of her shirt, pulled out a recent school picture of Jason and held it out to him.

Stephen took the picture and examined it for a minute while Paige tried to distract herself by rubbing Iris's belly. "What a handsome young man," Stephen said. He shifted his gaze to Paige. "He resembles you."

She swallowed the sob that bubbled up in her throat. "This is Jason. He's my son."

Stephen pursed his lips and nodded decisively. "Yes. I thought so." He took one last look at the picture before handing it back. "A very handsome boy, as I said. You should be proud."

Paige swallowed hard again. "You can keep it if you like."

Stephen lowered his eyes to the picture once more. A smile spread across his face. "I would like that very much. Thank you."

With a herculean effort, Paige held back her tears. "Can I get you anything? Something to drink, maybe, before I go?"

"How sweet of you to ask." He glanced at his watch, studied it for a moment while his mouth worked, then looked up again. "It should be time for my walk soon, but a cup of tea would be very nice."

"I'll get it for you." Paige rose. On impulse, she leaned forward and gave her father a hug. He responded to her affection by wrapping one arm around her back, his head just above her shoulder, his mouth near her ear.

Because of the proximity, Paige caught his softly whispered words. "You're my darling girl, Paige. You are." When she straightened, the vague look had returned to his eyes.

CHAPTER FOUR

PAIGE WAS RELIEVED that the nasty weather held off during her drive home. Emotionally and physically drained, she didn't think she was up to coping with treacherous road conditions. A couple of blocks from home, she pulled into a gas station and filled up the Honda. The least she could do was return it to Chelsea with a full tank.

She parked it in Chelsea's assigned spot, retrieved her overnight bag and headed inside. None too soon, as the first flakes of snow started to fall.

She dropped her bag inside the door to embrace Jason, who rushed into her arms. She held him tight and breathed in the baby powder fragrance of his shampoo. If there was a better feeling than holding her son, she couldn't imagine it.

Mrs. Bennett joined them by the door. Paige understood the silent support in her eyes and knew she wouldn't ask how things had gone with Jason in the room. She thanked Mrs. Bennett for taking care of her son.

"No trouble at all, my dear. We enjoyed ourselves. Jason, make sure you show your mother what you've been working on."

Jason did just that after Paige had put her things away. He'd painted a winter scape with a large snowman that looked a lot like Frosty.

"See?" He thrust out a printout of a photo. "It's the snowman Chelsea and I built!"

Paige examined the photo, then the painting again. The likeness was undeniable. Her son had a remarkable talent. "It's wonderful," she said. "You had a nice time while I was gone?"

"Yeah, Chelsea took the picture that I used for the painting," he replied, but the light in his eyes had dimmed.

Paige stroked his hair. "What's wrong, sweetie?"

"I was sick, Mom. Like before."

She immediately placed her palm on his forehead, checking for fever. Since Jason had started his treatments a few days earlier, they were both adjusting to the cyclical swings in his health. "How are you feeling now?"

"Better. Mrs. Bennett took my blood pressure, too. She said it was fine. She wrote it down in your journal."

Paige looked over the notes in the journal

she kept of Jason's health. With relief, she saw that everything seemed okay now.

He'd always had a hard time immediately after a treatment, especially with the nausea, but got progressively better. She knew from experience that the second week after a treatment was generally good for him. Of course, as the cycle progressed, the effects built up and he felt increasingly worse, particularly right after the treatments. Paige not only accompanied him when the new cancer drug was administered, but tried her best to stay home with him the day or two after, when he was feeling the worst. He was already missing a lot of school because of his various appointments.

She was very grateful for her friends in the building—Chelsea, Mr. and Mrs. Bennett, and her next-door neighbor, Mr. Weatherly. She could count on one or another of them to help out if she found herself in a bind.

The reality was that Jason needed her, and her whole world was Jason. Nothing mattered more than making his life easier and taking care of him when he was unwell.

Paige accepted this, and she had no complaints—if only Jason could be healthy again.

JUST THREE WEEKS before Christmas, and it had been one of those days, Daniel Kinsley thought as he let himself into his house. If his initial consult with a potential new client was any indication, there was another nasty divorce battle brewing. And she was young. In her twenties. She and her husband hadn't been married a full year!

They were using the standard "irreconcilable differences" argument. Did they even know what that meant in legal terms?

He'd finally gotten rid of Gloria Farnsworth. He'd transferred her case to one of his partners. The firm didn't want to lose the revenue they could generate if she did take her husband to court and there was a protracted legal battle. But now he had "Farnsworth lite" to contend with.

As dissatisfying as his work continued to be, there was one bright spot for Daniel. It had to do with a little boy named Jason.

Daniel had made his decision to sponsor Jason the day he'd spoken to Laura Andrews, but he hadn't had a chance to confirm it.

He sent Laura a quick email, letting her know his decision. By the time he'd fixed himself a Crown and Coke, set a fire in the fireplace in his home office and gone back to his laptop, she'd already emailed him a scanned copy of Jason's handwritten wish list. He chuckled as he printed it.

Daniel perused the list while he sat by the fire and sipped his drink. Much like the lists provided by the other families, Jason's consisted of basic items—winter clothes, a stuffed dog, a backpack for school, a sketch pad, a New England Patriots cap, a toy train and a book about circuses. Circuses—huh! Daniel remembered his own fascination with circuses when he was a kid, but they were more popular then. It was different now. He couldn't remember the last time he'd heard of one in the area. He wondered how the kid had developed an interest in circuses and felt a sudden connection with this boy he'd never met.

Daniel was particularly struck by the last item printed neatly at the bottom of the page.

Jason wanted to be a "normal" boy. What would that mean to a kid like him? To be healthy? To have a father?

Daniel stared long and hard at the list and the little boy's meticulously neat printing. Daniel might not be able to make Jason's last wish come true, but he resolved to take care of all the others on the list—and more.

THE NEXT DAY was no better for Daniel. By six-thirty, he'd had enough. After another discussion with his new twenty-something client, he'd hung up the phone, packed his briefcase and left the office. He hadn't planned to stop at Westfarms Mall. He just wanted to get home, have a light dinner and catch up on his paperwork. But as he was approaching the New Britain Avenue exit off I-84 W, he remembered that he needed refills for his electric shaver. He took the exit, regretting that decision as soon as he saw the packed parking lot. Who said there was anything wrong with the economy? Based on how full the lot was, half the population of Hartford must've decided to go shopping.

He *hated* crowds. That was one of the reasons he tried to avoid malls, especially at this time of year.

Well, he was here. If he could find a parking spot, he might as well brave the crowds. They certainly wouldn't decrease as the days before Christmas flew by. He reluctantly squeezed his Mercedes coupe into a tight spot between two hulking SUVs. He entered the mall by one of the main doors leading into an atrium. Jewel-toned Christmas lights shone everywhere. Children's laughter and the occasional wail mingled with the buzz of shoppers, all layered over traditional Christmas music. The smell of greasy fries and overcooked burgers wafted over to him from the nearby food court.

The atrium was filled with people, many of them kids. As he made his way in, he realized why. At the far end of the atrium, a very convincing Santa sat on his throne, surrounded by a half dozen elves. What person in his or her right mind would wear those green outfits with the green-and-black-striped tights and still be able to smile about it?

He couldn't say what compelled him, but he stopped to watch.

Santa had a little boy who couldn't have been more than five sitting on his lap. The boy was hunched in on himself and kept glancing with pleading eyes toward his mother at the side of the dais. Daniel felt for the kid. He looked painfully uncomfortable, but the mother seemed oblivious. She was preoccupied with capturing the perfect shot of him with Santa.

Daniel hadn't noticed how tense he'd become watching the poor kid until he heard his own breath hiss out when the kid was finally allowed to slide off Santa's lap. Was that how it had been for him when he was a boy?

Daniel was about to move on when he noticed the next kid in line to have an audience with Santa. She was all blonde curls and porcelain skin, and she wore a pretty, frilly dress. She reminded him of the child on the billboard visible from his office window. There was nothing shy about this kid. She clambered up on Santa's lap, took his face between her tiny hands and placed a smacking kiss—he could have sworn he heard it where he stood— right on Santa's big nose. As the child spoke intently, she used her pudgy little fingers to count, no doubt enumerating the things she wanted for Christmas. Daniel caught himself grinning. Self-consciously, he forced his lips back into a straight line.

He cast a glance at the girl's mother. Unlike the previous woman, this one was filled with pride in her daughter. If the look on the mother's face was any indication, the little girl would get everything she dreamed of for Christmas.

An image of a boy with a mop of blond hair, bright blue eyes and a smattering of freckles came to mind. Daniel thought of what Jason's Christmas would've been like if he hadn't agreed to sponsor him. He was glad it was a rhetorical question. He'd guarantee the kid wasn't disappointed.

Forgetting all about his electric shaver refills, Daniel consulted the mall directory and headed to a toy store.

A couple of hours later, carrying numerous shopping bags, he entered a hobby store. He was hopeful he'd be able to tick the toy train off his list, too. Finding the appropriate section, he stacked his bags in an out-of-the-way corner so his hands would be free. He began to examine the various toys neatly arranged on the shelves.

He picked up and examined a locomotive, then a caboose. He was fascinated by the perfectly crafted miniature pieces, but there were so many of them. When he was a child, his parents had encouraged him to play with educational toys. He'd never had anything as frivolous—or as much fun—as a train set. Perhaps because of that, he wanted to make this a special gift for Jason, but he had no idea where to start.

"May I help you?" Daniel nearly jumped when he heard the pleasant, cheerful voice behind him. He carefully replaced the caboose on the shelf and turned to see a lovely dark-skinned young woman with short, springy hair and an eager-to-help expression on her face.

Generally not one to ask for assistance, at this moment he considered the young woman a godsend. "If you know about trains, yes, I beg you to help me!"

"It's not my specialty, but I'd be happy to see what I can do. Are you interested in a particular piece or a set?"

The kid had asked for a toy train, but Daniel wanted to do more. "A set, I think." He gave her a grateful smile. "Something special."

After a brief discussion, the sales associate advised Daniel that the complexity of the set he was considering was beyond her level of expertise and said she'd fetch the owner of the store. With the owner's assistance, Daniel decided on a deluxe electric train set. He knew it was over the top, but somehow his own childhood's unfulfilled desire had become entangled with the kid's wish, and Daniel couldn't resist. He hoped Jason would be as excited about it as he was.

The challenge was that the set had to be custom manufactured, and the company was already backed up with orders. When Daniel shared Jason's story with the owner of the shop, the man made a firm commitment that he'd do whatever needed to be done and personally guaranteed that Daniel would have the train set in time for Christmas.

Another hour later and still without the shaver refills, Daniel was loading shopping bags into the trunk of his car. Doing a quick scan of his doors, he was grateful for small blessings that his car appeared to be undamaged. Shopping malls, especially during the hustle and bustle of the holidays, tended to put him in a sour mood. Yet he found his disposition decidedly brighter than it had been when he'd left the office. He paused. Had he *ever* been this happy and excited about Christmas?

At home, he took all the parcels into a spare bedroom. Despite his growling stomach reminding him that he hadn't had dinner, he unpacked the gifts. He read labels, examined assembly instructions and realized he felt like a kid himself.

He suddenly remembered that he was supposed to leave for Newport to visit his parents the week before Christmas. At the thought of spending a whole ten days with his family, he nearly shuddered–and immediately felt guilty. It wasn't that he didn't *love* his parents. There just wasn't any warmth in the relationship. Not like the depiction on the billboard across from his office.

He'd visit his parents. He was too much of a dutiful son not to. He'd spend the weekend, but he'd make excuses and return home before Christmas. That way, he'd be in Hartford to finish shopping for Jason—not that he hadn't already covered everything on the list—and he'd make the most of the holidays on his own.

CHAPTER FIVE

CHELSEA SAT ON a chair in Paige's living room, one leg dangling over its arm. She was dressed in her favorite color—black leggings, thick black socks and an oversize black sweater. Jason was sprawled on the carpet, reading a book. Paige was curled up on the sofa, her legs tucked under her. In contrast to Chelsea's dark, she was light. She wore faded jeans and a white long-sleeved T-shirt, and her blonde hair was pulled back from her face in a high ponytail.

Her friend studied her while munching on a carrot stick. "You look about eighteen, you know, with your perfect skin and that ponytail."

Paige flicked her ponytail over her shoulder. "I think that's a stretch, but thanks for the compliment."

Bobby Helms's "Jingle Bell Rock" started to play on the radio.

"Can you believe it's only a couple of weeks

until Christmas?" Chelsea exclaimed. "What are you guys doing this year?"

Paige glanced down at her son just as he turned his head and smiled up at her. "Jason and I discussed it. Although it would be great to be with Mom and Dad, we decided to spend Christmas here."

Jason pushed up into a sitting position and crossed his legs. "Yeah. That way I won't get as tired, 'cause I'll need all my energy for my next treatment right after Christmas."

Paige looked back at Chelsea. "The doctors timed his second treatment as far before the holidays as possible to make sure he'd feel the best he could for Christmas. But it means he'll get the following one on December 27."

Chelsea nodded in sympathy. "Bummer about not seeing your grandparents though, huh, Squirt?"

Jason lowered his eyes. "That's okay. I wanted to, but Gramps doesn't really remember me most of the time," he murmured, then brightened. "Besides, we can see you and Mr. and Mrs. Bennett, and Mr. Weatherly! You can all come over, and we can have hot chocolate and play games and stuff!"

Chelsea swung her leg to the floor and shifted in the chair. "Actually, I won't be here for Christmas. I'm taking Joel to spend the holidays with my parents in North Carolina. Things are getting serious enough that it's time they met him. We'll be gone from just before Christmas until the second of January." Chelsea shrugged apologetically. "Mrs. Bennett mentioned yesterday that they'd be spending Christmas with their daughter, her husband and the grandkids."

Jason looked crestfallen.

"Sorry, Squirt," Chelsea said. "At least Mr. Weatherly will be here."

A tap at the door had Jason scrambling to answer it. As if on cue, Mr. Weatherly stood in the doorway, holding a small plant, its pot wrapped in shiny red paper.

"Well, hello, Mr. Weatherly." Paige rose to greet her next-door neighbor. Harrison Weatherly was a very proper, middle-aged English gentleman. He was dressed, as always, as though he was off to have tea with the Queen. Today he wore gray tweed pants with an impeccable crease, a perfectly pressed white shirt, a black knit vest and a maroon bow tie. Paige knew he'd never been married and—because a young lady in his youth had broken his heart—he liked to boast that he was a confirmed bachelor. He didn't have family in the United States. It struck Paige that he seemed lonely. Gardening was his passion, and he made the most of the small outdoor space that came with his ground-floor apartment. Paige had a soft spot in her heart for Mr. Weatherly.

"Hey, Mr. Weatherly," Chelsea chimed in, waving at him.

"What's that?" Jason dashed over, peering at the plant.

"This is for you, young master Jason, and for your mother. It's a miniature spruce, all decked out for Christmas. Here you go." He handed Jason the small tree, which was decorated with tiny ornaments and a miniature star on top.

"It's cool!" Jason exclaimed. Catching his mother's look, he swiftly added, "Thanks."

Paige stood on her toes and gave Mr. Weatherly a kiss, bringing a bright red stain to his cheeks. "It's beautiful and very considerate of you. Thank you."

"I just thought it might be nice on your table. Perhaps as a centerpiece for Christmas dinner."

"It'll be perfect! Jason, why don't you take it over now? Mr. Weatherly, please come in for a cup of tea."

Mr. Weatherly followed Paige into the apartment and made himself comfortable on the sofa while Jason positioned the little tree in the middle of their dining table.

Paige paused at the doorway to the kitchen. "Speaking of Christmas dinner, we'd love to have you join us."

Mr. Weatherly smiled broadly. "What a kind invitation, but this year I'm going to New York City. I've always wanted to experience New York at Christmas. Attend a Broadway play, see the Christmas tree at Rockefeller Center. I finally decided to do it. I signed up for a New York Christmas excursion. I'm quite excited about it."

"That's wonderful," Paige said, but she shot Chelsea a quick glance and felt sad as she prepared the tea. Christmas was about spending time with loved ones—family and friends. She wondered again if there was any way she and Jason could spend it with her parents, but travel would be hard for him, and her father wasn't comfortable in places he didn't recognize. So this Christmas it would be just her and Jason. All the more reason she needed to make it a special one for him.

DANIEL WAS IN his office on a settlement teleconference call with opposing counsel for one of his clients. They were doing the customary dance, even though they both knew where they'd ultimately end up. It promised to be a long dance. He leaned back in his chair and spun it around to watch the snow falling outside while he listened to the opposing counsel list the multitude of alleged grievances against his client.

Daniel's gaze rested on the billboard with the Rockwell-like family. He focused on the flawless-looking parents, ostensibly so happy and in love. They seemed to exude tenderness for each other and their child.

It made him think of Jason's mother. How would she feel, having recently learned of her son's illness, alone and with obvious financial difficulties? Who would she lean on for support? Was there someone who loved her and would shower her with gifts on Christmas morning? He had no idea who she was, what she did for a living or what her dreams and desires were. But he could guess that her fears would all be concentrated on her son. He was equally certain that she'd be a good mother. The image of the boy in the picture Laura had sent him suggested a happy, well-loved kid.

Daniel's thoughts kept darting back to Jason's mother while he half listened to the other lawyer drone on. He'd had enough by the time they finally agreed on the settlement—a settlement he'd been so confident in, he'd already had the agreement drafted.

He turned to his computer and flipped through his contacts as he concluded the call. Rather than hanging up, he dialed another number. After two rings, the call was answered.

"Laura Andrews."

"It's Daniel Kinsley, and I'd appreciate your help with something."

"Sure, Daniel. I'd be happy to assist if I can."

"I need some information about Jason's mother."

A note of apprehension crept into Laura's voice. "Now, Daniel, that's against our policies. Most of our families are proud, hard-working people, and they don't feel good about needing assistance. We assure them that we'll keep identities confidential."

He chuckled. "Oh, I don't need to know her identity. Just a little about her."

"I don't understand…"

"It's nothing sinister. Based on what you told me, I figure she's unlikely to splurge on anything for herself. It occurred to me that I'd like to get a few things for her, too."

"That's very considerate of you. What do you have in mind?"

He chuckled again. "I haven't got a clue!" Whenever he'd dated a woman during the holidays, invariably the gift of choice had been jewelry. He was well versed in the cut and clarity of diamonds, although he'd always stayed clear of rings. But he didn't consider jewelry an appropriate gift for this particular woman. "That's where I need your help, Laura. Can you give me some ideas?"

"Let me think… Yes! I know exactly the types of things she could use."

Daniel made a list. It shocked him that he was looking forward to doing more shopping.

PAIGE WAS GRATEFUL that Jason was feeling better after his treatment. It had been his last before Christmas, and they were able to spend a quiet weekend at home. Mr. Weatherly's gift of a small Christmas tree aside, they had an agreement with their neighbors that they wouldn't exchange gifts, other than each of them bringing some small toy for Jason, and Jason painting everyone a picture. Since their neighbors were leaving for Christmas over the coming days, they all stopped by Paige and Jason's apartment to offer holiday greetings. First it was Mr. and Mrs. Bennett from across the hall, Mr. Bennett making a special effort to move around despite his severe arthritis.

Next it was Chelsea, brimming with excitement about introducing Joel to her parents.

Sunday morning, Jason was working with his watercolors at the dining room table. Paige sat down beside him, tilting her head to see what he was painting.

The background was a mottled green. The large form in the foreground was mostly filled with a pale burnt-orange wash, leaving some sections white. Jason was working with a fine bristle brush and undiluted black paint. As Paige watched, the form started to take the shape of a tiger—a rather well-executed one.

Where had her son gotten his talent? Neither she nor her ex-husband was artistic, but there was no denying that Jason had a gift. She began to say so when a knock sounded at the door. Jason was reaching over to put his brush down, but Paige laid a hand on his wrist. "You keep doing what you're doing. I'll get it."

"Good morning, Mr. Weatherly," Paige greeted him. He was dressed as spiffily as usual, with a vest under his houndstooth check jacket, a bow tie and a fedora.

"Hi, Mr. Weatherly!" Jason stuck his paint brush into the mason jar on the table and ran over.

"A merry Christmas to you, Jason." He handed Jason a package wrapped in gold foil with a big red bow. "Hold on to this until Christmas," he said with mock sternness. "Don't open it until then."

Jason shook the box gently and listened to the slight rattle.

"No trying to guess, either, young man!"

"Okay. And thank you. I'll go get your gift." Jason hurried to his room and returned carrying a large envelope, hand-decorated with a Christmas motif, and with Mr. Weatherly's name beautifully written on the front. "This is for you." He held the envelope out to Mr. Weatherly.

"Thank you, young man. If you don't mind, I'll wait to open this, too. Gifts should be opened on Christmas morning, don't you think?"

Jason nodded.

"Mr. Weatherly, would you like a cup of tea?" Paige asked.

"That would be lovely, thank you."

He followed Jason to the table, while Paige went into the kitchen. Their conversation drifted in to her as she made the tea.

"This is going to be a tiger, isn't it?" he asked Jason as he studied his painting.

Jason knelt on his chair and picked up his brush. "Yes. It's a Bengal tiger."

"I can see that. Well done. And you're painting it from your imagination?"

"From my memory! I saw one in a zoo
once."

"You *did*?"

"Oh, it was a long time ago." Jason added
a few more black stripes to the tiger's face.
"When my dad was still around."

He nodded. "What made you want to paint
it now?"

Jason moistened the tip of his brush again
and swirled it lightly over the cake of black
paint. He glanced toward the kitchen doorway.
Keeping his voice low, he responded. "Every
year, at Christmas, I make something for my
dad. Something he'd like. He really liked the
tiger at the zoo, so I thought I'd paint him a
picture of a tiger this year."

Hearing her son's words, Paige froze in the
doorway, a tray with cups, milk and sugar, a
pot of tea and a plate of cookies in her hands.
Jason took that moment to glance up again.
Their eyes met. Paige moved forward and
placed the tea service on the table. She poured
three cups of tea, passed Mr. Weatherly his
cup, and made hers and Jason's with a bit of
sugar and some milk.

They chatted until Mr. Weatherly finished
his tea and rose. "Well, I'd better be off now,

since I'm leaving for my trip soon." He held Jason's envelope in one hand, tapping it lightly on the palm of the other. "I thank you for this, and I know I'll love it. Merry Christmas to you both!" He gave each of them a stiff little hug, and they said their good-byes.

Paige cleaned up the tea service before rejoining Jason in the dining room.

She sat at the table, elbows resting on the surface, not quite knowing how to broach the topic of Jason's painting. "It's turning out really well," she began.

"Thanks, Mom," he mumbled, but he avoided eye contact.

Her heart had been aching from the time she'd heard Jason's admission to Mr. Weatherly, but fresh pain seared her now. She ran a comforting hand up and down Jason's back. "It's okay. You don't have to worry about what I heard."

His eyes darted to hers before he lowered his lashes again. "I'm sorry, Mom."

She took the brush out of his hand, placed it back in the mason jar, then drew him into a hug. "Oh, sweetie. You don't have anything to be sorry for." As his arms tightened around her waist, she rocked him gently. "I'd like us to talk about it, though."

He gave her one final squeeze before settling back in his chair, but he remained silent.

"Do you want to talk about it?"

Jason picked up his brush and fidgeted with it. "I know we'll probably never see Dad again," he muttered.

Paige felt the burn of tears.

"It's no big deal," he said quickly. He twirled the brush between his fingers. "But every year I make something for Dad. This year, it's the tiger. Just in case..." He shrugged. "After Christmas, I'll put it away. I have a shoe box I use for that. Last year I made him a candy dish at school."

Paige had wondered what had happened to the pretty blue-and-white dish.

"After Christmas, I'll put the painting of the tiger in the box, too."

Jason's eyes shone with some indefinable emotion when he looked up at her, "Then if I do see him again, the presents will all be there for him."

Paige's heart simply shattered, but she'd die before she'd let Jason see that. She smoothed his bangs back from his forehead and brushed her lips across his brow. "That's very thoughtful of you. It's a beautiful painting. I know your father would love it."

Jason straightened his shoulders and swirled

his brush over the cake of black paint. "Thanks, Mom." His voice soft, he added, "Maybe someday I *will* be able to give it to him."

DANIEL WAS ASTONISHED to discover that he actually *enjoyed* shopping for Christmas gifts despite the crowds, noise and general cacophony. He'd even taken care of all the wrapping. Well, not personally. That was beyond his capabilities or, perhaps more accurately, his patience. But he felt good about that, too, because he'd had everything wrapped by one of those charitable gift wrapping services in the mall.

He dropped off all the brightly wrapped packages for Jason and the few for Jason's mother at the Foundation's warehouse so they could be delivered the day before Christmas.

The only thing missing was the deluxe electric train set he'd ordered. Two days before Christmas, he called the hobby store's owner again to follow up on the delivery date.

"I'm so sorry for the delay, Mr. Kinsley, but the manufacturer didn't realize how popular train sets would be this year."

"But you told me—"

"I did, and I am a man of my word. I've contacted the manufacturer. He's working around the clock to fill all the orders, even though it's costing him more money and he likely won't make a profit on these remaining sets. I know that's not your concern, but I just want you to appreciate his commitment. He's promised to deliver all the train sets by Christmas. Yours was one of the last orders placed. Unfortunately, that means it's also one of the last being manufactured. He's trying for tomorrow, but if that's not possible, he will *absolutely* have it done by Christmas morning."

Daniel was somewhat reassured, but now he needed another favor from Laura. He knew this one would be a challenge for her. There was no point in delaying the inevitable, so he called her number next.

When she answered the phone, he began, "Laura, I've got a problem."

"Of all the people I know, I'd think you'd be the least likely to have a problem. Not one you can't resolve, anyway," Laura teased him.

"See, that's the thing about assumptions. They're often wrong."

Daniel summarized the situation, and the humor went out of Laura's voice. "I explained our confidentiality provisions before. If I'm not at liberty to give you a name, I certainly can't give you an address, especially without checking with Jason's mother."

"You *can't* check with her. I want it to be a

surprise for both of them. You should see this train set, Laura! The kid's going to flip."

"I really can't—"

"As for a courier, I've already looked into that without any luck. How about one of your staff, then? I really want Jason to have the train set."

After a brief silence, Laura responded. "I don't have anyone I could ask. They're mostly volunteers, and they've worked exceptionally long hours this year because of the large number of families needing help. I couldn't take them away from their families. I'd do it myself, but I promised my parents I'd visit them. I can't disappoint them."

"Then I have to do it. I'm a lawyer. That means I have a code of ethics that requires me to respect confidentiality. I just want the kid to have this train set, and there's nothing I can do to get it earlier. Believe me, I've tried."

"All right, Daniel. I'm breaking the rules here. I hope you know this could cost me my job, but you have a compelling argument, and you're not leaving me much choice."

"Thank you, Laura! You won't lose your job. I promise. If anyone gets any ideas about it, I'll get you the meanest, most tenacious employment lawyer in existence." He laughed. "Opposing counsel won't have a chance, but it won't come to that."

CHAPTER SIX

THE DAY BEFORE Christmas, Paige felt sluggish and achy. She'd been working long hours and odd shifts so she could take Jason for his various doctors' appointments. She had her checkbook, her phone and a pile of bills in front of her. Her bank balance had been teetering on the brink of overdraft for weeks now, but with the extra hours she'd worked, she'd been able to keep it in the black.

She slid another bill toward her. She paid it through the automated system and checked her balance—precariously close to zero. She would definitely be dipping into overdraft this week, and she'd barely done any Christmas shopping. Between work and taking care of Jason, Paige had had the chance to buy him only one gift so far. She'd wait until Jason lay down for his nap and call Mrs. Bennett to watch him for a couple of hours before their daughter picked them up. That way she could slip out for a bit and do some shopping.

She glanced up when Jason walked into the

kitchen. He was wearing his pale blue pajamas, adorned with Squidward Tentacles, Patrick Star and some of the other characters from his favorite cartoon. He wore furry dog slippers and had his teddy tucked under his arm. He was dragging his feet, a sure sign that he was tired.

Paige got up and went to him. Crouching down, she cupped his cheeks in the palms of her hands. She could see the sheen of perspiration on his face, and touched his forehead lightly, checking his temperature. He had a slight fever. She'd have to make a note of it in his health journal.

"Let's get you some juice before your nap, okay?"

He nodded sadly.

She poured him a small glass of orange juice, and she held his teddy while he drank it. Ill as he was, he still shuffled over to the sink and put his empty glass in it before reclaiming his teddy. With Paige's hand on his shoulder, they walked to his bedroom.

Paige tucked him in and lowered his blinds. She sat with him as he read aloud from *The Hobbit* until his eyelashes fluttered closed and the rhythm of his breathing changed. Paige dropped a kiss on his forehead and turned off his bedside lamp.

She watched him until she was satisfied that he was napping comfortably.

Closing his bedroom door, she started for the kitchen to call Mrs. Bennett. Suddenly, the room swam in front of her, and she leaned heavily on the doorframe to keep from falling. Brushing her hair back with her free hand, she noted that her own forehead was warm, too. She took a few deep breaths to steady herself. "Okay. I'm okay," she whispered. "Just a little tired."

She pushed away from the doorframe and moved slowly into the living room. Before she went shopping, she'd sit down and rest for a few minutes. She lowered herself gingerly to the sofa and sighed in relief as she rested her head against the cushion. She'd close her eyes for a little while, and she'd be fine.

She bolted up at the pounding behind her temples and winced at the sharp pain that followed it. She grabbed her head with both hands. When she heard the banging again, she realized with a measure of relief that the racket was *not* in her head but at her door. Disoriented, she checked her watch. It was well over an hour since she'd sat down and closed her eyes.

The knocking resumed. She rose as quickly as her throbbing head would allow, worried that the noise would wake Jason. Groggy, she swayed as she went to answer the door.

Two delivery men stood in the corridor. They held large cartons overflowing with Christmas-wrapped packages.

"Ah...may I help you?" she asked with some confusion.

The younger of the men jiggled the carton he was holding and leaned an edge against the doorframe. He flashed her a crooked smile. "Yes, ma'am. We have some gifts for you." He jostled the carton again and raised his right knee to balance it on his upper leg. "They're darn heavy."

"I don't understand..."

The two men exchanged a look. It was the other, older man who spoke. "Are you Ms. Summerville?"

"Yes," Paige replied hesitantly.

"These are for you, from the Wish I May Foundation."

Paige belatedly recognized the Foundation logos on their jackets and raised a hand to her forehead. "Oh, I'd forgotten. *This*..." She gestured at the large cartons. "This is all from the Foundation? For *us*?"

"Yes, ma'am."

"May we come in, please?" the younger

man asked again, obviously struggling not to drop his carton.

"Yes. Yes, of course." Paige stood back, opened the door fully and motioned for them to enter. As they did, she snuck into the kitchen to take a couple of painkillers for her headache. When she returned, she was surprised to find not only the two large cartons but also a smaller box of decorations, another box with some nonperishable groceries and a large cooler she assumed was filled with food. A bound Christmas tree leaned against her living room wall, and the two men were busy assembling a tree stand.

With everything else on her mind, she *had* forgotten about the Wish I May Foundation. Clearly its executive director, Laura, had delivered on her promise. Paige shook her head in amazement at all the boxes in her living room.

"Where would you like your tree?" the older man inquired.

A tree was something else Paige had planned to get that day. Dazed, she looked around the room and pointed to the corner behind the armchair. "Over there, please."

"Good choice. That way you can see it from your sofa and your dining room."

"Can I get you some coffee or juice?" Paige offered.

The older man glanced at his partner, who shook his head. "No, thanks. We're fine."

They spread out a large sheet to keep the pine needles from getting all over the floor and began unwrapping the tree and setting it up.

The tree was absolutely beautiful! It had to be at least seven feet tall. In the stand, it nearly reached the ceiling.

Finished with the tree, the men gathered up the twine, the packaging for the stand and their tools and moved to the door. "Have a merry Christmas," they said with cheerful smiles.

"Oh, wait. Just a minute, please." Paige rushed into the kitchen, returning a moment later, rummaging through her handbag. "Here." She pulled out a twenty-dollar bill and held it out to the older man. She couldn't really afford the tip, but they'd taken such care and effort setting up the tree, and it was a blessing to have received so much.

The older man raised both hands, palms out. "That's very kind, but no, thank you. It's been our pleasure." They both wished her a merry Christmas again as they left.

Paige turned and leaned against the closed

door. She steepled her fingers and held them in front of her mouth. Her gaze roamed from carton to box to cooler to the Christmas tree. "Oh, my goodness," she whispered.

Although she felt much better after the nap and the painkillers, she certainly didn't need to go shopping now. She checked her watch again. Another thirty minutes had passed. Jason usually didn't nap longer than two hours. She probably had about thirty minutes to get things organized. Her lips trembled as she smiled, and she gave silent thanks to Laura and the Wish I May Foundation.

Unsure of where to start, she looked in on Jason first. He slept peacefully, one arm around his beloved, slightly frayed teddy bear. Paige backed quietly out of his room to get to work. She could hardly wait to see his reaction when he woke up.

Paige put away the food from the cooler first, then unpacked the gifts. She was surprised to discover that, at the bottom of one of the cartons, there were a few presents with her name on the tags.

After the gifts were neatly stacked and the cartons collapsed and stored by the apartment door, she put away the nonperishable food. Just as she finished, Jason padded into the living room. He still wore his pajamas and clutched his teddy tightly to his chest. He looked around the room, his eyes wide. "Mom…?"

Paige held out her hand. When he put his small one in hers, she led him to the tree. "How about we make hot chocolate and decorate our tree?"

His eyes lit up at the mention of hot chocolate before his face turned serious again. "Mom, where did all this come from?"

As much as Paige tried to shelter her son, she knew he was astute enough to understand that they couldn't afford such luxuries. "Santa?" She tried for levity, knowing he hadn't believed in Santa for a couple of years.

"Mooom…"

She thought of Laura and improvised. "A wonderful angel."

The little boy in him prevailed, and a smile spread across his face.

For those precious hours—as they drank hot chocolate, decorated the tree and arranged the presents beneath it—Paige was able to forget about her son's illness and her financial woes. Jason's cheerful laughter, something she so seldom heard these days, warmed her right down to her toes.

At the end of the evening, they were curled up on the sofa together, sipping more hot chocolate and watching *A Charlie Brown*

Christmas—one of Jason's favorite holiday shows. When the closing credits rolled, it was well past his normal bedtime. Paige turned off the television and took their empty mugs into the kitchen. By the time she returned, Jason's head had drooped to the side, and he was sound asleep. The glow of the Christmas tree lights—the only illumination in the room—gave his face a rosy tint, masking the paleness of his complexion. In sleep, a smile tugged at the corners of his mouth; a bit of cocoa was smeared on his upper lip. Jason looked so healthy, happy and normal, Paige wanted that moment never to end. He stirred, seeming to grope for his teddy, before his hand fell limply onto his lap again.

Paige lowered herself beside him and watched him breathe. Such a simple thing, really, but to see him do it without strain was its own kind of miracle. She rested a hand on his narrow shoulders. When he stirred again and reached for her, she gathered him in her arms, then lifted him up and carried him into his bedroom.

CHAPTER SEVEN

"MOM? MOM!" JASON stroked Paige's face.

Despite their late night, Jason was up early on Christmas morning and clearly eager for Paige to wake up, too.

Paige yawned and stretched. She rolled over on her side and tucked one arm under her head. "Good morning, sweetie." He was already dressed in jeans and his favorite blue sweater.

"Mom! C'mon. It's Christmas!" He yanked at her other hand. "You *have* to get up. We have *presents* to open."

Paige stifled another yawn and smiled. "Yes. We do." She thought of the three beautifully wrapped packages with her name on the gift tags. They were entirely unexpected, as Laura hadn't said anything about gifts for her. She felt a thrill of anticipation. "Go get a glass of milk, and I'll be out soon."

By the time Paige entered the living room wearing jeans and a pale yellow shirt, Jason had settled by the tree. There were two glasses of milk on the coffee table, one nearly empty, the other full. She surmised that the full one was for her. How sweet of him.

Jason glanced up as she approached. Scooting around, he tucked his legs under him and sat back on his heels. "Can we open the presents now?"

Paige bent down beside him. "I don't see why not. But you have to give me a hug first."

"Yay!" he proclaimed as he threw himself in her arms and briefly buried his face in the crook of her neck.

She stroked his mop of hair as she stood up. "Decide which one you want to start with while I go get a garbage bag for the wrapping paper, okay?"

When she returned, Jason was bubbling with excitement. In no time at all, most of the presents were open and piled around them. Jason had gotten almost everything on his wish list: a sketch pad, winter clothes, a New England Patriots cap, a picture book about circuses, a stuffed dog and a backpack for school. The only thing missing was a toy train, but he didn't seem to mind. There were too many other exciting gifts he hadn't even asked for.

"Look, Mom!" Grinning, Jason showed her an electronic tablet. "And *this*!" He held up a kid-size Patriots jacket that came with the cap.

"I see, sweetie!" She playfully tugged the cap down over his eyes. "Santa's been good to you, huh?"

Santa had been good to her, too. The packages with her name on them had contained lovely things she would never have spent money on. She'd received a soft-as-a-cloud fleece bathrobe that would replace her well-worn terry-cloth one and would come in handy with the cool winter temperatures. She'd also received a beautiful lilac wool sweater. She assumed Laura must have thought of her and given their sponsor an accurate guess as to her size, since both the bathrobe and sweater were a perfect fit. The third package contained a fancy coffeemaker. She hadn't had one since she was married. She'd made do with instant. The coffee machine had come with an ample supply of coffees, teas and hot chocolate that would last a long time.

They'd each also received a few small gifts from Paige's parents.

Now there were only two packages left under the tree: Jason's gift for Paige, and hers for him. Paige had kept them back on purpose. "Why don't you open yours first?" she encouraged him.

She didn't have to ask him twice. Jason

pulled the rectangular box toward him and looked up at her. "It's heavy."

"Uh-huh." She knew he was trying to figure out what it was. This was the only gift she'd bought herself. She'd purchased it nearly a month ago, when she got a special customer service bonus from her employer. She had wanted Jason's present to be special, and she hoped he'd like it, especially after all the other gifts he'd received through the Foundation.

Jason was busy tearing the shiny wrapping paper. He ripped off a piece that revealed the writing on the carton. "Whooaa!" he exclaimed and quickly tore away the rest of the paper. He opened the cardboard container just as quickly and lifted out a wooden artist's box. Unlatching the top, he examined the paints and pencils and brushes, taking them out and replacing each with great care. Closing the lid, he threw his arms around Paige's neck.

"Thanks, Mom!" There was no doubt that this gift was from her.

Jason reached for the last gift and handed it to Paige. "Now you have to open mine."

"Okay." She started peeling the wrapping paper off very slowly. Jason squirmed impatiently. "C'mon, Mom!"

Under the wrapping paper, she found a tissue box. "You got me a box of Kleenex—just what I need at this time of year!" she teased.

"Mooom..." He was bouncing with excitement.

Paige loved that he was as excited to give gifts as he was to receive them. She pulled off the tape and a protective piece of cardboard. Inside the box was a lovely heart-shaped ceramic case. It had a pale-yellow background and was decorated with delicate flowers. She took it out carefully with both hands. "You made this for me?"

"Uh-huh. The art teacher let me go to a class with the older kids. We were doing pottery, and most of the kids made bowls or mugs and stuff, but I wanted to make you something special. I had to fire it—that's what they call it when you put the clay in this oven to bake on the colored glazes. I had to do it once for each color. I used yellow as the background, 'cause it's your favorite.

"Some kids had their stuff break when they fired them too much, but the teacher helped me, and mine didn't. I remembered how you used to collect shells and keep them in that box you had. This is so you can collect things again." Paige recalled the pretty jewelry box she'd had. She'd used it to store all the shells and other bits and pieces she'd collected over the years. She had no idea what had happened to the case, let alone its contents, but it was odd that Jason had remembered it.

Tears gathered in her eyes. "It's beautiful." She leaned forward and slipped her arms around Jason. "And very special. Thank you."

AFTER THEY'D PILED all the gifts under the tree, they started preparations for dinner. Paige was standing by the kitchen sink, peeling potatoes. Jason was kneeling on a chair by the counter, basting the huge turkey they'd received through the Wish I May Foundation.

"It's too bad Chelsea, Mrs. Bennett and the others aren't here," Jason remarked.

Paige glanced at her son. He had his head bent over the turkey, methodically brushing it with oil. "It's a little quiet this year, isn't it? But our friends have their own families to visit."

"Yeah." Jason dipped the brush into the small bowl of oil and continued basting. "I miss Grandma and Gramps, too."

Paige wiped her hands, moved to stand beside Jason. "That part we can fix. Why don't we call them once we've finished up in here?"

After Paige slid the roasting pan with the turkey into the oven, they called her mother and father using the speakerphone. They chatted at length with Charlotte and briefly with Stephen. Jason thanked them for the gifts they'd sent him, and Charlotte praised Jason profusely for the beautiful picture he'd painted for them of Iris sitting on the lawn in front of their house.

The turkey had been in the oven for hours, filling their apartment with its delicious aroma, by the time Paige and Jason were settled in the living room again. They'd made more hot chocolate and were playing one of Jason's new games when someone knocked on the door.

Thinking it might be one of her other neighbors, Paige was surprised to find a tall, attractive man at her door. He was easily over six feet, with an athletic build. He had well-cut, thick black hair, a strong face and friendly, vivid green eyes. He wore black slacks and a weathered black leather bomber jacket over a white shirt. He had a grin on his face and a large, cheerfully wrapped box in his arms.

Paige held the door ajar but blocked the opening with her body. The man didn't appear threatening, but she believed in being cautious, especially where Jason was concerned.

"Are you Ms. Summerville?"

"Yes, I am."

He braced the package against the doorframe and held out a hand. "I'm Daniel Kinsley."

Paige glanced at his hand but kept her own on the doorknob. The name meant nothing to her. She had no idea who this person was. Just because he was unreasonably attractive and well-dressed didn't mean he couldn't be a threat. She remembered hearing about a man who dressed up as Santa Claus with a bag of gifts to get into people's homes to rob them. "I'm sorry, but should I know you?"

"No, not directly. I'm your sponsor from the Wish I May Foundation." He continued to smile.

The warmth of his smile made it hard to imagine he could be dangerous, but...

"I asked Laura Andrews for your address," he explained. "So I could bring Jason a gift."

"Oh," was all Paige could manage, since this did nothing to dispel her unease. They'd already received the delivery, and she knew the Foundation protected the families' identities.

Peering into the living room and at a wide-eyed Jason, Daniel waved to him. "And that must be Jason!" He lowered his voice conspiratorially. "I'm sorry to show up unannounced on Christmas Day. I realize it's unusual, but these are special circumstances. This is his last Christmas gift. Jason wanted a train, and I ordered this for him." He nodded at the large package in his arms. "But it didn't arrive until this morning, too late to deliver it with the rest of the gifts. I wanted to make sure Jason got it."

Paige studied the box. "That's much too big for a toy train."

Daniel laughed. "It's a train, all right. It just happens to be a complete, deluxe electric train set," he whispered.

"Oh, Mr. Kinsley—"

"Daniel. Please."

"Okay, Daniel. You didn't have to do this." Paige's unease was subsiding. There was a genuinely disarming quality about the man. Then she felt her eyes go as wide as Jason's. Her embarrassment at having to accept charity from a stranger warred with her gratitude for all he'd done for them—essentially giving them Christmas. Flustered and a little uncertain, she motioned behind her with her arm. "You mean *you* are responsible for *all* of this?"

He laughed again. "Guilty as charged." Sobering, he added, "How could I not do it after learning about Jason?"

His laughter and obvious sincerity further lessened her discomfort. Their eyes held for a long moment. Something warm, something elemental—a shared understanding, perhaps—passed between them.

With her eyes still on his, Paige broke the silence. "Mr. Kinsley—Daniel," she corrected herself before he could. "I don't know how to thank you. Come in, please."

As Daniel stepped inside, Jason dashed over. "What's that?"

"Jason! This is Mr. Kinsley."

"Sorry, Mom. Hello, Mr. Kinsley. Um, what's that?" he asked again.

"It's a gift for you." Daniel glanced at Paige. "Where should I put it?"

Paige looked around the living room. "How about here?" she suggested, leading him to the coffee table. When the oven timer dinged, she excused herself.

She opened the oven door and checked the turkey, which was coming along nicely. She realized that it, too, was courtesy of their Wish I May Foundation sponsor. The person who was currently in their living room. The person who'd already been so generous to them and had come to deliver another gift. It was hard to believe. She tried again to push aside her reservations about receiving charity.

Not wanting to leave Jason with a stranger for long, regardless of how trustworthy he seemed, Paige rushed back to the living room.

Colorful wrapping paper was scattered everywhere. The large box was open and stood next to the coffee table. Daniel's jacket was slung over the back of the sofa. His sleeves were rolled up, and he was removing pieces of the set.

Jason beckoned to her. "Look, Mom! Look at *all* these pieces!"

She joined them. "I see."

"Mr. Kinsley is helping me. Is that okay?"

Paige's eyes met Daniel's. She'd never seen eyes that shade of green, and they shone with pleasure. "Sure. We shouldn't keep him too long, though. I'm certain Mr. Kinsley has plans."

"I've got time, if you don't mind me helping Jason put the train set together."

Paige hesitated. "All right. I'll just finish getting dinner ready." Still cautious of a stranger with her son, she turned back to Jason as she was about to enter the kitchen. "Call if you need anything."

Paige prepared the vegetables, got the makings for the salad ready and continued to marvel at Daniel Kinsley. She hadn't known his name until he introduced himself. All she'd known from her discussions with Laura Andrews was that Jason's sponsor was a lawyer with an important firm in Hartford, Connecticut. This had to be highly unusual, a sponsor delivering gifts personally, but Paige was sure Laura wouldn't have given him her address if she didn't trust Daniel.

Paige scooped the cranberry sauce into a small serving dish. She'd made all the dinner preparations she could for the time being. She put the oven mitts back in the drawer next to the stove and stepped through the kitchen doorway into the living room.

Kelly Clarkson's melodic voice singing "Silent Night" flowed through the room. All the wrapping paper and packaging from the train set had been cleared up and stuffed inside the box, which stood next to all the other collapsed cartons beside the apartment door. Jason and Daniel were sitting side by side at the coffee table with their backs to her. The top was covered with the discarded cardboard from one of the cartons, and the train set components sat on the cardboard. Daniel and Jason's heads were bent together as they worked on assembling the pieces.

Jason suddenly gestured wildly with his arms, and they both laughed. Their laughter was infectious, and Paige couldn't help grinning.

They seemed to be having a wonderful time putting the set together, so immersed in the task that they were oblivious to all else. To see her little boy so animated, so joyful, meant the world to her.

Paige leaned against the doorjamb and folded her arms.

Working as a team, Jason and Daniel tested the fit of a car on the track before starting to assemble the next one. Daniel sent one car rolling down the track, then turned and said something to Jason. Jason grinned and nodded energetically. As if he sensed her watching him, Daniel twisted his head further toward Paige, a smile on his face.

Above Jason's head, their eyes met. Paige felt that odd little connection again, the way she had when she'd first opened the door to him. There was so much warmth and kindness in his eyes.

Wistfully, Paige wondered what Christmas would've been like if Jason had a father who was still part of his life. Part of *their* lives. Someone they could share Christmas with. Instead, here was Daniel Kinsley, a big-shot lawyer, helping a very excited Jason assemble his train set.

Paige's smile wavered. In response, Daniel gave her a questioning look. She thought he might have been about to speak, but Jason hooted gleefully and nudged him. "Look, Mr. Kinsley, it worked! Just like you said!"

In the face of Jason's obvious delight, Paige's momentary sadness—or perhaps longing—was gone. After a final, probing glance, Daniel turned back to Jason.

Paige wiped her suddenly damp palms on her jeans and strolled over to where they worked. "Would you railway engineers like something to drink?"

"Apple juice," Jason responded. At her pointed glare, he quickly added, "Please. See, Mom?" He gave a car on the track a slight push and sent it gliding smoothly around. "That's the engine car. The pieces are so well-balanced, and the track's so smooth, it goes all that way on its own. Mr. Kinsley says that's iner…inertia. When something that's moving wants to keep moving." He glanced at Daniel for affirmation.

"Correct, my little conductor." Daniel said and ruffled his hair.

Jason beamed. He picked up the car and held it out for his mother to examine. "And see, this here?" He indicated the pointed front of the piece. "It's called a cow catcher." When she raised an eyebrow, Jason giggled and went on. "Don't worry, Mom. It doesn't really *catch* cows. It's just a name for it. It pushes stuff from the track that might cause the train to go off the rails. I bet Mr. Kinsley knows why it's called that!"

They both looked at Daniel. He shrugged. "It's because in the early days of the railroads, there were cows wandering across the tracks." When Jason returned his attention to the train set, Daniel held Paige's gaze. "What can I say? I know all sorts of useless things. Sometimes it actually comes in handy."

"I can see that. Can I get you anything to drink? A coffee, maybe?" She hesitated. "I'm afraid I don't have any wine."

Daniel glanced up. "No problem. I'll have what the kid's having."

"Okay." She turned and went to the kitchen. Moments later she was back with two tumblers of apple juice, which she placed on coasters on the small end table. "Dinner's nearly ready. Jason, when you're finished, can you set the table, please?"

Jason scrambled to his feet. "Sure. We're done." Grinning at Daniel, he asked, "Can we start it?"

Daniel nodded. "You're the conductor. Start it whenever you're ready."

"All right. Watch, Mom!" Jason threw the switch. He did a triumphant little dance—like a football player after a touchdown—as the train chugged around the track. All three of them cheered and clapped. Jason's face was flushed, and there was a sparkle in his eyes. "Isn't it great, Mom?"

"It's wonderful, sweetie." She bent to give him a hug, then a gentle swat on his behind. "Now the table, please."

Daniel rose, too. To Paige's surprise, Jason threw both arms around him. "Thanks. Thanks so much!"

Paige was grateful to Daniel not only for his generosity with the gifts but also for helping Jason with the train set. Mixed with her gratitude was guilt that they'd kept him from his own Christmas celebrations for so long. Although she was positive he'd be anxious to leave, it was nearly dinnertime. Since he *had* supplied all the food, in addition to everything else, the least she could do was ask him if he'd like to join them for dinner.

"I'd love to stay, if it's not an intrusion," he responded to Paige's utter shock. He went on to explain that his parents were in Newport, and he had no plans of his own.

It hadn't occurred to Paige that he would actually accept her invitation. She'd been certain that Daniel would be celebrating Christmas with family and friends, perhaps a girlfriend. Even more unexpectedly, she felt a surge of happiness that he'd be staying with them a while longer. He seemed like such a kind man, and he was a natural with Jason. She couldn't remember a time she'd seen her son happier.

"Paige?"

She'd been so deep in thought that she'd missed what Daniel had said. Disconcerted, she fixed a smile on her face. "I'm sorry, I didn't hear that."

"I said, if you're going to feed me, I should help set the table."

"Oh, that would be nice. Thanks."

Jason looked up at his mother. "Mom, before we do, can I show Mr. Kinsley some of my paintings?"

Paige nodded. "Of course, if he's interested. We still have some time." And it would give her a chance to let the peculiar flutter in her stomach settle.

Jason reached for Daniel's hand and tugged with excitement. "Come and see!"

Daniel glanced over his shoulder at Paige as Jason pulled him toward his room. Paige returned his smile with an unsteady one of her own before they disappeared into Jason's bedroom.

JASON'S SMALL HAND in Daniel's, holding tightly, gave him a warm feeling and an uncharacteristic sense of yearning. For what exactly, he wasn't sure.

He didn't spend a lot of time with kids. His main exposure was through the kids' softball team he coached. Even that he'd been coerced into by the partners in his law firm. The son of one of his partners played on the team, the firm was the official team sponsor, and his partners knew about his affinity for baseball. They'd cajoled and pushed and prodded until he'd finally agreed to be an assistant coach. Once he got involved, he discovered that he enjoyed it and that he *liked* kids.

Even so, he couldn't remember ever holding a child's hand before.

His palm felt cold, decidedly empty, when Jason withdrew his hand.

"Look!" Jason pointed to the paintings affixed to the corkboard over his desk.

"You did those?"

"Yeah!"

Daniel stuck his hands in his pockets and bent forward. He examined each painting carefully. He focused on one in particular, with an orange-and-black tiger nearly filling the page. The tiger's long tail was curled, his face turned toward the viewer, mouth open in a snarl. He seemed ready to pounce. Vertical black lines represented the bars of a cage.

The overall impression was of a tiger caged but not conquered. As Daniel moved his head sideways, the tiger's eyes seemed to follow his. "This one." Daniel pointed to the painting. "The tiger looks ready to spring, not quite accepting that he's captive."

Jason nodded, his face flushed. "Yes! Yes, that's exactly what I wanted to show."

Daniel gestured to another picture. "And this one. It looks like the acrobat *is* swinging from the trapeze." The corded muscles, the extended neck, the apparent sway of the body with the rope. Jason had talent, remarkable talent for a kid of his age. He knew how to capture details and movement. "These are great!"

Jason's face turned a bright shade of pink. "Thanks. I like to paint."

A number of the paintings were circus-themed, and Daniel remembered wondering when he'd read Jason's Christmas wish list how he'd developed a fascination with circuses. "Have you ever been to a circus?" he asked.

Jason shuffled his feet. "Nah. I've wanted to go since I was little, but Mom says they aren't around anymore."

"So, where did you get the ideas for the paintings?"

"I had a toy circus when I was a kid. I still

have some of the pieces. And I got books from the library." In a more subdued tone, he added, "Except the tiger. I saw him at the zoo."

"Your paintings are very good," Daniel repeated. "I do like the tiger the most."

"Would you like to have one?" Jason asked.

"You worked very hard on these. Are you sure you want to give one away?"

"Yeah. Like a Christmas present. You got us a whole bunch of stuff, but we didn't get you anything. So I can give you a painting. I painted pictures for our neighbors, too, for Christmas. And for Grandma and Gramps."

"Okay. Which one would you like to give me?"

Jason's brows drew together, and he pulled at his upper lip as he contemplated his paintings. His face was very serious when he looked up at Daniel. "The tiger. You said you liked it best."

"Yes, I do."

Jason scrambled up on his chair and carefully unpinned the painting. He climbed down and rummaged through a desk drawer, taking out a large envelope. Then he slid the painting into the envelope and handed it to Daniel.

"I really appreciate this, Jason. Thank you. It's the best gift I've received this year."

Jason's cheeks darkened from pink to red, and his chest swelled as they left his room.

When they rejoined Paige, she looked at her son, then at the envelope in Daniel's hand. "What's that?"

"It's one of my paintings," Jason said. "I gave it to Mr. Kinsley. As a Christmas present."

Paige's gaze moved from her son to Daniel and back. "That's nice of you."

"Jason is very talented. I'm honored that he'd give me one of his paintings. They're all excellent, but I did favor this one."

Paige smiled at Jason. "Which one did you give Mr. Kinsley?"

Jason stared down at his socks and scuffed his toes on the carpet. "The one he liked best," he said evasively.

"It's the painting of the tiger," Daniel supplied.

"Oh." Paige's smile faltered. She turned questioning eyes on her son.

Jason was still preoccupied with his socks. Daniel noted the expression on Paige's face. It showed surprise and something more. He surmised there was a greater significance to the gift than he'd presumed, and he hoped he hadn't done anything to create friction, however slight.

"Mr. Kinsley said he liked the tiger best." Jason shifted his feet. "I *want* him to have it. Okay?"

Mother and child exchanged a look that Daniel couldn't interpret. "Of course." Paige opened her arms, and Jason stepped into the quick embrace. There was no mistaking the affection they shared.

Daniel was glad that whatever had caused concern for Paige had passed. "Thanks again." He ruffled Jason's hair, which had the little boy grinning up at him so naturally and openly, it seemed to surprise his mother. Daniel dropped his hand lightly onto Jason's shoulder. "How about we set the table now?"

THEY SAT DOWN to dinner not long after, and the conversation flowed comfortably, mostly about Jason, his school and his art.

As they were finishing dessert, Jason could barely keep his eyes open. Paige had begun brewing coffee in her new machine, but she asked Daniel if he wouldn't mind waiting for the coffee so she could help Jason get ready for bed.

When Paige returned, the dining table had been cleared, and Daniel was in the kitchen, dirty dishes stacked on one side of the sink and his hands in soapy water.

"Oh, my gosh!" Paige rushed over. "You shouldn't be doing that."

She reached for the dishcloth, but he easily resisted her effort to grab it. "You made dinner and were kind enough to ask me to join you and Jason. The least I can do is clean up."

Flustered and embarrassed by having a near-stranger and a guest washing dishes, Paige held out her hand for the dishcloth. "I appreciate it, but I can finish."

Daniel kept washing the dishes. "Why don't you make the coffee? When you're done, you can help me dry."

Speechless, she did as he suggested, giving Daniel the Christmas mug Chelsea had presented her with last year.

They'd nearly finished their first mug of coffee by the time the dishes were washed, dried and put away. She topped off both their mugs, and they carried them into the living room.

Paige sank onto the sofa, dropped her head back and let out a long sigh. Remembering she wasn't alone, she abruptly sat up. "I'm so sorry..."

Amusement and understanding danced in Daniel's eyes. "Don't be. You've had a long, eventful day, following what I'm sure have been quite a few trying—and tiring—days."

He started to rise with his mug in hand. "I should go and let you get some sleep."

Paige lightly touched his forearm. "No. Please stay. Finish your coffee."

Daniel watched her for a moment, as if having a silent debate with himself, then nodded and sat back down. He took a sip from his mug. "Thank you again for a wonderful dinner."

"I'm glad you could be here. It meant a lot to Jason." She smiled down at the train set on the coffee table. "I don't think we could've figured out how to put it all together, or not in the time it took the two of you." She set her mug aside, linked her fingers and looked down at her hands. "Thank you for all the gifts. The ones for me were totally unexpected, unnecessary, but very much appreciated. I frankly don't know what I would've done without your generosity."

Daniel began to protest, but Paige shook her head.

"I don't have the words to adequately thank you for what you've given Jason, and I don't just mean in a material sense." She raised her eyes to his. "You've made him very happy and taken his mind off…everything, other than the sheer joy of Christmas. He doesn't have too many opportunities to be a carefree little kid.

Today, he was nothing but. I'm more grateful than you can imagine."

DANIEL GLANCED AROUND the room at the many caring touches everywhere—small scented candles burning, the warm, fluffy throw draped over the back of the sofa, the framed photos of family on tables and walls. Through the opening to the kitchen, he could see some of Jason's drawings attached to the front of the refrigerator with animal-shaped magnets. It all showed love and devotion, something that had been lacking in his own childhood.

Daniel placed his mug next to Paige's and laid his hand on top of hers. "It meant a lot to me, too. Thank you for sharing your day with me." He chuckled. "I've never enjoyed Christmas much, but today, you and Jason brought new meaning to it for me."

With a small laugh of her own, Paige drew back her hand and picked up her mug. "Listen to us! I'll be in tears in a minute if we don't change the subject, and that would just embarrass both of us."

He thought otherwise, but he didn't want to cause her any distress and changed the subject, as she'd suggested.

"I noticed how many of Jason's paintings had to do with circus acts. I used to love circuses as a kid, but they aren't popular anymore. How did Jason become so fascinated by them?"

"Oh, he's always liked animals, but mostly it has to do with a circus set that he had as a toddler."

"He mentioned that. Interesting he'd remember that far back."

"I remember it, too. It was a Fisher-Price play set." Paige hesitated and wrapped both hands around her mug. "It has particular significance for Jason because it was the last thing his father gave him."

"Oh, well… Please thank Jason again for the painting."

Paige looked away briefly. "He…he really wanted you to have it."

Daniel raised his eyebrows. He *had* caused her discomfort, unintentional though it was, but he didn't understand why. "Is there something I should know about the painting?"

Paige fidgeted with the handle of her mug. With her thumbnail, she scraped at a nonexistent flaw on the handle. "I thought he'd painted it for someone else."

Daniel reached for the envelope on the sofa next to him and held it out to Paige. "If it's a problem, I won't take it."

"No, it's not a problem," she was quick to reassure him.

When Daniel still seemed uncertain, she pushed the envelope toward him. "Please, keep it. Just know it means a lot that he wanted you to have it."

IT WAS PAST midnight when Paige tried unsuccessfully to stifle a yawn. Checking her watch, she was surprised at how quickly the night had passed.

"This time I really will go and let you get to bed."

Paige rose and gathered up the mugs. Daniel rose, too. "Let me help you with that."

She smiled warmly at him. "Please let's not go through that again."

She took the mugs into the kitchen and walked Daniel to her apartment door. She retrieved his jacket from the hall closet and handed it to him.

He shrugged into it. "Thanks again for dinner."

She shook her head and smiled. "Oh, no. I should be thanking you." She swept an arm around the cheery room, the Christmas tree lights still glowing and candlelight flickering. "For everything."

"It was my pleasure. Really. Jason's a great kid. You've done well with him."

The simple words of praise meant more to her than he could imagine. "Thank you," she whispered.

Their eyes held, and they stood in silence for a long moment. Eventually, Daniel stepped forward and rested a hand on Paige's shoulder.

She felt that odd flutter in her stomach again. She wanted to look away, but she was mesmerized by his deep green eyes.

"I enjoyed myself very much. Thanks for sharing Christmas with me." Daniel took another step closer, hesitated. He squeezed her shoulder lightly, then stepped back and grasped the doorknob. "I wish you and Jason the very best. You both deserve it."

Before Paige could say anything else, he'd walked out of her apartment and closed the door behind him.

CHAPTER EIGHT

DANIEL WHISTLED AS he used his key card to open the door to the law offices of Lindstrom, Kinsley and McGuire.

He paused as he pushed through the large mahogany door. Whistling? Him? Really?

He couldn't remember having whistled in his life. Well, to call his dog when he was a kid, or to get someone's attention, yes. But whistling to *himself*? Never before. "Hmm. Odd," he murmured.

He made sure the door closed and latched behind him. The day after Christmas wasn't a statutory holiday in the state of Connecticut, but like many other employers in Hartford, he and his partners offered it as a paid holiday to their staff. For Daniel, it was just another work day. Christmas had never been a happy time for him, and he'd always preferred to have it over and done with and get back to work. He knew he was the exception, and he'd be the only one in the office today.

But why had he been whistling?

He gave it some thought. It was simple. He was in a good mood! The hours he'd spent with Paige and Jason the day before were the most enjoyable he could remember in years.

He stopped abruptly and stared down at his feet. Had he been almost *skipping* to his office? He looked around quickly to be absolutely certain there was no one watching. Well, he wasn't *skipping*, but he'd definitely had a spring in his step.

He unlocked his office door, placed his briefcase on his desk, hung up his coat and headed to the kitchen to make a pot of coffee. As the coffee brewed, he rummaged through the cupboards, searching for something to snack on. He hadn't bothered with breakfast that morning.

It was his lucky day. A box of raspberry-flavored breakfast bars was hiding behind the boxes of single-serving sugar and non-perishable creamers. He grabbed two and slid them into his shirt pocket. Leaning against the counter, he folded his arms and thought about the night before.

Paige was beautiful. No question about that. With her flaxen hair—long, straight and glossy. It surprised him how much he'd wanted to run his fingers through it to see if it felt as smooth and silky as it looked. And her eyes.

Big and blue, heavily fringed by long lashes, and so gentle and expressive. He couldn't remember the last time he'd seen a woman without a touch of makeup, and yet her lashes, mascara-free, seemed longer and thicker than they had any right to be. And those lips. They weren't pouty, what he thought of as Angelina Jolie lips, but they were so appealing, especially with those little smile lines at the corners. And when she smiled? Her straight, white teeth lit up her entire face. She just didn't smile enough.

His bright mood darkened slightly—understandable under the circumstances.

At some point during the evening, after Jason had gone to bed and they'd been sitting on the sofa, talking, he'd started to focus on her lips. As he was saying good-bye, he'd wanted nothing more than to kiss her. To brush his lips lightly across hers to see what she tasted like. He'd considered it, seriously, as he was leaving.

But he hadn't done it. Resisting the urge had taken everything in him, but a kiss wouldn't have been smart…or fair. She was brave, extremely courageous, in fact, and had so much to deal with. What would it have accomplished to give her a good-night kiss?

Okay, it would've satisfied his curiosity,

but then what? He would've been taking advantage of the situation. He was just there to drop off a Christmas gift, and she'd been kind enough to ask him to stay for dinner at a time that should have been reserved for family. Especially if... No, he wouldn't even consider the possibility that this could be Jason's last Christmas.

She'd asked him and he'd stayed. And he'd had a great time. The kid was impressive— funny and bright. Daniel shook his head. He'd never see the kid, or his mother, again. Daniel happened to be a sponsor for Jason this year. That was the extent of it. He was not relationship material, and he was absolutely certain that Paige wouldn't be interested in casual dating. When the coffee machine beeped, he poured himself a cup and returned to his office.

Settling behind his desk, he took a sip of the hot, strong coffee. He should really do something to show his appreciation for Paige's hospitality. It was the polite thing to do. Leaning forward, he set his cup on the coaster next to his computer and did a web search. He had no trouble finding the florist Selena, his executive assistant, used whenever they needed to send flowers or a gift basket. With a name like Flowerfully Yours, how could he forget? And they had an online order form. Convenient.

He scrolled through the many flower arrangements. Wanting to keep it friendly, he decided on an arrangement called "Garden Delight," consisting of a variety of colorful flowers. A little bland, but he wasn't going to the "Romance" collection. He didn't want to give Paige the wrong impression. It was a simple thank-you gesture. That was all. With Jason in mind, he added an optional stuffed bear.

Then he contemplated what to put on the enclosed card. He tried several different messages, but none sounded right. Finally, he came up with, "Thank you for letting me share Christmas with you and Jason." When he was halfway through inputting his personal and credit card information, he abruptly exited the form and went back to the previous screens. He made some quick adjustments, adding a dozen yellow roses and modifying the message, moved forward to the payment screen, then completed and submitted it before he had a chance to rethink it again. He closed his browser, took a large gulp of coffee and got to work.

PAIGE DIDN'T WORK the day after Christmas because no one was available to take care of Jason. The following morning, they took the bus to the hospital for his treatment and, since he was feeling well afterward, Mrs. Bennett offered to take him to the afternoon matinee at the local theater so Paige could work half a day.

Paige and Jason arrived home at nearly the same time. Paige had made what she called a turkey roll for dinner—basically leftover turkey, stuffing and cranberry sauce, rolled into a piece of flaky dough. She sliced the top of the dough and crisscrossed the strips before putting the whole thing into the oven to bake. While they ate dinner, Jason told her excitedly about the movie he and Mrs. Bennett had seen.

As much as she enjoyed this precious time with her son, her gaze kept drifting to the empty chair at the other end of the table, the chair Daniel had occupied during Christmas dinner. It had been so nice to have him join them—to have some adult conversation at the dinner table and later in the evening. She immediately felt ashamed at the thought. She would give up anything and everything to be able to spend all her dinnertimes with Jason.

As if Jason could read her mind, he stopped his recounting of the movie and asked, "Will Mr. Kinsley have dinner with us again?"

Paige's jaw nearly dropped. *Out of the mouths of babes...* She took a long drink of water to moisten her suddenly dry throat. "I don't think so."

Jason looked crestfallen. "Why not? Didn't he have fun?"

Why not, indeed? "I'm sure he did, but he's a very busy man. And he lives in Connecticut."

"That's not far," Jason rationalized.

"I know, but he was really just here to drop off your train set."

"Can't you invite him back? Didn't you like him?"

She wasn't sure what to say. Unfortunately, yes, she did like him, but she also knew his visit was merely a pleasant memory to file away, and they'd never see him again. Daniel had certainly made an impact on Jason.

She was saved from answering his question by a knock on the door.

"I've finished my dinner, Mom. I'll get it!" Jason was up and racing to the door. She was glad he was doing so well—and made a mental note to record it in his journal—but she worried that his enthusiasm to answer the door was driven by an irrational hope that it would be Daniel. She realized she'd also felt a similar surge of hope. Ridiculous. Daniel stopping by unannounced, as he had on Christmas day, was a one-time occurrence.

She heard Jason's voice behind her. "Hi, Chelsea."

Paige glanced over her shoulder. Seeing her friend with her arms full of flowers, she got up, too.

"Hey, Paige. Can you take these from me, please?" Chelsea held out the large vase, and Paige reached for it.

"I thought you were supposed to be away until after New Year's Eve?" Paige asked.

"Yeah, well, plans change. It was great seeing Mom and Dad, but Joel and I decided we wanted some time on our own." Chelsea winked at Paige.

Jason pointed to the flowers. "Who're they for?"

"For your mom, Squirt."

"They are? Why?" He glanced at his mother, brows raised. "It's not your birthday or anything." He looked back at Chelsea.

Chelsea threw up her hands and laughed. "Don't ask me! I didn't open the card." Her eyes met Paige's, and there was an impish gleam in them. "I considered it. But I didn't."

"Oh," was all Paige could say.

"I was on my way in when the delivery guy was at your door. Since you weren't home, he asked if I knew you and if I could accept the delivery."

Jason danced around Paige. "Come on, Mom. Open the card!"

Jason's train set still occupied their coffee table, so Paige put the arrangement on the dining room table.

"Interesting that it has those long-stemmed yellow roses in there with all the other colors and greenery," Chelsea observed while Paige loosened the cellophane wrapping and pulled out the card on its plastic spike. She noted that there was another spike stuck in the arrangement with a little brown bear laced to it with raffia. She held the card with one hand, removed the bear with the other and handed it to Jason. "I think this must be for you."

"Thanks!" Jason exclaimed as he unwound the raffia to release the bear.

Chelsea stood on her tiptoe and tried to peek over Paige's shoulder. "Sooooo, open the card and tell us who it's from."

The envelope had her name and address neatly printed on the front. She slipped out the card and turned it over.

Jason tugged at her sleeve. "Who sent it, Mom?"

She reread the card, looked at Chelsea, who was watching her expectantly, then glanced at her son. "It's from Daniel."

"*Yesss!* What does the card say, Mom?"

"It says he enjoyed dinner with us, and he thanks us for inviting him."

"I bet we'll see Mr. Kinsley again!" he said, apparently satisfied. "Can I go to my room and play the SpongeBob game he gave me?"

"Sure, sweetie."

When they were alone, Chelsea wiggled her eyebrows. "Do tell! You've been holding back on me, Paige."

"You might as well make yourself comfortable and have a coffee. It's a long story."

"I'm all ears," Chelsea assured her as she followed Paige into the kitchen. "Hey, that coffee maker's new!" She ran a fingertip along the brushed metal surface of the unit. "Fancy. Where'd you get it?"

"Like I said, a long story. Why don't you go into the living room, and I'll join you in a minute."

As they enjoyed the excellent coffee, Paige related the story of Christmas Day and Daniel. Chelsea had a wide grin on her face. "Mr. Tall, Dark and Wonderful, huh?"

"I didn't say that!"

"No, you didn't. I paraphrased. Am I right or wrong?"

Paige still felt decidedly uncomfortable. "You're not wrong."

"Then I'm right. What else did the card say?"

"What makes you think it said anything else?"

"A guy doesn't send a lady roses just to thank her for dinner." She gave Paige a friendly poke on the shoulder. "And the look on your face when you were reading the card."

"Chels, yellow roses signify friendship. Nothing more."

"And the card?" Chelsea persisted.

Paige lifted the card from the table and read it again. "He wants to know if I'll have dinner with him. He's included his home and office numbers."

Chelsea did an energetic fist pump. "Whoo-hoo! I knew it!"

Paige glanced toward Jason's room. "Shh. Keep it down."

"Why? From what I saw, Jason really likes the guy."

"Yes, he does. That's why I don't want him to get excited about this."

"Why?" Chelsea repeated. "He'll find out sooner or later."

"*If* I go."

Chelsea stared at her. "*If?* You're kidding, right?"

Paige shook her head. When Chelsea only gaped at her, Paige added, "I'll think about it."

"Wait! You get an invitation to dinner from a rich, good-looking guy who's great to you and terrific with Jason, and you're going to *think* about it? When's the last time you went on a date?"

Paige had gone out briefly with an ex-colleague about a year after Jason's father had left them. Their short-lived relationship had been a disaster. Although he'd initially been friendly toward Jason, he'd ended up resenting the demands Jason made on her private time. Jason was devastated when it ended. She hadn't gone on a date since. She did a quick calculation. "Over three years ago."

"Seriously? Sorry, I didn't mean that to sound the way it did. But *seriously*? You're a beautiful, young, single woman. I can understand why you're not interested now, with Jason sick again, but what stopped you before?"

Paige shrugged. "Jason, especially now." She paused. "The one time I dated after Mark and I split was a catastrophe. He was a co-worker at the financial services firm when I was the office manager there, so Jason and I had known him before I started dating him. Jason liked him, and he grew attached to him.

When it didn't work out, and with Jason's father leaving us still fresh in his memory, he took it very hard."

"Aw. That must've been a bummer. But it's been ages. From what you said, Daniel strikes me as a responsible person, and Jason is older now. Why don't you give it a shot with Daniel?" Her voice dropped. "Paige, you're an incredible mom, but you deserve a life, too."

Paige reached for her coffee mug and toyed with the handle. The image of Jason and Daniel, heads bent together, assembling the train set, came to mind. She gave the locomotive sitting on the track a little push. She couldn't ignore the fact that Daniel's generosity had made it possible for Jason to have a special Christmas.

"Why are you hesitating?" Chelsea prompted her.

"I don't know. I worry about Jason. I worry about him becoming attached to another man and that man leaving us." She sighed. "I seem to worry about everything these days."

Chelsea patted Paige's knee. "Wouldn't it be nice to share that worry with someone else now and then?"

Paige laughed. "Yeah. Yeah, it would."

Chelsea took another sip of coffee. "Have

dinner with the guy. What have you got to lose?"

Her heart. "I'll think about it."

PAIGE DID THINK about it. All night. Finally, she'd run out of excuses. The more she thought about it, the more she wanted to see Daniel again. She'd have to accept that they'd only be friends. That seemed to be the way he wanted it, if the yellow roses were any indication, and she had Jason to consider. If they were friends, their relationship didn't have to end.

The next morning, she pulled the card out of her wallet and dialed the number on it. A very businesslike female voice answered. "Mr. Kinsley's office. May I help you?"

"Um, yes. I'd like to speak to Mr. Kinsley?"

"May I ask who's calling, please?" She gave the assistant her name.

"I'll see if he's available. Just a minute, please." There was a click, and Paige found herself listening to elevator music. It didn't last long.

"Paige?" Daniel sounded happy, surprised but happy. "I'm glad you called. How's Jason?"

That he asked about Jason first scored major points with her, and she felt that flutter in her stomach again. "He's fine. Thanks. His treatment went well."

"I'm glad," he said again. "Since you called, does that mean you'll have dinner with me? We could make it a threesome. Or, if you prefer, we could take Jason to a movie."

The flutter intensified. "You're giving me a lot of options." His offer to spend time with Jason truly touched her heart but confirmed her assumption that he just wanted to be friends. Yet it was her excitement over having dinner with him that had motivated her to finally make the call. If she said she wanted to see him alone, would he think she was a bad mother? She didn't know what to say.

"Why don't we do this? Let's have dinner tonight, just the two of us. If all goes well, we'll plan an outing with Jason. How does that sound?"

He'd solved her dilemma, and in a considerate way. "I'd like that."

CHAPTER NINE

PAIGE HELD AN unsteady hand to her tummy. It felt as if there were a thousand butterflies flitting around inside. She was thankful that Chelsea had insisted on helping her get ready for her dinner date with Daniel. Chelsea had also offered to lend her a dress, which Paige greatly appreciated, as her own wardrobe was limited.

A sharp, keening sound distracted Paige. She glanced at the window behind her. Even though it was shut tight, she could hear the howling of the wind.

Why did there have to be a winter storm, of all things, on the night of her date with Daniel?

"Paige, are you listening to me?"

"Sorry. What?"

Chelsea held up a bright red dress on a hanger and wiggled it. "What about this one?"

It was a great dress and it suited Chelsea to perfection, but it was a little too loud for Paige's taste. "It's nice, Chels, but I don't think so."

Chelsea continued to hold the dress in front

of her and turned around to look at herself in the full-length mirror on the back of the closet door. She poked at her hair with her free hand. "This is what I'll wear next time Joel takes me out. Which reminds me... Never mind. We can talk about my love life later. Tonight is about you." She tossed the dress on the bed and selected another. "Here." She held it out to Paige. "I think this is it. You *have* to try this on."

The dress was a deep ultramarine-blue jersey. Paige liked that it was cut in a simple style with a rounded neckline and long, straight sleeves. There was nothing fussy or over-the-top about it. Chelsea might have been right on this one. She hoped so. Checking her bedside clock, Paige saw that that she was running out of time. Daniel was picking her up in less than an hour.

She accepted the dress from Chelsea and took it into the bathroom to try it on. She emerged a couple of minutes later, tugging at the hemline.

"That's it! That's what you're wearing." Chelsea turned Paige toward the mirror. Stretching up on tiptoe, she rested her chin on Paige's shoulder and peered into the mirror with her.

Paige examined herself critically. The dress

fit her well. She was slimmer than Chelsea and—since Chelsea preferred her clothes to be a bit tight—the dress flowed smoothly over her torso and hips and flared into a flirty A-line at the bottom. She reached for the hem again and gave it another tug. "It's nice, but it's too short." She might have been slimmer than Chelsea, but she was also a good three inches taller.

Chelsea swatted Paige's hand away and adjusted the hemline herself. "That's crazy. Look at *those* legs! If I had your legs, I promise I'd be wearing dresses a *lot* shorter than this."

Paige glanced at the mirror. Mark had always said she had nice legs, although why she'd think of him now was beyond her. She turned to the side and craned her neck to see. The skirt really wasn't *that* short. The issue was just her own comfort and modesty.

"Wait. Wait!" Chelsea squealed. She dashed out of the bedroom. A few seconds later, Paige heard her apartment door open and close. She went into her bathroom and played with her hair, trying to decide how she should wear it. She had it half pinned up when Chelsea rushed back in.

"Here." She held out a pair of mile-high black stilettos. "You have to try these."

Paige eyed the shoes warily. It'd been a long

time since she'd worn high heels. She was five-eight, while Mark was around five-eleven, so even when she had worn heels, they'd tended to be on the low end. She had to admit that these looked sexy. "They're going to be too big," she said. Chelsea's shoes were a full size larger than Paige's.

"No problem. We'll stuff some tissue in the toe. It's better than being too small. Here." She pushed the shoes toward Paige.

Paige slipped them on and turned back to the mirror. She giggled nervously. "Wow!"

"Wow is right!" Chelsea pretended to pout. "It's *my* dress. *My* shoes. And they've never made me look so drop-dead gorgeous."

Paige felt a silly grin spread across her face. "Not bad, huh?" Another whistle rattled the bedroom window, and her smile dimmed. "There's a storm out there. I can't wear these shoes." Paige knew she sounded embarrassed as she asked, "Chels? You wouldn't happen to have a pair of dress boots, would you? I only have my everyday, practical ones."

Chelsea considered for a few seconds. "I think I have a pair that would work. Let me get them."

Chelsea brought the boots, and when Paige tried them on, she loved them. They had a mid-height heel and worked well with the dress but weren't excessive. Paige gave Chelsea a hug. "Thank you for lending me your stuff. Without you, I have no idea what I would have worn."

"Mom?" Jason stuck his head in the bedroom door.

"Come in, Jason."

Jason walked hesitantly inside and stared open-mouthed at his mother.

Paige did a little pirouette. "What do you think?"

"Jeez. You don't *look* like a mom."

"It's unanimous!" Chelsea interjected, but Jason still seemed uncertain.

"Come here, sweetie." Paige bent down, held her arms open for her son and hugged him. "It doesn't bother you that I'm going to dinner with Daniel, does it?"

He shook his head. "Then what's up?"

He thought about it. "You just look…different. Like ladies do in the movies." He reached out to play with the side of her hair she hadn't clipped up yet. "You look really pretty."

"Thanks." She gave Jason another hug, rubbing his back. Her eyes met Chelsea's over his head, and they both smiled.

"C'mon, Squirt. Let's go play a game while your mom finishes getting ready. Might as well get started, since you're stuck with me tonight." Chelsea held a hand out for Jason.

"Don't forget to use that makeup I brought you," she said to Paige as they left her bedroom.

Thirty minutes later, Paige emerged. Jason's pride and joy—his train set—had been moved into his own room. Jason and Chelsea sat by the coffee table playing Scrabble. They stopped when she walked in.

"Well?"

Chelsea got to her feet. "The guy doesn't have a chance." She glanced at Jason. "Oops. Sorry. So, anyway…" She hurried over for a closer inspection. "The makeup is perfect, natural but sexy. And I love what you did with your hair." It was piled on top of Paige's head in a loose knot, with a few wispy strands left to frame her face. "Kind of mussed and elegant at the same time."

Before Paige could respond, Daniel was at the door.

Paige felt a mixture of nerves and excitement. "It's showtime." Chelsea made scooting motions with her hands. "Go get the door."

"Right." Paige took a quick peek in the hallway mirror, smoothed her hair, then ran her hands down the length of the dress before opening the door.

"Hi." Daniel stood in the doorway. He was dressed in a navy blue suit with subtle pinstripes, a pale blue shirt open at the collar, and a charcoal-gray coat. There was a large bouquet of yellow roses in one hand and a magazine in the other. He offered the flowers to Paige.

"Thank you." She raised the bouquet to her nose and inhaled deeply, the sweet scent making her smile. "Mmm. There's nothing like the smell of roses." They were yellow again, a sign of friendship—but she pushed that nagging thought aside. "Please come in."

As Daniel stepped inside, he ran his gaze over Paige. "You look stunning. Great boots."

Paige and Chelsea exchanged a conspiratorial grin, and since Daniel's back was to Chelsea, she gave Paige a quick thumbs-up.

When Paige had made the introductions, Daniel turned to Jason. "I brought you something, too." He handed Jason the magazine. "It's on train sets. It has ideas about how to change the configuration of your set, parts that you can get online, stuff like that."

Jason held the magazine reverently and flipped through a few pages. "Cool."

"Jason…" Softly spoken, Paige's single word had the desired effect.

"Thank you, Mr. Kinsley."

"I'll just put these in water before we go," Paige said.

Chelsea stepped forward and took the roses from Paige. "Jason and I will take care of it. Have a terrific time."

"Shall we?" Daniel asked.

Paige pulled her coat out of the closet and Daniel helped her into it. They said good-bye and walked out the front door of her apartment building, into the sharp pinpricks of freezing rain. Daniel placed his hand lightly on her arm. Even through her heavy winter coat, she seemed to tingle where he touched her. He gave her elbow a squeeze. The tingling sensation intensified and spread. "Wait here and I'll get my car."

"You don't have to bother. I can just go with you."

"It's no problem. You shouldn't have to trudge through all the slush. I'll be back in a minute."

He raised the collar on his coat and headed briskly toward the visitors' parking area. A couple of minutes later, a late-model midnight-blue Mercedes coupe stopped at the curb. Daniel was out of the car and by Paige's side in no time at all. When he took her hand to help her into the low-slung car, she felt that tingle again.

Was she being foolish? she wondered as she fastened the seat belt. She thought of the yellow roses. Here she was, feeling hopeful and dreamy, and the only thing he wanted to be was friends. He felt sorry about her circumstances, that was all, and he figured a nice dinner out might be a friendly gesture. She reflected on everything he'd done for her and Jason. There was no question that he was a giving and considerate man. That just made it more likely that this, too, was an act of charity.

Why hadn't she thought of that before? Of course she was grateful for everything Daniel had done, especially on Jason's behalf, but how humiliating if this, too, was done out of sympathy.

Daniel slid into the driver's seat and secured his own seat belt. Turning to her, he smiled. "All set?"

She forced a smile in return and nodded.

Had she made a mistake in accepting his invitation?

CHAPTER TEN

THE FREEZING RAIN persisted. It coated the roads and sidewalks with a thin layer of ice. Daniel's Mercedes might have looked sporty, but it handled well on the slippery roads, and they were in Hartford and at the restaurant in under an hour. Daniel pulled up to the curb by the entrance, where the burgundy canopy and vigilant staff kept the sidewalk free of ice and snow. An attendant assisted Paige out of the car. Daniel handed over his keys and joined her a moment later.

The double doors of the restaurant were stained glass in rich mahogany frames. On either side of the entryway, small spruce trees swathed in a myriad of twinkling white lights stood sentry. Daniel held the door open for Paige.

The blast of warm air as they stepped into the foyer felt heavenly.

A hostess with the voice of a lounge singer and the look of a runway model greeted Daniel. "Mr. Kinsley. It's good to see you again."

Gracious and hospitable, she turned her attention to Paige. "Welcome to Pietro's." She dispensed with their coats, then lifted two leather-bound menus from the stack on a pedestal. "Your table is waiting. Please follow me."

The restaurant's lighting was subdued, the interior decor tasteful, elegant and evocative of a winter wonderland. Seating areas were separated by potted birch trees, their bare branches twined with more glittering fairy lights. Rich, dark wood and stained-glass inserts contrasted with crisp white linen, fine bone china and sparkling crystal. Large poinsettias graced some of the pedestals and counters. Efficient waiters and waitresses entered and exited through swinging doors.

Paige tried hard not to stare. She couldn't remember the last time she'd been to a restaurant that wasn't part of a fast-food chain.

The hostess led them to a table in a quiet corner. A large leaded-glass window was beside them on one wall and a fireplace with a smoldering fire in the hearth on the other. Paige chose to face the fire, and Daniel held her chair out for her.

Their waiter appeared, placed their napkins on their laps, and inquired about their drink order. Daniel asked him to give them a minute. When the waiter was out of hearing range, he turned back to Paige. "Would you like to share a bottle of wine or would you prefer a cocktail, or a nonalcoholic drink?"

She realized Daniel was being considerate to ask. He wouldn't know whether she drank alcohol or not, since she hadn't had wine in her apartment at Christmas. She appreciated his thoughtfulness and smiled. "I'd love some wine."

He nodded. "Do you have a preference?"

Paige chuckled and felt the heat rise from her neck to her cheeks. "No. Not really. It's not often that I indulge in wine these days." Her smile wavered.

Daniel held her gaze for a moment before signaling the waiter and accepting the wine list from him.

"Is something wrong?" he asked after the waiter had left.

"No." Her face still felt hot, so she knew there must be vivid color on her cheeks. She glanced down and straightened her cutlery. "It's just that it's been a long time since I've done any of this." With a sweep of her hand, she indicated their surroundings. "The beautiful restaurant. A bottle of wine." *A date with an attractive, intelligent man.*

"Then I'm especially glad you said yes to

dinner, and I hope you'll enjoy yourself. I've always found the food here excellent," he added as they perused the menus.

The waiter returned with an ice bucket containing a well-chilled bottle of wine. He lifted out the bottle, wiped it with a napkin and held it for Daniel to examine.

Daniel tested and approved the wine, and the waiter filled their glasses. He took their orders before withdrawing again.

Paige took a sip, closed her eyes and made a sound that was almost a purr. When she opened her eyes, she saw Daniel grinning at her. Feeling her face flush again, she decided to get onto a safe topic. "Thank you for thinking of Jason. He'll have his nose buried in that magazine for weeks."

"I hoped he'd like it. He's a terrific kid."

"What you did for us at Christmas meant a lot to him." Paige leaned forward. "It meant a lot to *me*."

"It was my pleasure. It also saved me from an uncomfortable Christmas with my folks."

"Oh?"

"I shouldn't have said that. My parents are good people. I just wouldn't characterize our relationship as warm, and Christmas can be a little awkward."

"I…I'm sorry." Paige thought of her own

parents and how much they meant to her. She couldn't imagine having family and not sharing a close, loving relationship with them.

Daniel drank some wine and waved her concern away. "Don't be. We make it work."

They paused while the waiter served their appetizers and topped up their glasses.

When they were alone, Daniel asked, "What about your family?"

Paige's smile was bittersweet. "My parents are incredible."

"Tell me about them," Daniel encouraged her as he tasted his smoked salmon.

"I'm an only child. Like you, I think."

He nodded.

"My parents met when my mother was in high school. My father is eleven years older than my mother. Although they say it was love at first sight, my father waited a couple of years to ask my mother out. Until it was no longer 'improper'—his word—because of the age difference. Once they got married, they took the time to enjoy each other and had me later in their lives. I couldn't have asked for better parents."

"Where are they now?"

"They retired years ago to Great Barrington, in the southwest part of Massachusetts. Have you been there?"

"I've driven through."

Paige tried a piece of calamari. "Mmm. This is delicious. Great Barrington is a quaint little town. We used to vacation there when I lived at home. After all these years, they're still madly in love." Her eyes clouded. "Except now Dad doesn't always remember Jason and me. He developed Alzheimer's shortly after they moved."

"I'm sorry," Daniel said simply.

Paige slid a piece of calamari around on her plate with her fork. "They were looking forward to retirement so much, but they hardly had any time to enjoy it together before Dad was diagnosed. Now Mom does the best she can, but it's a struggle for her to take care of my father, and it's not getting easier. His condition is deteriorating." She skewered the calamari, dipped it in the cocktail sauce and popped it into her mouth.

"That's why you weren't with them at Christmas?"

"That's right. It was hard on us, but with my schedule, Jason feeling ill from treatments and the difficulty my father has with travel, we just couldn't make it work."

"It's unfortunate that you can't rely on them more for assistance with Jason."

She felt a sudden defensiveness, but it was

extinguished as quickly as it had appeared. She realized there was no criticism in Daniel's words or in his tone. "Mom wants to help with Jason." Paige glanced down at her plate and played with her food again. "But she can't leave Dad, and financial help is out of the question. It would mean mortgaging or selling their bungalow, which is now the only place Dad knows."

Paige met Daniel's eyes. "That's too much of a sacrifice. But Mom's just a phone call away." She sighed heavily and took a sip of her wine. "Yes, I've often thought how wonderful it would be to have them close by, but that's not possible right now."

She stabbed the last piece of calamari and was surprised to find she'd cleaned her plate while they'd been talking.

The waiter removed their empty plates and replaced them with their main courses.

"And Jason's father?" Daniel asked once they were on their own again.

"Oh, he...he's been gone a long time," Paige said vaguely.

"I remember you mentioning that the last thing he'd given Jason was the circus set, and that's why Jason's so interested in circuses."

"That's right." Paige sipped her wine. "I suppose because Jason was so young and he associates that circus set with his father, his preoccupation with circuses helps him keep the memory of his father alive."

"That makes sense." Daniel took a bite of his steak Diane. "So, tell me more about your work. You said on Christmas Day that you work in a call center for a collections agency. That can't always be fun."

She laughed. "That's an understatement. People can be downright mean."

"How did you get into it?"

She toyed with her wineglass. "I needed something that gave me a certain degree of flexibility with my hours, something that would allow me to take time off whenever I had to. I understood how collections worked from my previous job, and they liked that."

"What did you do before?"

"I was an office manager for a financial services firm," she explained. "My degree is in business. My next step with the company would have been chief administrative officer."

He looked impressed. "That's a major responsibility. You enjoyed it?"

"Yes." She smiled. "The partners were wonderful to work for. They gave me lots of opportunities for learning and advancement. When Jason was first diagnosed with cancer, I took a leave of absence from my job. The partners were very supportive. They told me to take all the time I needed." She broke eye contact and watched the embers glow and sputter in the fire. "Unfortunately, they never counted on the amount of time involved. After...we lost Mark, I needed to ask for even more days off, since I had to be there for all of Jason's treatments and other appointments. It was a small company, and ultimately their business had to take priority. I understood that, and to be fair, I quit.

"I was fortunate to get the job at the collections agency right away. As long as I give them sufficient notice, I can set my own hours."

"Sounds workable."

"It is, from that perspective. Unfortunately, the call center's competing with offshore, low-cost companies, so both my income and health care coverage are much lower than they were, just when I need them the most. To save money and be closer to work, we moved to Camden Falls." She brightened. "The move turned out to be the best thing that could've happened to Jason. Yes, it meant that both he and I had to leave our friends behind, but Jason was young, so he adapted quickly, and he loves his school. It's perfect for him, because it's a progressive school that offers more advanced art classes for kids his age."

"And what about you?"

"The distance and my preoccupation with Jason's needs caused me and my friends to drift apart over time. That was hard for me at first, but there's always a silver lining. Many of the people in our apartment building have become good friends."

Daniel cut another bite of his steak. "With everything you've been through, I admire your positive outlook, your optimism."

Paige swallowed a forkful of her veal parmigiana and chuckled. "Thank you, but I just do what I have to. We love our apartment and our wonderful neighbors. One of the things that drew me to this place is the fact that it's on the ground floor. If we can't have a house with a yard, Jason can at least play outside on our little patio. I also like that the building is so small. I love the informality of it, and we know everyone who lives there. Like I said, our neighbors are a terrific support system."

"Chelsea's an interesting person. Vivacious."

Paige nodded. "She's a sales associate at the Sinclair Art Gallery. Then there's Mr. and Mrs. Bennett across the hall. They're retired. Both Mrs. Bennett and Chelsea have done so much to help us over the years. I don't know how we would've gotten by without them. And our next-door neighbor is Mr. Weatherly. He's such a sweet man, so proper and polite. He's a true British gentleman." She gave a small laugh. "You'd never guess he manages a supermarket. It's a good thing he's on the ground floor, too, as he's an avid gardener. He helped us get a little garden going on our patio. It's not much space, but Jason adores it."

"Jason gardens?"

Paige laughed again. "Not exactly. Jason used to love playing in our yard when he was a toddler, and I think he misses it." She twirled pasta around her fork. "I'd love to be able to give him that again. A house with a yard and a garden. A tree house in the back, maybe a wading pool, and a puppy for him to play with."

DANIEL COULD VISUALIZE the house and the yard. He could feel the sense of welcome, of belonging. Paige was a terrific mother. It was obvious.

Despite all the adversities Jason had to face, he was well adjusted and happy. Daniel was certain a lot of that had to do with Paige. She was smart, committed, nurturing. Paige smiled, saying, "We'd love the proverbial white picket fence, of course."

Her comment made him think of family. He

could envision Paige and Jason in that house. But as compelling a picture as she painted, a white picket fence wasn't for him. He *liked* her. Add beautiful to all her positive qualities, and what was not to like? But he wasn't looking for more than a casual date. He didn't have it in him. He was resigned to staying single. His parents' relationship and his work were justification enough.

There was no house with a white picket fence in his future. Maybe he'd made a mistake taking Paige to dinner if she was thinking white picket fences. He should've known better and gone with his initial instincts, but the truth was, his emotions were already invested, and that worried him. He barely knew her.

He'd just have to stay off the subject of white picket fences and everything they implied. With that in mind, he turned the discussion to lighter topics.

As they shared tiramisu, Paige glanced out the window. "Oh, look. It's snowing. I love those big, fluffy flakes! When it's so still and calm, they take forever to float down, and you can catch them on your tongue."

They watched together for a few minutes as the flakes shimmered in the glow of the Christmas lights and drifted lazily to the ground. After they finished their dessert and coffee, Daniel settled the bill and pulled Paige's chair back for her.

It was relatively mild outside, and the huge feathery flakes of snow continued to fall.

"Would you like to go for a walk?" Daniel asked before the valet could retrieve his car. Despite his reservations, he wasn't quite ready to have the evening end.

She buttoned the collar of her coat and raised her face to his. "That would be nice."

They strolled past shops and restaurants still decorated for Christmas. Soon their hair, as well as the shoulders of their coats, were dusted with snow. Paige pointed excitedly at window displays, laughed at the antics of a young couple's puppy and recounted Christmas memories from her childhood.

At some point, Daniel took her hand in his, and she didn't resist.

He'd bought her an expensive dinner, yet she seemed more alive, more joyful now, enjoying the simple pleasure of a nighttime walk, their joined hands swinging with each step.

She turned her face to his again, and a gentle smile curved her lips. Her eyes were clear and tranquil. The worry lines he'd too often seen on her brow were, for the moment, nonexistent. Whatever his concerns, Daniel loved to see Paige so happy and carefree, even if just for a short time.

Had he ever known someone who got such pure pleasure out of something as simple as walking in softly falling snow? Not likely. The women he normally dated would've been horrified by the thought of it. They'd fuss about getting their designer shoes soiled or their hair wet. He had to admit he'd always been shallow enough to enjoy their beauty and ignore the rest.

"Is everything okay?"

Daniel looked at Paige. "What?"

"You made a noise."

He'd been so absorbed in his thoughts, he hadn't realized he'd snorted. "Yes. I'm fine. I was just thinking what a nice time I'm having with you." He gave her hand a little jerk. "Ready to go back?"

Daniel's car was waiting for them when they returned to the restaurant.

The snowfall was much heavier when they reached Paige's apartment building. Daniel parked at the curb. He skirted the front of his car, opened the passenger-side door and extended his arm toward her. She placed her hand in his and swung her legs out. He steadied her, but with the slick sidewalk, she slipped, and one leg nearly shot out from under her.

Daniel managed to grab her, or she would've ended up unceremoniously on her backside.

Her arms went instinctively around his neck. In the process, her body bumped up against his, and their lips were a hairbreadth apart.

"Oh." Paige's breath fluttered across Daniel's parted lips.

Time seemed to stop, but the snowflakes continued to drift down, transformed into minuscule beads of moisture as they alighted on Paige's skin. A few cotton-soft flakes glistened on her long eyelashes, and Daniel yearned to kiss them away.

Instead, he dropped his gaze to her mouth. Big mistake. For a moment, he allowed himself to consider kissing her. He more than considered, he *longed* for it. This wasn't just a physical pull. That he could've dealt with. His emotions getting all caught up with her was exactly what had worried him in the restaurant. That and the complications a relationship would bring.

He forced his gaze back up. Her eyes were fixed on his, drawing him in deeper. He felt the warmth of her breath again.

It seemed his emotions were already involved, but he could still do something about the complications. He lowered her gently to her feet.

"Let me see you to your door."

Paige gave a nervous laugh. "Technically, I *am* at the door. I can make it safely to the apartment from here." He stepped toward her, and a blush crept up her cheeks. "Thank you for dinner and a lovely evening."

"I'm glad you enjoyed it." Daniel didn't want to ask if they could do it again. He wasn't sure he wanted to. More accurately, he *wanted* to, but he wasn't sure he *should*. Even if he resolved that dilemma, he wasn't at all certain she'd agree. He sensed a reserve in her that he was unaccustomed to.

She was about to turn away when she paused and closed the gap between them once more. She set one hand lightly on his chest. "I had a wonderful time, Daniel. Thank you." She placed a feather-light kiss on his cheek, smiled a melancholy smile and with a wave walked through the door.

WHY HAD SHE done *that*? Well, for a couple of reasons. First, she was sincere about what a good time she'd had. She would never have imagined it would be possible to actually *relax* and enjoy herself. And she'd done both those things. Daniel had transported her away from her worries, even if it was just for an evening. Second, she was attracted to him, no question about it. She couldn't remember feeling such an attraction since…maybe never.

Had she felt like that about Mark? Yes, in some ways. He had dazzled her. She had fallen head over heels in love with him. But Daniel? It was an entirely different feeling. Yes, there was the physical attraction, but there was something so steady and solid about him, it stirred feelings deep inside her. Someone she could lean on? Unquestionably rely on? Those had been her thoughts during the drive home. As she was about to walk away, she realized it was a fantasy to think there could be anything between her and Daniel. He had his work and his life, and she was a single mom with a very sick child. And why would a man like Daniel, who had the entire world at his feet, want to get tangled up in a situation like that? She suspected dinner was simply another kind gesture from Daniel, and she was romanticizing it.

But she couldn't resist allowing herself that one indulgence, that kiss on his cheek. Something to take away and hold dear, a memory to cherish.

She knew she'd surprised him. Stunned him, actually, if the look on his face was any indication. But what she understood—and perhaps he didn't—was that the kiss had been a thank-you *and* a good-bye. She couldn't possibly get involved right now, when Jason wasn't only the center of her universe but her *entire* universe. Nor would she expose Jason to possible disappointment.

She let herself into the apartment, took off the beautiful boots and tiptoed into the living room.

Chelsea was curled up on the sofa, sound asleep.

Paige nudged her shoulder.

Chelsea made a little groaning sound, and she twisted in a way that reminded Paige of a cat roused from sleep. Stretching both arms above her head, she yawned. Opening one eye, she stared up at Paige. "You look good," she observed. She opened the other eye, then pushed herself up into a sitting position. "But you don't look like you've been messed up by a hot guy with a steamy good-night kiss."

"That's because I wasn't."

"Aw. Too bad." Chelsea shoved aside the throw that had been covering her and patted the sofa. "Sit down and tell me about it."

"Chels, it's late."

Chelsea checked her watch. "Seriously? It's just after ten. C'mon. Tell me how it went."

Paige gave in to the desire to talk about

Daniel and her evening, and dropped down on the sofa next to Chelsea.

"Sooooo?" Chelsea prompted.

Paige rested her head against the cushion. She turned slightly so she could see her friend. "It was an incredible evening. Daniel is a considerate, intelligent, funny, wonderful guy..."

"You left out gorgeous. Still, I can feel a 'but' coming."

"But...it can't go anywhere."

"What?" Chelsea shot upright. "What do you mean? You meet a guy who sounds like Prince Charming and it *can't go anywhere*?" With the last three words, she did an uncanny job of mimicking Paige.

"Let's get real." Paige counted off the various points on her fingers. "He lives in Connecticut. He's a partner in a busy law firm, which demands a lot of his time. He doesn't have a great family history with relationships. And his lifestyle is nothing like mine."

Chelsea was silent for a long moment. Finally, her eyes sad, she asked, "Those are just excuses. What's *really* bothering you?"

Paige picked up a coaster from the coffee table and turned it over and over in her hands. "I can't get involved right now. Jason's sick. He's my absolute priority. He needs all my time and attention, and all my love. There's no room in my life for a relationship, especially one just starting out. I couldn't do either Jason or a relationship with Daniel justice. Also, Jason already likes Daniel a lot, and if things don't work out, I don't want him getting hurt."

"But—"

"But if the circumstances or the timing were different, well, then maybe…"

Chelsea reached for Paige's hand. "We live in a complex world. The timing and circumstances are never perfect when it comes to a new relationship, but we're given very few opportunities to get it right. If you think it could be right with Daniel, don't turn away. Give it—*give him*—a chance."

"Thanks, Chels. I appreciate the advice, and I'll think about it. You're one of the smartest people I know." She drew her hand away and rose. "And thanks for taking care of Jason tonight."

"I'm always happy to do it." Chelsea rose, too, and straightened the bottom of her hoodie. "But if I'm so smart, why does Squirt always beat me at Scrabble?"

Later that night, lying in bed with sleep eluding her, Paige thought about Chelsea's words. She'd made an excellent point, but try as she might, Paige couldn't see how she could introduce a relationship into the very delicate balance she'd been able to establish among Jason, her family and her work.

CHAPTER ELEVEN

ON THE DRIVE HOME, Daniel mulled over the evening. He realized that he was shy of commitment and he understood why. Consciously or not, that was the reason he'd always sought out what he knew were shallow, superficial relationships.

He'd learned tonight that, in contrast, Paige had the benefit of her parents' loving, loyal and committed relationship. As family-oriented as she was, it must have been extremely hard for her to have lost her husband. Based on what she and Jason had said, it was a sudden loss. She didn't say how it had happened—an accident, perhaps? She didn't appear comfortable talking about it. As both she and Jason still seemed to bear the scars, he'd let it go. But he sensed that she'd be the type of person who didn't take marriage vows lightly. When she'd said "I do" to her husband, she would have expected it to be forever. Losing her husband, and so early in their marriage—so early in his life—must have been devastating for her.

Not only that, she'd implied it had been at a time that was already excruciatingly hard for her, during their first battle with Jason's cancer.

He couldn't remember the last time he'd felt toward a woman what he was starting to feel for Paige. If ever. He just wasn't sure exactly what he was feeling—or what to do about it.

Once inside his house, he checked his voice mail. He had two messages. The first was from one of his partners, suggesting they grab a beer on Sunday. He was considering it as he played his second message.

He heard his mother's voice. "I thought I'd find you in, Daniel." Why did those few innocuous words spark such a sense of guilt in him, as her comments so often did? "You're just like your father." And she made that sound like the greatest of sins. He put the call on speakerphone. It was easier to listen to the message with a bit of distance. Automatically, he started to leaf through the papers on his desk to clear up what he could. "And where is he? Not at home. Not with me."

Daniel paused. Was she suggesting that his dad was cheating on her? Impossible. Whatever problems his parents had in their marriage, his father would never do that.

"Oh, I know he'll come rolling in around

midnight, smelling of cigar smoke. He went to that cigar place again with Harold. He knew perfectly well I wanted to go to the club for dinner tonight. Pamela and her new husband were going, and with all the rumors about how much younger he is, I wanted to have a look for myself."

Daniel snorted. His mother shouldn't have been surprised. If his father's first option was dinner at the club with his mother, he was a wise man to choose an alternative. Daniel listened to the rest of his mother's message and deleted it almost before she'd finished saying good-night.

His parents had been married for, what, forty-three years now? Not much had changed in all that time. They tolerated each other's presence, often went their separate ways and never showed much emotion. Despite his mother's words, her voice had been matter-of-fact, not suggesting any great concern. What kind of life was that—devoid of mutual enjoyment and love?

He sat down heavily in the leather chair behind his desk. The mellow, happy mood he'd been in had evaporated. But his mother had bent his ear at exactly the right time. He rested his head against the back of his chair and stared up at the ceiling.

During dinner, had he really thought, however fleetingly, of a house with a white picket fence, and what it would be like to share it with a wife and kids? Specifically with Paige and Jason? Thankfully he'd come to his senses quickly. And yet…he wanted to see her again. He might have dropped her off a short while ago, but he found he *missed* her. He'd be her friend. But his policy about not getting involved was a sound one. He didn't want to set himself up for a cold, loveless marriage like his parents', or a heated, unpleasant one, the kind he saw all too often in his practice.

Was he jaded? Cynical? Yeah. But who could blame him?

He'd help Paige any way he could. She deserved that. After all, he had other female friends, didn't he? Well…to be honest, not really. Any women he'd considered friends had invariably become dissatisfied with the boundaries he'd put on the relationships. They'd either drifted away, or the relationship ended in harsh recriminations about how he'd misled them. He snorted again. Was there no winning?

Yes, having a drink with one of his partners on Sunday was a great idea—a much safer bet. It would help him put things back into perspective.

PAIGE AND JASON were on the train, heading home from the hospital after Jason's MRI scan. As brave as he tried to be, it always took a lot out of him. He was leaning against Paige, his head on her shoulder. She knew he was drifting in and out of sleep, as his body would jerk every once in a while.

Christmas was behind them. That brief period when Paige and Jason's troubles had been magically suspended, thanks in large measure to Daniel. For a while, they could focus only on what was good and happy. Soon enough, reality had intruded again. Paige was stubborn; she readily admitted it. Sometimes— okay, *most* of the time—it was a fault. Hadn't her stubbornness contributed to the breakdown of her marriage? Mark had said as much when she'd taken such a firm position with respect to Jason's health and treatments. But she *had to do* what she believed was best for Jason. In the end Mark couldn't accept her decision to proceed with treatment and ultimately surgery.

But occasionally stubbornness, especially combined with her almost limitless optimism, could be a strength. It meant that she wouldn't give up, regardless of how daunting the odds might be.

She was determined that they'd beat Jason's illness, whatever it took. But she had challenges. Big ones. Not the least of which was money. With her health-care plan's specific exclusion of experimental treatments and limitations on other benefits, she didn't know how she'd find the money for Jason's ongoing treatments, as well as surgery, if they went that route. But she'd do it. Even if it meant appealing to Mark. She'd swallow all her pride, if she had to, in the interests of Jason's welfare.

She and Mark had cut their ties cleanly and completely, because she needed sole legal custody of Jason to be able to do what she considered best for him. Mark couldn't handle what lay ahead for Jason, and as a consequence, he'd withdrawn totally from their lives. They hadn't had any contact since the legal documents were signed four years ago, to the point that she had no idea where he was living.

It saddened her that two people who had loved each other and had a child together could lose all contact, but there didn't seem to be any middle ground at the time. But regardless of what had happened between them, if she needed money for Jason, she would locate Mark and do whatever she had to do. As long as he didn't think that if he gave her money, she'd have to do what *he* wanted.

But first, she had a bigger question to answer.

The risks associated with surgery were significant. She'd taken some time alone with Jason's oncologist that morning to discuss them. She wanted to fully understand the facts and the options they had. She needed to know the unvarnished truth about Jason's chances—with and without surgery. The information wasn't encouraging. At this point, surgery wasn't an option because the tumor was too large. The hope was that the experimental drug would shrink the tumor. If they then opted for the surgery, and Jason survived it, brain damage was an added risk due to the location and size of the tumor. Without surgery, he had months at best. There were a lot of *if*s involved.

She *had* to keep believing, despite the odds. She would *not* accept that this Christmas could be his last.

She thought about Mark again and wondered what his reaction would be. She knew she should tell him what Jason was facing, but she didn't think she could handle another heated argument about treatment options and the right one for her son.

"Mom?" Jason's voice was barely a whisper.

She closed her eyes and rubbed her cheek against his soft hair. "Yes, sweetie?"

"When are you going to see Mr. Kinsley again?"

Paige stilled. "Oh, I don't know if I am."

Jason snuggled in a little closer and tilted his face up. "Why?"

Her voice was gentle when she answered him. "We've been through this. He's busy. And I have you."

"Did *he* say he's busy?"

"No. I just assume he must be. He's got a very important job."

Jason seemed to consider this for a while. "I like him," he finally said. "Maybe we could both see him." The last sentence was slurred as he drifted into sleep again.

Jason's words brought to mind Daniel's promise that the three of them would do something together. Daniel must've changed his mind, since he hadn't mentioned it during their dinner.

Jason was tired and feeling queasy the next morning. Paige kept him home from school, and Mrs. Bennett agreed to stay with him again so Paige wouldn't have to take more time off work.

"How is he?" Paige asked Mrs. Bennett when she got home.

"Oh, he's a little trooper." Mrs. Bennett placed a hand over her ample bosom. "My heart just goes out to him. He's resting now."

Paige pointed to a large envelope on the dining room table. "What's that?"

"Oh, it's a card Jason made for Mr. Kinsley. Isn't he clever? He even made the envelope out of his sketch paper, since you didn't have one large enough."

Paige picked up the envelope. It was addressed in Jason's neat, precise printing to Daniel at Lindstrom, Kinsley and McGuire. "How did Jason get the company name and address?"

"As I said, he's a clever lad. He found the information on the internet."

Paige pursed her lips. "Huh." She turned the envelope over to pull out the card, but the back of the envelope had been glued shut. Feeling a little awkward, she put the envelope back on the table, thanked Mrs. Bennett again and saw her out.

When Paige asked Jason about the card later that evening, he said only that it was to thank Mr. Kinsley for all the things he'd bought him.

Paige put the appropriate amount of postage on the envelope, and they mailed it on their way to Jason's school the next morning.

"WHAT'S THIS?" DANIEL asked when Selena handed him a large homemade envelope.

"Since I *obviously* haven't opened it, I don't know. But it doesn't seem to be business-related, so I thought you might want to do the honors."

Daniel slid his letter opener under the flap of the envelope and neatly sliced it open. He removed the folded sheet of cardboard with the colorful painting on the front. He didn't have to read the inside to know it was from Jason. The painting was distinctly his and beautifully executed. Daniel had a hard time believing a seven-year-old had painted it.

It was a Christmas-themed picture. A couple sat on a sofa, a Christmas tree glowing behind them, and a young boy knelt on the floor, playing with a train set. The blonde woman was laughing and the dark-haired man had one hand resting on the boy's shoulder. There was a broad smile on the boy's face.

Daniel easily recognized Paige's living room, and there was no doubt that the woman, man and child were the three of them. The kid had captured them well.

With the card still in his hand, he abruptly swung his chair around. He stared at the Norman Rockwell–like billboard. Somehow—in comparison to Jason's painting—the billboard family struck him as artificial and stilted, their smiles forced.

He looked down at Jason's work again. The three of them seemed completely at ease with one another. Daniel scrutinized his own likeness more closely. He appeared relaxed, comfortable. Genuinely happy. Was that how the kid had seen him?

An uneasy feeling crept through him as he continued to stare at the painting. He had never imagined himself married and with a family; he was not a picket-fence type of guy. It already worried him that he was developing a soft spot for Paige—not to mention her son—and in such a ridiculously short time. But in Jason's painting, he looked disconcertingly right, as if he belonged there. *They* looked right together.

He opened the card. Jason's careful handwriting flowed across the page.

Mr. Kinsley,

Thank you for everything you did for Mom and me, for all the gifts and for sharing Christmas with us. It was fun.

Mom works really hard, and she worries about me even if she tries not to show it. At Christmas, you made her forget to worry. You made her happy. You made me happy. I hope you were happy, too.

I made this painting for you so you can remember how much fun we had.

I hope we see you again soon.

Jason Summerville

P.S. Just so you know, Mom makes the absolute best mac and cheese in the world! You should ask her to make it for you sometime.

Daniel swung around and stared at the billboard again, then down at Jason's card. One image was stiff and contrived, the other relaxed and natural. A few days ago, he'd thought nobody lived like the family in the billboard picture. He'd always focused on the negatives in relationships; it was the nature of his life. Intellectually, he knew there were just as many happy marriages. Paige's parents were one example, and he guessed Paige's own marriage was probably like that, too. Until her husband died.

Wasn't life about taking chances?

He might have to find an opportunity to try Paige's mac and cheese. After all, hadn't he promised Paige a date for the three of them?

CHAPTER TWELVE

"I'LL GET IT, MOM." Jason answered the phone, and his face lit up as he greeted the caller. Paige dried her hands on the dish towel and headed toward him. She paused midway, as the call appeared to be for him. Whoever it was certainly knew how to put a smile on Jason's face.

"Yeah. It's really cool…Yes, thank you so much…Uh-huh. No, I just drew it from memory…Aw, thanks!…Uh-uh…Okay." He held the phone away from his ear and called, "*Mooom*, it's for you."

"Who is it?" she asked, surprised that it was for her.

Jason handed her the phone, grinning. "You'll see!"

Paige took the receiver.

"How are you, Paige?"

"Daniel?" Jason was bouncing from foot to foot beside her, hanging on her every word. "Hold on a minute, please," she said before covering the mouthpiece. "Jason, either sit down or go to your room."

"He's gonna ask you out again, Mom. I know it!" Jason whispered.

It was hard not to get caught up in Jason's enthusiasm. Where did this giddy schoolgirl excitement of hers come from? She tried to keep her face from showing any emotion and pointed toward Jason's room. "Go, please." She could hardly keep from laughing when he did a little dance, followed by a butt wiggle just before he went through his door. She smiled, shook her head.

"I'm sorry to keep you waiting, Daniel." She knew her voice was much warmer than it had been when she'd first taken the call.

"I'd like to follow up on our agreement. How would you and Jason like to see a show tomorrow? Jason can pick the movie. The new Disney movie is playing at the Camden Falls Cinema, if he's interested in that sort of thing. It's getting great reviews."

Paige plopped down on the sofa, opened her mouth, then closed it again. He hadn't forgotten his promise.

"Paige?"

"Yes. Sorry, I'm here."

"How about it? We could see the New Year's Eve matinee."

"Um, sure. I know he'd love it. That's very nice of you."

"Don't say that too fast. There's a condition."

"A condition?"

"Jason and I discussed it, and we hope you're okay with it, as it's nonnegotiable. You have to make us your famous mac and cheese for dinner afterward."

"How did you…?" She chuckled. "Never mind. Jason told you. I accept the condition. What time should we be ready?"

Before Daniel had a chance to respond, an excited "Yesssss!" emanated from Jason's room.

Paige was laughing when she spoke into the phone again. "I guess it's a date."

IT WAS NEW Year's Eve day. Daniel was taking them to a matinee, and she was making dinner afterward.

Jason had agreed enthusiastically with Daniel's suggestion of the Disney film.

All Jason had talked about since the call the day before was seeing the movie with Daniel. Paige couldn't deny that she shared Jason's excitement. In her case, it had less to do with the movie and more to do with seeing Daniel.

In the morning, she did all the shopping for their dinner. With Jason's help, she prepared everything she could in advance. When they returned from the movie, she'd only have to put the casserole in the oven, warm up the garlic bread and put together their salad. She still couldn't believe that the second meal she'd be cooking for Daniel was mac and cheese, but he'd insisted.

She'd picked up some sparkling grape juice so they could toast the new year. She'd splurged on a couple of small party favors, too. Jason loved the kind that you blew into, and they whistled while the coiled-up plastic strip shot out. She was looking forward to celebrating New Year's and hoped fervently it would be a good one for Jason.

DANIEL ARRIVED PRECISELY at three. He wore dark jeans, a slate-blue crewneck sweater and his leather bomber jacket. Paige was dressed similarly in her faded jeans, the beautiful lilac sweater Daniel had given her for Christmas and a ski jacket. Her hair was pulled back in a ponytail. Her skin had a youthful, healthy glow.

Jason was wearing his Patriots jacket and cap. Daniel made a big deal of it, causing the boy to strut around proudly.

At the theatre, Daniel bought them buttered popcorn and sodas. After much affable debate, they decided to sit in the middle of the front row on the upper tier. This gave them a great view, unobstructed for Jason, and Daniel could still stretch out his legs. After a little more debate, Jason won out on the seating arrangement, which resulted in Daniel sitting in the middle.

The movie had barely begun when Jason glanced over at him.

Daniel held out the bag of popcorn. "Would you like some more?"

"Thanks." Jason reached in and took a large handful, but he continued to watch Daniel.

Daniel leaned over and whispered in Jason's ear. "Don't you like the movie?"

"The movie's great!"

"Then what's up?"

Jason snuck a peek at his mother, then held a forefinger to his lips. "Shh."

Daniel lowered his voice even further. "Now will you tell me what's on your mind?"

"Okay," Jason murmured. "But it's a secret."

Daniel gave him a solemn nod, and crossed his heart with his forefinger. Jason giggled. Paige looked over at the sound and smiled at her son trying to stifle his laughter. Daniel maintained an expression of pure innocence until Paige turned away. "You nearly blew it there, pal. So, go ahead. Spill the beans."

"This is kind of like a date, right? You and Mom? I just happen to be along?"

Daniel responded with a cautious, "Uh-huh."

"So, we're sitting here in a dark theater…"

"Uh-huh."

Jason rolled his eyes. "Do I have to tell you *everything*?"

Daniel's lips twitched, but he held back his grin. "It might be best if you did."

Jason leaned in a little closer and whispered conspiratorially. "Shouldn't you be holding Mom's hand or something, like the guys do in movies?"

Daniel stared down at Jason. The light from the movie screen flickered, casting him in alternating brightness and shadow, but there was no denying the eagerness on his face. "Pretty smart, aren't you?"

Jason grinned. "Yup, that's what my teacher told Mom. Now, are you going to hold her hand or what?"

"In my own time, pal." With mock seriousness, he nodded. "These things can't be rushed."

Good to know, Daniel thought, turning back to the screen. Jason had made it clear that he wouldn't have any concerns if a relationship developed between Daniel and his mother. On the contrary, Jason seemed to be all for it. It was hard to concentrate on the movie, with

Jason's frequent surreptitious glances and his own thoughts about Paige.

When she put her soft drink container in the cup holder on her armrest, Daniel saw his opportunity. Shifting the bag of popcorn, he reached over the armrest, placed his hand on Paige's and closed his fingers around hers. He felt a slight jolt from her, but she didn't withdraw her hand. She looked up at him, her eyes questioning, and he smiled reassuringly.

Hesitantly, she smiled back and turned her hand over, linking her fingers with his.

A few minutes later, out of the corner of his eye, Daniel saw Jason wriggle in his seat. The kid had a huge grin on his face and gave him a thumbs-up. Clearly, he approved.

IT WAS DUSK when they left the theater. They strolled to the town square in front of city hall to have a final look at the enormous Christmas tree that would be dismantled soon. Daniel bought them roasted chestnuts, and Jason fed some to the ever-present squirrels.

As they meandered along the paths blanketed with snow, Jason scooted out from between them to Daniel's other side. When Jason yanked on his sleeve, Daniel glanced down. Jason made a comical gesture—holding one hand in the other—and grinned. Daniel had to laugh. He'd never needed a seven-year-old matchmaker before, but the kid had another good idea. He clasped Paige's hand. She pulled it away and looked over at Jason. Seeing him peering at her, a grin on his face, she gazed back at Daniel, who shrugged and reached for her hand again. This time she curled her fingers around his.

Hand in hand, they walked back to Daniel's car and piled in. At Paige's building, he let them off at the front door and went to park.

WHEN PAIGE OPENED the apartment door for Daniel, he handed her a brown paper bag and said, "For later."

Paige pulled out a bottle of Dom Pérignon. She had an idea how much real champagne cost. "Thank you. This will put the sparkling grape juice I bought to shame. Come in and make yourself comfortable while I stick this in the fridge."

With her preparations complete and twenty more minutes to go before the pasta was ready, they moved to the living room. Giving Jason the option of what game he wanted to play, he opted for Go Fish. Neither Paige nor Daniel intended to lose, yet Jason walloped them.

When the stove timer chimed, Paige threw

down her cards good naturedly. "Saved by the bell! Let's go eat."

Dinner conversation centered mostly on Jason, his art and schoolwork. Jason told Daniel about his desire to become an architect when he grew up, but he also questioned Daniel about his job. After dessert, Jason and Daniel helped clear the table, but Paige insisted that the dishes be left until morning.

As it was nearing nine o'clock, Jason changed into his pajamas, and they moved to the living room to watch *Rudolph's Shiny New Year* on television. It was another of his favorite holiday shows. Jason was wrapped in a throw and cocooned on the sofa between Paige and Daniel. He managed to stay awake for the entire program, but by the end, he was yawning incessantly and couldn't keep his eyes open. As the credits rolled, Paige was about to lift him into her arms. Daniel tapped her shoulder. "May I do it?"

Paige paused, then nodded in agreement.

Daniel tucked the throw more snugly around Jason and gently picked him up. Jason's head rested against Daniel's chest, just under his chin. Daniel inhaled deeply, and Paige was certain he got a whiff of Jason's shampoo. The smile it brought to his face moved her in a way she hadn't thought possible. Jason moaned in his sleep, nestled closer to Daniel and slipped his arm around Daniel's neck.

Paige stood transfixed, her hands pressed together in front of her face. Her eyes filled with tears. There was something poignant about the large, fit man holding her small, fragile child in his arms so lovingly.

Lovingly.

The word echoed in her mind. Could this man she barely knew care about her child that much in such a short time? And, if so, what did it mean? She gave her head a quick shake. She was romanticizing things again. There wasn't any room in her life for that. She could blame her crazy daydreams on the time of year and her own emotional state.

She followed Daniel into Jason's room.

And stopped short. Daniel was tucking Jason's teddy in the crook of his arm and pulling the blanket over him. She raised a hand to her heart in a futile attempt to still its rapid beating.

She backed out and returned to the living room. Changing the television to a local station that would be broadcasting a countdown to midnight, she adjusted the volume for background music.

"Are you up for some champagne?" Daniel asked when he rejoined her.

Still unsteady from the realization that she was falling for Daniel, she cleared her throat and hoped he wouldn't notice the quaver in her voice. "That would be nice. I'll get it." She hurried into the kitchen to try to regain her balance.

She took the bottle from the refrigerator and, on impulse, held her hand, chilled by the bottle, to her forehead. That cooled her flushed skin. Feeling a little steadier, she grabbed two wineglasses from a cupboard and took them and the bottle to the living room. She handed the bottle to Daniel and placed the glasses on the coffee table. "I hope you're okay with these. I don't have champagne flutes."

"They'll do just fine. Ready?" Daniel asked as he was about to uncork the bottle.

They both laughed when the expulsion of the cork made the customary popping sound. Daniel filled their glasses, and they toasted to the new year.

The next two hours slipped by as they talked about their childhoods, their jobs and Jason.

Barry Manilow's "It's Just Another New Year's Eve" was playing, the last song before the official countdown to midnight, when Jason's door opened. With his teddy bear clasped under his arm, he shuffled into the living room.

Paige was up and rushing toward him immediately. "What's wrong, sweetie?"

"Nothin'," he responded, still groggy. "I just wanted to be up for midnight. I set my clock. I have something for you."

The final chords of the song faded, and the host started the countdown. "Ten…nine…"

"You need to sit on the sofa next to Mr. Kinsley, Mom."

The last vestiges of sleep gone, Jason dashed behind the sofa. "C'mon, Mom. *Hurry!*"

"…seven…six…" the host counted.

On five, Jason moved his other hand from behind his back. He clutched a sprig of mistletoe. "You know what this is for, right?"

"…three…" He held it over the space between Daniel and Paige's heads and giggled.

"…two…" Paige sent Daniel a silent apology, but his expression was amused.

"…one!" At the blast of horns and noise makers on the television, Daniel cupped Paige's cheek in the palm of his hand and leaned in for a kiss. Paige closed her eyes and leaned in, too, as if irresistibly drawn by a magnet.

Jason whooped loudly.

The kiss was light and brief, but it gave her a little jolt. When she opened her eyes and gazed into Daniel's, she could see in the expression on his face that he'd felt it, too. The sweet taste of the champagne lingered on her lips as it did on Daniel's. She ran her tongue over her upper lip, savoring the flavor.

"My work here is done," Jason declared cheerfully, his words followed by a huge yawn. He kissed his mother on the cheek. "See you in the morning, Mom. Good night, Mr. Kinsley." Jason held up his hand, and Daniel high-fived him. "Happy New Year!" he called, waving the bear over his head, as he trotted back to his room.

After his door closed, Paige could almost hear the ticking of the clock over the soft music that was now playing on television. Then they both began to speak at once. "You first," they said in unison, and laughed.

Aerosmith's "I Don't Want to Miss a Thing" was playing in the background. Daniel rose and held out a hand to Paige. "How about this instead? Dance with me."

Paige hesitated only for an instant before placing her hand in Daniel's and letting him draw her up and into his arms. "I love this song," she murmured.

With Daniel's arms encircling her waist, and hers draped over his shoulders, they moved to the rhythm as the poignant words flowed over them.

When the song ended, Daniel lowered his mouth to hers. They kissed gently, tenderly. And this time it was their own decision.

CHAPTER THIRTEEN

As THE WEEKS PASSED, Paige's feelings for Daniel were undeniably growing. It meant a little more juggling of her time, but for the most part Jason was included in their plans.

Jason seemed pleased about their budding relationship, and there was no question that he was developing a strong attachment to Daniel. Paige smiled at the thought of her son taking every opportunity to encourage her and Daniel to see each other. When they weren't with Daniel, Jason was constantly talking about him. She was certain he would've slept in his Patriots ball cap and jacket if she'd let him.

Which just gave Paige a whole new set of things to worry about. She assumed that part of the reason Jason was growing so attached to Daniel was the total absence of a father figure in his life. Jason had no idea why his father had left them; he just knew Mark wasn't part of their lives. All his friends had a father who was still around, even if their parents were divorced.

Paige also continued to worry that if and when the relationship with Daniel ended, Jason would be devastated. He had so much to deal with already. She couldn't imagine how he'd handle Daniel's disappearance from their lives. With Jason's increasing needs, the day would come when it would no longer be fun for Daniel. He'd leave them, just as Mark had…and just like the guy she'd dated briefly the year after. Most distressing, she worried that Jason's desire for a father figure pointed to her own failure as a parent. She couldn't keep back a groan.

Jason looked up from his painting. "You okay, Mom?"

"Oh, yes, sweetie. Sorry to interrupt you." She ran a hand over his mop of blond hair. When had she turned into such a pessimist? She'd always considered herself the opposite. But she'd sustained some hard hits, and Jason's illness overshadowed everything.

She should be thrilled about Daniel being in their lives. He was wonderful to them, caring, considerate and so splendid with Jason. It didn't hurt that he was tall and gorgeous, and just being near him made her blood pressure skyrocket and her heart race like a jet engine.

Yes, she should be over-the-moon happy. To be able to discuss her worries about Jason with him, and have him truly listen and support her was an unexpected gift. He took a real interest in Jason and how he was doing. But a niggling doubt tried to worm its way back into her consciousness. *And when he left them, where would they be?* But she refused to dwell on the possibility. It was hard to believe that Daniel had been in their lives for more than three months now. Time was certainly flying by.

WHEN CHELSEA CAME HOME, Mr. Weatherly held the door open for her. "You're back from work early today."

"Yeah. The gallery is changing some of the exhibits for the weekend, and we got a head start to make sure we're ready by Saturday morning. It's nice to be done so early." They walked through the foyer together. "It seems such a waste not to enjoy the sunshine when the days are still so short."

"Well then, this might be the opportunity I've been waiting for." Glancing at his reflection in the mirrored wall next to the mailboxes, Mr. Weatherly straightened his bow tie. "I'll fix you a cup of tea. There's something I've been wanting to discuss with you or Mrs. Bennett."

Chelsea looked at him curiously, and he added, "It's about our Paige."

She grabbed his arm. "Did anything happen? Is it Jason?"

He was quick to reassure her. "No, no, no. I've just been thinking about something."

Comforted, Chelsea followed him into his apartment. She unwound her scarf and stuffed it into her coat pocket. Mr. Weatherly took her coat and hung it up, along with his own.

She helped him make the tea, and they took their cups to sit side by side at the small patio table in his sunroom.

"Here's the thing. I know I have no right, but I think of our Paige as…if not a daughter, as a younger sister."

Chelsea leaned over and gave him an affectionate kiss on the cheek, causing vivid color to bloom on his face. "Aw, that's sweet. Of course you have a right to feel that way, and she'd be touched by it."

Slightly embarrassed, he cleared his throat. "She's been through so much, and now she has Jason's illness to worry about. I just don't want to see her hurt."

"Why would she get hurt?"

"This Daniel Kinsley chap. He's been around a lot lately, and I worry about both Paige and Jason getting too attached to him."

Chelsea raised her eyebrows. "Why would you feel that's a bad thing? I think it'd be great if Paige could have the love and support of a wonderful man, especially now."

Mr. Weatherly stabbed a finger in the air to emphasize his point. "See? That's just it. We don't know anything about this Kinsley chap. I've met him only in passing. He seems pleasant enough, but that's just on the surface. You may have spent more time with him, but what do we really know? How can we be sure he's a good man? One who'll stick by her?"

Chelsea's laugh bubbled out. "Are you kidding? Daniel's a gem. He's decent, kind, has a good job and seems pretty stable to me. I wish I could meet someone like him!" She clapped a hand over her mouth. "I didn't mean that. Joel is wonderful…in his own way."

Mr. Weatherly's shoulders sagged, and he shook his head. "I'm just saying."

"Oh, I'm sorry. I didn't mean to hurt your feelings. Paige is very lucky that you care about her as much as you do. I care about her, too, and I haven't seen any red flags with Daniel. He seems solid, and he treats both her and Jason so well."

Mr. Weatherly lifted his cup, sniffed the tea and took a sip. He put it back on its saucer. "What do you or any of us really *know* about

him? How do we know he's not your proverbial axe murderer?"

Chelsea stifled a giggle. She took a sip of her
own tea. "True. But what can we do about it?"

"We could make sure he's everything he
says he is."

She hesitated. "How could we do that, besides
looking up the usual corporate stuff online?"

"We could keep an eye on him. Maybe dig
deeper when you check him out on that fancy
computer of yours."

Chelsea put her cup down. "I don't know,
Mr. Weatherly. I realize you mean well, but I
don't think either Paige or Daniel would appreciate it if we interfered."

"And what if he's not all he seems to be?
What if he hurts her at such a vulnerable time
in her life? How about Jason? The young man
is developing quite an attachment to Kinsley,
from what I gather. How would it affect him
if something went wrong?"

"Hmm." She hadn't considered that angle.
Daniel's presence seemed to be lifting Jason's
spirits, providing a distraction. How upsetting
would it be if he hurt them? She remembered
that Paige had raised the same concern. "You
may have a point," she conceded.

"I heard Paige mention that he coaches kids'
baseball on Saturday mornings at the Camden

Falls fairground. The spring season hasn't officially started yet, but he supposedly holds practices for his team when the weather's good. Let's start there."

They put their plan into action the next day. It was a brilliant early-April morning, and the sunshine took the edge off the cool temperature. Mr. Weatherly's 1965 buttercup-yellow Mustang convertible—his pride and joy—was buffed to a sparkling shine, as always. They both wore dark glasses, worthy of any respectable sleuth, as Mr. Weatherly pulled out of the parking lot.

Four hours later, they pulled back into the lot. Mr. Weatherly shut off the engine, crossed his arms over the steering wheel and tapped his fingers on the braided leather cover. "That wasn't any great revelation."

"Oh, I don't know about that." Chelsea nudged his shoulder. "We found out he drinks his latte without froth."

Mr. Weatherly guffawed. "We did, didn't we?"

She rubbed his arm. "Don't look so disappointed. We should be glad we saw him with the baseball team. We want him to be who he says he is. We want him to be good for Paige."

He nodded.

"Why don't we stick to internet searches

from now on, until you're satisfied?" Chelsea suggested. "Or maybe you should get to know him. You might like him."

He nodded again.

SUNDAYS WERE SPECIAL days that Paige, Daniel and Jason spent together. This Sunday, Daniel was driving Paige and Jason to Great Barrington to visit Paige's parents. Since they hadn't seen them at Christmas, a visit was long overdue, and Paige's mother had often told her how eager she was to meet Daniel.

The drive passed quickly. Jason was bouncing in the backseat as they pulled up outside his grandparents' house. He rushed up the front steps ahead of Paige and Daniel. As soon as his grandmother opened the front door, Jason threw himself into her arms. He greeted her parents' little sheltie, Iris, next. Wanting his undivided attention, Iris pranced and leapt excitedly around Jason's legs.

When his grandfather walked into the vestibule, Jason seemed a little uncertain but gave him a big hug. Paige breathed a sigh of relief that her father didn't reject Jason's affection. Jason, for his part, seemed to take his grandfather's forgetfulness in stride.

Daniel accepted Charlotte's warm embrace rather awkwardly. Paige knew that outward signs of affection didn't come naturally to him. Although he and her parents hit it off from the start, Daniel seemed just a bit too formal and reserved, especially next to her warm and easygoing parents.

Her father's Alzheimer's wasn't a factor in Daniel's interactions with him. Since it was their first meeting, there was no shared history that had been forgotten. Paige was overjoyed to see her father's good spirits. She marveled again at her mother's strength and dedication in the face of her father's illness.

The company and conversation proved to be tiring for Stephen. After an early dinner, Charlotte helped Stephen settle down for a nap.

"Where are Jason and Daniel?" Charlotte asked when she rejoined Paige in the kitchen.

"They're in the yard playing with Iris." Paige glanced over her shoulder and smiled as she finished wiping the counter. "You have no idea how much I wish I could get him a dog."

"Until you do, he's welcome to play with Iris anytime you like. Paige…?"

Paige draped the dish towel over the handle of the oven door and turned to her mother.

"Honey, there's something I'd like to talk to you about."

"Sure, Mom."

Charlotte poured two cups of coffee and handed one to Paige. "Let's sit down."

Paige sat at the kitchen table across from her mother. "What's up?"

"I need to talk to you about your father."

Apprehension formed a hard ball in Paige's stomach. "Okay."

"I don't know how to tell you this…"

"Mom, what is it?"

"I can't believe I'm saying this, but I'm worried about how much longer I can take care of your father at home. I just went to the corner store last week to get some milk and eggs. Oh, Paige. When I got back, he was gone."

"*Gone*? Why didn't you call me?"

"I didn't want to worry you. Thank goodness, I found him. He'd wandered over to Jim and Heather's place. You know them, our next-door neighbors? But…" Charlotte raised a hand to her throat. "You have no idea how scared I was. If I can't leave him alone, even for such a short time, I don't know what I'm going to do."

Paige stared at her—stricken yet understanding.

"Paige, honey. I don't want to do this, but I'm worried I'll have no choice other than to put him in a long-term care home." Charlotte's face showed her anguish. "I feel so awful saying this, but it's becoming too much to continue caring for him at home. I can't leave the house. I can't sleep. I'm just so worried about him."

Paige squeezed her mother's hand and swallowed hard to clear the huge lump in her throat. She'd known this heart-wrenching day would come. She just hadn't expected it this soon. "Try not to feel bad, Mom. You need to do what's best for Dad. I'll do everything I can to help."

"You already have your hands full with Jason."

"But you can't do this on your own."

An excited Jason rushed into the kitchen, the little dog at his heels. Daniel followed at a more leisurely pace. "Hey, Mom! You'll never believe the neat tricks I taught Iris!" The moment Paige met Daniel's eyes, he sent her a questioning look. Paige shook her head, letting him know she didn't want to discuss it in front of Jason or her mother.

A distinct pall had fallen over the afternoon, and Paige, Daniel and Jason said their good-byes shortly after.

Appearing a bit self-conscious, Daniel initiated a good-bye hug with Charlotte and accepted her kiss on his cheek.

THE MOMENT THEY were in the car, Paige fastened her seat belt, leaned against the headrest and closed her eyes.

Daniel thought of Charlotte's whispered words as she'd kissed him good-bye. *Take care of my little girl, will you? She may not admit it, but she needs you.*

Daniel felt his heart twist. Paige looked so sad, so forlorn. Something was clearly wrong.

He raised his hand. Not knowing what he'd intended to do, he withdrew it without touching her. He glanced in the rearview mirror to make sure Jason had his seat belt on, then started the engine. He couldn't ask her what was wrong with Jason in the backseat, so they drove to Camden Falls in silence.

"Would you like me to come in?" he asked as he pulled into the driveway of her building.

Her eyes were apologetic. "Is it okay if you don't? Jason's had a long day, and I'd like to get him into bed."

"Aw, *Mom*!" Jason complained from the backseat. "I'm not *that* tired."

"Don't sweat it, pal." Daniel reached back and pulled the bill of Jason's Patriots cap over his eyes. "I'll see you guys again in a couple of days."

By the time Daniel had hopped out of the car, Paige had already climbed out and was holding the seat forward for Jason.

Daniel drew Paige into a hug, and she wound her arms around his waist and held tight. He stepped back and, his voice low, asked, "Would you like to discuss it later?" He could see her distress, but she shook her head. He brushed his lips lightly across hers, but disappointment left a bitter taste in his mouth.

Daniel bent down to give Jason a hug. He waited until Paige and Jason were inside the building before he slid back into his car and drove away. He couldn't get the wounded look in Paige's eyes out of his mind. It couldn't have anything to do with Jason. Her father, maybe? Whatever the reason for her distress, Daniel cared. Didn't she realize that?

How was he supposed to help her if he had no idea what was going on? When was she going to trust him and understand that he *wanted* to help?

Daniel's concern turned into frustration, and he fumed about it for the whole drive home. Why did she have to be so stubborn?

At home, he tossed his coat over the back of a chair instead of hanging it up, and grabbed his iPhone. He did a directory search. When he found the number he was looking for, he punched it in.

"Charlotte?" he inquired when a woman's voice answered.

"Yes?"

"It's Daniel Kinsley."

"Oh, Daniel. Is everything all right?" She sounded anxious, and he realized belatedly that of course her first thought would be that they'd been in an accident on the drive home.

"Yes, everything's fine. Paige and Jason are home safe, but I need your help."

"My help?"

"Yes. I'd like to know what happened today."

"What do you mean?"

"Paige was obviously upset when we left. It had to do with something you two talked about while Jason and I were outside. Can you tell me what it is?"

"Paige didn't tell you?" There was hesitancy in Charlotte's voice.

Daniel considered making excuses about Jason's being with them, but he couldn't lie. "No, she didn't. Look, I'm worried about her, and I'd like to help if I can."

There was a pause.

He was almost certain the problem, whatever it was, had nothing to do with Jason. Still, he wanted confirmation.

"I might as well tell you. It concerns Stephen, and you'll find out sooner or later anyway."

Daniel had begun to suspect this, so he wasn't surprised. While Charlotte explained the situation to him, he fixed himself a drink. He sat on a kitchen chair, his elbow resting on the table, his forehead in his hand, as he listened to her. No wonder Paige was so distraught. He couldn't imagine having to make a decision like that about one of his parents.

"Have you considered home care?"

He heard a huge sigh. "Oh, yes. Believe me, I looked into it. It would've been my first choice. But to get someone with the right qualifications…it's not possible. The cost would be too high. We just can't afford it."

Daniel would've expected a nursing home to be as expensive, if not more so, but Charlotte explained the funding structure and their retirement benefits. She said that if Stephen lived in a nursing home, she'd sell their house, freeing up capital.

Daniel thought of the warm, tranquil house into which Charlotte and Stephen had welcomed him. He remembered all the charming touches she'd so lovingly added, and how contented and settled Stephen seemed there. He pictured Stephen sleeping in his big chair in the den, a small smile on his lips, his hands linked over his stomach. There'd been a fire in the hearth, and the little sheltie had lain at his feet, snoring softly. Daniel had concluded that, despite his illness, Stephen was happy and comfortable.

He drummed his fingers on the table. This must be tearing Charlotte apart. Paige, too. He wanted to help, but even though he'd just met Charlotte, he guessed she'd probably be as stubborn as her daughter. He thanked her for trusting him with the information and assured her again that he'd do whatever he could for Paige.

Maybe there *was* something he could do. He finished his drink, checked the time and went to his office to do a bit of research on his laptop.

Deciding on the company he was interested in, he looked up the name and number of its CEO, Dr. Margaret Winter. Knowing she wouldn't be in on a Sunday, he left a message, asking her to call him at his office the next day.

The call came in around noon.

"Thank you for getting back to me so quickly, Dr. Winter."

"No problem. I don't know what your call's about, so I'd appreciate your enlightening me."

Her voice sounded defensive and distant. He wondered if he'd made a mistake selecting her organization, despite the Oakridge Seniors' Center's excellent credentials and references.

He'd expected the CEO to be friendly, compassionate. His voice cooled in response. "Certainly. I'd like to find out about your services."

"Our services?" He heard a soft chuckle, and a distinct change in her tone. "I'm sorry. When I got the message that you were calling from a law firm…I may have misinterpreted."

"My call has nothing to do with my practice. I should've made that clear. It's a personal matter. I want to talk to you about somebody who could benefit from your home care services."

An hour later, Daniel felt he *had* found the right company. He also understood why Dr. Winter—or Margaret, as she insisted he call her—had been apprehensive about being contacted by a law firm. The Oakridge Seniors' Center was experiencing some short-term cash flow issues due to a bad debt they'd incurred. She'd worried that, committed though they'd always been to their suppliers through good times and bad, their slower-than-normal payments had caused one of their suppliers to follow through on threatened legal action.

The issue that remained was how Charlotte would be able to afford the extra cost of home care for Stephen. Then—as Daniel thought about the organization's financial dilemma—an idea occurred to him. He made another call to Margaret Winter. Now he just had to find a way to execute his plan without letting Charlotte or Paige know he was involved.

CHAPTER FOURTEEN

CHELSEA SET HER laundry basket on top of a washing machine when she saw Mr. Weatherly in the laundry room. "I'm so glad you're here," she whispered urgently. "I tried your apartment, but there was no answer. I need to speak with you. I think I discovered something." She glanced around the laundry room, empty expect for them, and went to close the door. She returned to where Mr. Weatherly was folding his clothes and hopped up to sit on the low counter. "I can't believe this. *You're* not going to believe this." She threw her hands up. "Oh, my gosh! What are we going to do?"

"Well, it's rather difficult for me to say, not having the faintest idea what you're talking about."

Chelsea squirmed a bit. "Oh, right. I did another online search. I came up with the usual information for Daniel Kinsley in Hartford, where he lives. You know, telephone directory, LinkedIn, that sort of thing. But as you suggested, I dug deeper. I found an online article from a community paper in Hartford about a Mr. and Mrs. Daniel Kinsley attending a charitable event and making a sizable donation."

Mr. Weatherly straightened. Shock was evident on his face. "He's *married*?"

Chelsea nodded slowly. "Looks like it. How horrible for Paige and Jason. As cautious as she was at first, Paige has really fallen for him."

"Are you positive it's him? Could it be a relative? His father maybe?"

"I'm afraid it's him. His parents live in Newport, Rhode Island. The article was about what it called 'Hartford's elite.' I checked the local directory, and there's only one Daniel Kinsley. Besides, how many rich Daniel Kinsleys can there be in Hartford?"

"This is terrible! I didn't really expect to find anything when I suggested we look into him. It was just…an abundance of caution, to make sure our Paige wouldn't get hurt." Mr. Weatherly spread his hands. "Now look at the mess we're in."

"That, that…goat!" Chelsea said vehemently. "How do we tell Paige?"

Mr. Weatherly lifted his newsboy cap and scratched his head. "I don't know. Any way we do it, it's going to hurt her. Just what I wanted to avoid. Poor little Jason."

Chelsea pushed off the countertop. "Let's talk to Mrs. Bennett. She may have an idea."

Mrs. Bennett made loud *tsk*ing noises. "How could you interfere with Paige's personal life like that?"

"We didn't interfere," Chelsea insisted. "We just wanted to make sure she and Jason wouldn't get hurt."

"And is your mission accomplished?"

They shook their heads in unison.

"Exactly the opposite, I'd say." Her voice held a note of censure.

"But he's *married*!"

"Hush," she scolded Chelsea, then turned to Mr. Weatherly. "I would've expected better of you, Harrison."

A flush rose to his cheeks. "I just wanted to protect her. The same as you."

"That may be, but I don't follow people around and do computer searches on them."

"But what do we do now?"

"Nothing."

They both gaped at her. Chelsea found her voice first. "What do you mean, *nothing*?"

"I don't believe for a second that Paige's Daniel is married. Keep your day jobs, you two—you'll never make detectives. You really should have more faith in people. And if not in people overall, look at how good Daniel's been for both Paige and Jason. Can you honestly believe that same man would have a wife and be cheating on her?"

Neither responded, but Chelsea felt more than a little embarrassed.

"Harrison, I'm surprised at you. By your own admission, you don't know Daniel. Why wouldn't you have taken the time to get to know him a little?"

Again, neither Mr. Weatherly nor Chelsea had a word to say.

"Hmm. I think it's time we *all* got to know Daniel better—and not because I give any credence to your suspicions. So, this is what I'm going to do. I'm going to host a dinner for all of us. Daniel will be our guest of honor. And the two of you," she said, wagging a finger at them, "are going to help me."

A FEW DAYS LATER, Chelsea sat in front of her laptop. Mr. Weatherly was hunched behind her. They both peered intently at the screen. Despite Mrs. Bennett's admonitions, Mr. Weatherly wanted to finish what they'd started. It didn't sit right with him, not knowing for certain about Daniel's marital status.

"Come on, come on," Chelsea implored as her emails downloaded. She glanced over her shoulder. "Mrs. Bennett will skin us alive if she finds out we're doing this."

Mr. Weatherly straightened, then adjusted his vest. "In for a penny, in for a pound, as they say. We've come this far. We might as well satisfy ourselves if we can. What is it you said you're waiting for?"

"I reached out to the editor of the community paper that ran the article. She told me they didn't print any pictures of the charitable event, but they had some on file. She's sending me one of Mr. and Mrs. Kinsley."

"Just like that?"

"I did get a little creative. I might've implied that there was an, um, interest in possibly recognizing them. You know, like an award." Chelsea glanced up, a grin on her face. "I didn't exactly lie. That *is* our interest. Recognizing them—just not in the way she would've assumed." Chelsea clicked on refresh again and did a fist pump. "Here it is!"

Mr. Weatherly leaned forward. "Well, let's see it."

With a couple of clicks, she opened the file. They both held their breath until the image appeared on the screen.

"Well," Mr. Weatherly declared.

"I guess we have our answer now," Chelsea added.

"Should we let Mrs. Bennett know?"

"Are you kidding?" But as Chelsea rose, she hugged Mr. Weatherly, who staggered back. "Boy, aren't we lucky we didn't say anything to Paige?"

Mr. Weatherly stepped back and brushed nonexistent lint off his vest. "Yes, indeed."

Chelsea took another look at the picture on her computer screen. "Who do you suppose *that* Mr. Daniel Kinsley is?"

"It doesn't matter, now that we know it's not *Paige's* Daniel Kinsley."

Chelsea shrugged. "There's no other Daniel Kinsley listed in the area." She studied the photograph again. "But they look old enough to be his parents." She studied the photograph closely. "The comment about Hartford's elite could've been a generalization. Especially if they used to live there."

Mr. Weatherly stroked his chin as he scrutinized the picture. "That may be, but it doesn't matter to us."

"I'm just wondering…"

ALTHOUGH MOST OF Paige's neighbors had already met Daniel at one time or another, Paige was touched that Mrs. Bennett wanted to host a dinner for all of them. Mrs. Bennett said she wanted something celebratory to say good-bye to winter, but also to give some of the most important people in her life an opportunity to get together and, in Daniel's case, get to know each other.

They were all gathered around Mrs. Bennett's large dining table with Mr. and Mrs. Bennett at either end. Chelsea was seated next to Daniel. Paige could've sworn that Chelsea had maneuvered the seating arrangements to put herself in that particular spot.

"Sooooo, Daniel," Chelsea began, obviously trying to get his attention.

Daniel was talking to Jason about the chances of the New England Patriots making it to the Super Bowl the following year, but he turned to Chelsea. "Sorry, I didn't hear what you said."

Chelsea lifted her glass of apple juice. "I'm just curious. Have you always lived in Hartford?"

"No, not as a child." He was about to turn back to Jason, when she spoke again.

"But you've lived there for quite some time?"

"Yes. Since my partners and I established our law practice."

"And your family? Do they visit often?"

"They're in Newport. They come here occasionally, but I usually visit them."

Sitting across from Chelsea, Paige was on the verge of giving her a kick under the table. She could see that Daniel was getting impatient with this line of questioning. Chelsea should've known by now that Daniel was a private person and not keen on talking about his family.

Yet she persisted. "How do they feel about supporting charities?"

Before Daniel could respond, Paige had had enough and interjected, "Chelsea, can you come and help me in the kitchen, please?"

"Sure. In a minute."

"No. Now."

"Oh, okay." She flashed Daniel a smile and followed Paige into the next room.

THE MOMENT THEY were inside the kitchen and out of hearing range, Paige demanded, "What was *that* all about?"

"Just trying to make friendly conversation," Chelsea muttered.

"Chels, I know you better than that. And *you* know Daniel doesn't like to talk about his family."

She broke eye contact. "Yes, I do."

"Then what were you doing?"

"Oh, like I said, just making conversation."

Paige glared at her friend.

Chelsea gave up. "Okay, okay. A Mr. and Mrs. Kinsley attended a big-deal charitable event in Hartford recently. I wondered if they were his parents."

"How would you even know about a charitable event in Hartford—and that a Mr. and Mrs. Kinsley attended?"

"Oh, well…" Chelsea glanced toward the doorway, wishing her partner in crime, Mr. Weatherly, would miraculously appear. After all, the whole sleuthing thing was his idea to begin with. But no Mr. Weatherly. No white knight appeared in the doorway, either, and she'd backed herself into a corner. With her head lowered, she looked up at Paige through her eyelashes. "Because I searched the internet."

"And you just *happened* on a Mr. and Mrs. Kinsley at a charitable event?"

"Um, no. Not exactly."

"Then what?" Paige asked, tight-lipped, stirring the pasta sauce.

Chelsea sucked in a breath. "I was looking for them."

The serving spoon clattered in the pan as Paige turned around. "You were looking for a Mr. and Mrs. Kinsley? Why?"

Chelsea glanced at the doorway again, willing Mr. Weatherly to come to her rescue. "Oh, heck." In the absence of any assistance, Chelsea relayed the whole story.

"Chels, *seriously*? What were you thinking? I don't know if I should yell at you for interfering or hug you for caring so much." She went with the latter. "But don't *ever* think of doing anything like that again, or I *will* yell at you."

CHAPTER FIFTEEN

THE SUN WAS shining brilliantly. It cast a dappled patchwork of light and shade as it filtered through the pale green buds of leaves yet to unfurl on the massive red oaks edging Daniel's backyard. The smoke wafting from the stone barbeque on the flagstone patio carried the tantalizing scents of bacon and barbecued ribs.

It was unseasonably warm for mid-April. An ideal jeans-and-sweater day after the long, harsh winter. The timing couldn't have been better, since the weather allowed Daniel to move the get-together outside and have a barbecue, rather than the more formal sit-down dinner he'd originally envisaged.

Unexpectedly, as he wasn't big on parties or other social gatherings involving lots of people, he'd enjoyed himself at the dinner the Bennetts had hosted. So much so that he wanted to return the favor. Before he left, he'd extended an invitation to everyone to dinner at his house. He'd also invited Charlotte and

Stephen and had arranged private transport for them.

Daniel knew that Jason had been through-the-roof excited, and he could hardly wait for the day to arrive. To make it more enjoyable for Jason, Daniel suggested he bring a friend. Paige's parents brought Iris, and Jason and his friend were alternately chasing or being chased by the little dog. Their giggles and Iris's yips reverberated through the yard.

Daniel glanced around. Paige was sitting on a stone step near her mother and father. They were having a small celebration of their own; Charlotte had confided in him that through Stephen's family practitioner, they'd found a highly qualified home-care service, the Oakridge Seniors' Center, and—surprisingly—they could afford it. This meant that Stephen didn't have to move to a long-term care home. Daniel could see that it was a huge weight off both Charlotte and Paige's shoulders. He smiled a secret smile, knowing exactly how that had come about.

The Bennetts and Mr. Weatherly were engaged in a game of cribbage. Good thing he'd kept that old game without realizing people still played it.

Chelsea had offered to be sous chef and took her duties seriously. She was standing next to him and had taken over the preparations other than barbecuing the ribs and steaks. Daniel was adamant that he wasn't giving that up.

"Thanks for this. It's such a nice break for all of us," Chelsea said as she lifted the barbecue lid. "Especially for Jason. It was terrific of you to suggest he bring a friend." They watched as the two boys chased Iris around the yard, trying to get her to surrender the soggy tennis ball in her mouth. Chelsea pointed with the large fork. "Look at him! Sometimes it's hard to believe he's sick."

"Yeah. He looks perfectly healthy. If his father could see him today, even he would think Jason's fine."

Chelsea moved to the barbecue and poked a baked potato with the fork. "Well, of course he would. He doesn't know that Jason's sick. Paige hasn't told him."

Daniel turned Chelsea's words over in his mind, trying to understand what she'd just said. Finally, he asked, "What do you mean she hasn't *told* Jason's father?"

Chelsea stabbed another baked potato and glanced over at Daniel. "She hasn't told him Jason has cancer again."

Paige hadn't *told him*? What was Chelsea talking about? Was it possible that she would be as close to Paige as she was and not know that Paige's husband was dead?

Or was he? Daniel tried to recall the exact discussion he and Paige had about it months ago. Hadn't Paige said Jason's father was dead? No. Maybe not in so many words. But it was certainly implied. Otherwise, why would he have believed it? Besides, what other possible reason could there be for a father's complete absence from his son's life? "Where *is* Jason's father?"

Chelsea lowered the barbecue lid. She put the fork down, placing her hands on her hips. "I'm not sure. I know he's not in the state." She compressed her lips and shook her head. "Paige may have mentioned it, but I can't remember."

"Does he have any contact with Paige and Jason?"

Chelsea shrugged. "I doubt it."

Daniel lifted the wine bottle from the table and splashed more wine into Chelsea's glass. "Why's that?"

He noticed that she glanced over to where Paige was sitting with her parents. Then she shifted her gaze to Jason as he threw the ball to Iris again. "You should ask Paige about that."

"When I've asked, there hasn't been much discussion."

Chelsea sighed, took hold of the mother-of-pearl pendant hanging around her neck and ran it along its gold chain. "I imagine not."

"I'm just trying to understand." He heard the frustration in his own voice.

Chelsea nodded, and Daniel could see the hard set of her face. The silence hung heavy between them. She raised her chin and continued to fidget with the pendant. "You'd have to ask Paige," she repeated, reaching for her glass.

Daniel didn't know if he could've gotten Chelsea to say more on the subject, but just then Jason rushed over. Rising up on the toes of his sneakers, he braced himself on Daniel's knees. "Did you *see* Iris run after the ball? She caught it in midair!"

"I did. I also saw you throw the ball." He playfully squeezed Jason's bicep. "You've got quite an arm. I coach a kids' softball team. We should ask your mom if you could come out and play with us."

"Yeah! That would be great. When I'm feeling good," he added. He snuck a look at his mother, who was approaching them. "My birthday is coming up," he confided. "It's May second. Do you think Mom would get me a puppy? If we could get one, I'd take good care of it."

"Jason…" Paige had clearly overheard her son's last comments. She tried to sound firm, but there was humor in her voice. Then she looked from Jason to Daniel to Chelsea, and her smile faded. "Did I miss something?"

"No. Not at all," Chelsea responded.

"Just getting better acquainted," Daniel said.

Daniel didn't press Chelsea further. Nor did he raise his concerns with Paige that afternoon. It was a lot for him to digest. He mulled it over all through dinner. He couldn't shake the sense of frustration. He was falling in love with Paige. In fact, he was probably already in love with her. Now two of the things he admired most about Paige—her honesty and her integrity—had been brought into question. She might not have lied to him, but had she deliberately misled him? And if so, why? If the boy's father was alive, was she intentionally keeping Jason from him?

Knowing Paige, he found the idea hard to believe, but in his law practice, he'd learned that when it came to cases of marital discord or custody disputes, nothing surprised him. He considered himself relatively flexible and open-minded, but the law was the law. And parents, regardless of the circumstances, had their rights. He knew without a doubt that

Paige would never do anything that wasn't in Jason's best interests. Her fathomless love for her son was another thing he admired about her.

Would she do something illegal? Perhaps to protect her child? Okay. Maybe he could accept that. But there'd been no indication in his discussions with Paige, or anyone else, that suggested Jason's father was a threat to either of them. Nothing in her manner said she was afraid of him or even resentful. Mostly she seemed sad.

Once more, he shifted his gaze to where she sat with her parents. He wondered what had driven her to withhold Jason's illness from his father.

He knew this gathering—this brief sense of normalcy—meant a lot to Paige and even more to Jason. He cared too much about both of them to cast a shadow over it. He had to put his questions aside for the time being. At the first opportunity, he needed to learn from Paige what the facts were. He felt conflicted by his strict code of right and wrong and his deepening feelings for her. As a lawyer, he made decisions based on facts, and at the moment, he felt he didn't have them.

He'd gleaned a new piece of information, though. He'd learned that Jason had a birthday coming up. A puppy was out of the question. Paige had already told him dogs weren't allowed in their apartment building. He'd have to find another way to make this birthday special for Jason.

When Daniel said good-bye to Paige that night, there was a remoteness he couldn't mask. He knew she sensed it. He saw the bewilderment—and, yes, the hurt—in her eyes.

THE OPPORTUNITY TO discuss the matter came two days later. Jason was at an after-school spelling bee practice and Daniel met Paige at the end of her shift. They were picking up Jason together and having dinner. They had some time before Jason's practice was over, so Daniel suggested they go for coffee.

The coffee shop was empty except for them. They took a table by a window.

Daniel tried not to sound like a lawyer doing an examination for discovery, but some things were deeply ingrained, and he couldn't help it. He put the question to her bluntly.

"No." Paige shook her head, eyes slightly narrowed. "Jason's father didn't die. Where did you get that idea?"

"From you."

She raised her brows. "I didn't say that. I'm

sorry if I left you with that impression. I didn't intend to."

"Okay. But you haven't told me anything about him. I would've thought, especially under the circumstances, that he'd be very present in Jason's life. Does he know about Jason's condition?"

"No."

Daniel already knew as much from his conversation with Chelsea, and he let that go for the time being. He reached for her hand, squeezed it. "You've got to trust me at some point."

In an edgy gesture, Paige pulled her hand away, linked her fingers and placed her hands on the table. "Jason was only three when Mark left."

"That's when he was first diagnosed with cancer, wasn't it?"

"That's right."

"He just left?"

Paige nodded.

Daniel couldn't imagine any human being abandoning his or her family during a crisis, but he didn't voice his opinion. He'd never met the man, but if that was what he'd done, he was developing a strong dislike for him. He rose, needing to move. He strode to the window, his back to Paige.

She sighed. "I know it sounds terrible, but don't judge him too harshly. He had his reasons."

Daniel spun around. "Reasons? What possible reason could a man have for leaving his family, his *child*, at a time like that?"

"Mark was simply incapable of dealing with Jason's illness. Since he was a child, Mark has had a fear of hospitals. Perhaps understandable, based on what he went through as a kid, but he couldn't—or wouldn't—put his fears aside to do what needed to be done for Jason."

Daniel continued to stare at her, unable to understand.

"It was the first time in our marriage that I didn't back down. That I didn't concede to him when we had a difference of opinion. Based on the very best medical advice, it was clear what Jason needed medically. Mark didn't want to subject Jason to anything other than proven drug therapies, and certainly not to the risk of surgery. I must've seemed like the proverbial fierce lioness protecting her cub. He ultimately gave up fighting me. What I didn't realize at the time was that by making him give in to me about Jason's medical care, I'd chased him away."

Daniel's anger was ready to boil over. "Now you're making it sound as if it was your fault."

"Maybe it was." She held up a hand. "Please, let's not argue about that. Let me try to explain. Mark couldn't deal with the possible consequences. He was so terrified of the potential outcome, he cut all ties with us. I assume he believed that what he didn't know wouldn't hurt him. Does it seem rational and sane to you and me? Probably not. But it was part of his nature."

Before Daniel could say anything, she went on. "A weakness. A flaw? Call it what you will, but Mark was a damaged person. I hadn't known that when I married him." Paige shrugged. "Not that it would've made any difference. I was naive and in love. I thought love could change the world. If I'd known about his circumstances at the time, it still wouldn't have made a difference to me. I still would've thought love could fix that, too." A smile played briefly at the corners of her mouth. "But it wasn't enough. He was terrified of loss, and he compensated by being controlling. Wanting everything his way. With the best of intentions, to protect and preserve what was his."

Daniel shook his head. "But—"

"I tried to be there for him," she broke in, "to talk things through and support him. I suggested counseling, and I got him to go once.

Nothing seemed to help, though, and the longer we were married, the more controlling and emotionally inaccessible he became. Admittedly, when Jason was first diagnosed with cancer, I was so focused on him and his needs, I couldn't help Mark with his issues at the same time."

Daniel shook his head again and sat down. He reached for her hand. Her fingers were cold.

"Whatever *issues* he had, it's irrelevant. Jason and his needs should've taken priority, and he should've been there for both of you."

"As I said, it's not that simple. Mark had his own demons from his childhood."

"I can't imagine anything that would justify walking away from his family like that."

"He had his reasons." Paige closed her eyes. Based on her expression, Daniel assumed she was having an internal debate about how much she wanted to share with him. He was about to interject when she continued. "As a young child, Mark idolized his older brother, Chad. Mark was so much younger, but he always wanted to prove to his brother that he was all grown-up. That he was worthy of doing things with his brother and his friends. Of being included."

Daniel nodded, not sure how else to respond.

"One day, he hid in a motorboat his brother and a friend had taken fishing. He was just climbing out from under a tarp when they hit a large wave caused by the wake of another boat. The boy who'd been steering must have overcompensated, and Mark was knocked off balance. He tumbled over the edge, and his brother dove in after him, but the friend panicked and steered the boat around. The hull caught Chad hard, resulting in serious head trauma requiring surgery.

"The surgery was bungled, and Chad became disabled and ultimately died. Mark's parents were awarded a large sum of money, which Mark inherited as a college student when his parents died in a single-car accident. His parents had been drinking. Mark connected their drinking to the loss of their son. He was probably right about that."

Paige paused, but resumed the story a moment later.

"It was too much for Mark. He dropped out of school and let the money define him. As a child, he'd felt he had no control over anything. He couldn't change being the youngest son. He couldn't change his brother not accepting him. He couldn't change losing his brother and his parents."

"So…"

"So money became a means to an end for Mark. A way to control people and manipulate them. He tried to exert that control over me. The money had never mattered to me. But over the years, he'd insidiously taken control of our lives. I could no longer make decisions about anything. Until Jason was diagnosed with cancer."

"And then?"

"I had to put a stop to it. The situation wasn't just about me any longer, accepting whatever Mark wanted, even if it conflicted with my wants. I had to do what I considered right for my son. Nothing took priority over that. Mark didn't want to hear about any treatment or surgery that had risks. Of course, that included virtually everything the doctors recommended. Mark and I clashed over it. Despite the best medical advice available to us, he was terrified by the thought of surgery. For him, I think the fact that the tumor was in Jason's brain connected it more directly with what had happened to his brother."

She shook her head. "He made it clear that if I pursued the recommended course of chemo and possible surgery, he wouldn't have anything more to do with Jason…or me."

"I still don't understand how it's possible for a father to walk away from his son."

"Mark always said it had to do with his past. What I just explained to you. He didn't want anything to do with Jason once he became ill. At the time, I couldn't understand it, either. But now… Mark saw his brother's decline… and then lost him *and* his parents. I don't think we can appreciate what that would do." Paige dropped her head in her hands, running her fingers through her hair.

With her head still lowered, she murmured, "I don't know. Mark loved Jason. There was no question about that. He doted on him. I guess he couldn't deal with losing someone he loved again. By shutting us out, he wouldn't know, and he wouldn't have to deal with…things not turning out well. If the chemo hadn't worked, surgery was the next step. Mark drew a hard line there. We weren't even at the decision stage, but the thought of it, and my being adamant that if surgery was what was needed, that's what we'd do, seemed to be the final straw."

She shook her head again slowly. "I just don't know if I let Mark down in some way. If I could've helped him with his problems…"

Daniel clenched his fists and felt a quick flash of anger, but he knew that wouldn't do her any good. Fighting back his irritation, he relaxed his fists and placed a hand on her forearm. "Paige, you can't feel guilty about what happened...about what *he* did."

"If I hadn't pushed...if I'd been more willing to talk things over...if I'd been more supportive..."

Daniel raised his hand to cup her face. "Paige, no. Don't beat yourself up over this." When she finally looked at him, he held her gaze. "It's *not* your fault. No," he cut her off when she was about to protest. "In no way was it your fault." He felt he now had the facts about her husband's departure. But he still had an equally important question, one he needed an answer to. "Under the circumstances," he began, trying to soften the blow, "have you been keeping Jason from his father?"

"What?" Her head jerked up. She grabbed the edge of the table. There was a hot fire in her eyes. "My son *always* comes first with me," Paige said vehemently. "I did what I had to for the sake of his health. To break free from Mark's control, I accepted an agreement surrendering all financial support in exchange for sole legal custody of Jason."

"Paige—" he interjected.

She held up her hand. "I know what you're going to say. That what I did wasn't smart. No. Wait." She forestalled him again. "I *needed* to be able to make decisions in Jason's best interests on my own. You can't know what's smart or what's right unless you were in my shoes at the time.

"If I wanted money from Mark, he would've had to be involved. He would've had to know what the money was for. I already explained to you that he wouldn't support surgery or even some of the experimental drugs the oncologist was recommending. It was hard enough trying to figure out what the right thing was. I couldn't compromise my ability to do what I considered best for Jason by letting Mark have his say. Just the extra time to work through everything with Mark could have cost Jason his life."

Tears welled in Paige's eyes and spilled over. She brushed them impatiently away. "Jason is *everything* to me. Right or wrong, I did what I felt I *had* to do. But whatever the circumstances, whatever the relationship between Mark and me, I wouldn't have deprived my son of his father, or kept Mark from knowing his son." Her eyes shimmered with emotion. "To answer your question, no, I never would've kept Mark from Jason. That would have been cruel and unforgivable."

Daniel rose and went to Paige, his arms open. "I'm sorry."

Paige rose, too, but kept her distance. "So am I. I'll get Jason myself tonight." She turned and walked out of the coffee shop.

PAIGE WALKED BRISKLY toward Jason's school. She'd wanted so much to step into Daniel's arms, have him hold and comfort her, but she couldn't. He hadn't trusted her. He'd questioned her motives. Worst of all, he'd thought that she'd robbed her son of having a father. And that hurt to the core.

With a little distance and a lot of agonizing, Paige started to understand why he'd asked the questions he had. She hadn't meant to be secretive about Mark. It was simply an aspect of her life she hardly ever talked about. Call it a survival mechanism. She hadn't been forthcoming, and Daniel could've seen that as being secretive. If he'd believed Mark was dead, only to learn that he wasn't but had no role in Jason's life, she couldn't fault him entirely for jumping to conclusions.

She needed some time. Not because she wanted to punish Daniel. She just had to get over the hurt of Daniel's not trusting her and thinking she'd do something as abhorrent as keeping her son from his father. What she hadn't counted on was how saddened Jason would be by the rift between her and Daniel, by not knowing when they'd see him again. That only served to reinforce her worries about how Jason would take the end of her relationship with Daniel, should it come to that. But she had to admit, she missed Daniel, too.

It was obvious that Daniel was giving her the time she needed, but he'd sent her a beautiful floral arrangement by way of apology. It had lilies and chrysanthemums and baby's breath—and at least two dozen long-stemmed yellow roses.

"We're back to yellow roses again," Paige observed to Chelsea when the arrangement arrived.

"Not everyone thinks about the symbolism of flowers. I doubt that's the message he's sending you."

"What does that mean? Symbolism?" Jason asked.

"It means something representing or standing in for something else," Paige explained.

"What do the flowers symbolize? You were talking about the flowers, and Chelsea said not everyone thinks of them with symbolism."

Paige laughed. At times, she had to remind

herself that Jason was only seven years old. "We were talking about the yellow roses. You know when Daniel sends me flowers there are always yellow roses in the arrangements? Yellow roses symbolize friendship. So my point was that for Daniel to send me yellow roses, he must want to be friends."

Jason had a thoughtful expression on his face and nodded. "It's nice that he wants to be your friend. But that's not why he gives you yellow roses."

"It's not?"

"No. He does it because yellow is your favorite color."

True. Yellow *was* her favorite color, but it had to be a coincidence. She'd never mentioned it to Daniel, and he had first sent her flowers after they'd spent most of Christmas Day together. He didn't know much about her then, and certainly nothing as trivial as her favorite color. "I'm sure that's not the case."

"Uh-huh. It is. He said your shirt was pretty when he was here at Christmas. Your yellow one. And I told him it's your favorite color. Then he sent you yellow flowers. See! I *am* right."

Chelsea nudged Paige on the shoulder and smirked. "I was right, too!"

PAIGE DECIDED SHE'D been foolish to hold off seeing Daniel as long as she had. The chance to make amends presented itself when she received a call from Jason's oncologist. At Jason's last appointment, he'd asked her if she'd like to meet with other parents who had gone through circumstances like the ones she was facing. She welcomed the opportunity, feeling it might help with her own decision about surgery for Jason. The oncologist connected her with the mother of a child who'd had the surgery he was recommending.

Paige could meet with the woman one-on-one, and have an open and candid discussion with someone who must have experienced the same hopes and fears. The little girl had her surgery nearly eighteen months earlier, and she'd been cancer-free ever since.

The family lived in Hartford. Since Paige was going to be in the city anyway, it was the perfect opportunity to see Daniel.

Mr. Weatherly insisted that she take his Mustang—probably because he still felt guilty about his misplaced suspicions. Her only restriction was that she had to be back by four to pick Jason up from school.

Daniel enthusiastically offered to take her for lunch when she mentioned the possibility of seeing him.

Since Paige couldn't predict how long she'd be with the woman she was meeting, she and Daniel agreed that she'd go to his office when she was done.

Paige was encouraged by her discussion with the young cancer survivor's mother. Her morning had gone very well, and just before one in the afternoon, she walked into the plush reception area of Lindstrom, Kinsley and McGuire.

A receptionist, petite with a sweep of shoulder-length sable hair, was seated behind a low counter. "May I help you?" she inquired cheerfully.

When Paige informed her that she was meeting Daniel, the receptionist said someone would be with her shortly.

The woman who came to greet her a few minutes later reminded her of the voluptuous redhead on *Mad Men*. There was a smile on her face, but her eyes were shrewd and appraising. Paige rose and smoothed her skirt. She felt gauche in her simple skirt and sweater, next to the gorgeous woman in her impeccably tailored sapphire-blue suit. The woman extended a hand, introducing herself as Selena Wharton, Daniel's executive assistant.

She and Paige shook hands, and the smile spread from Selena's lips to her eyes. Paige had the odd feeling that she'd just passed some kind of test, but she wasn't sure what—or why.

Paige followed Selena down a couple of long corridors. The walls were muted gold and subtly textured. Framed paintings hung between doors opening into large offices. At the end of the second corridor, Selena shifted to the side and gestured for Paige to step into an even larger corner office.

Daniel was sitting at an expansive desk, his fingers flying over the keyboard of his computer. Selena motioned for Paige to enter, and she disappeared silently back down the corridor. Since, oddly, Selena hadn't announced her, and Daniel hadn't yet noticed her presence, Paige took a moment to absorb the grandeur of his office.

The walls were papered in a luxurious material she presumed to be silk, and they were lined with bookcases in the same wood as Daniel's desk. One wall had a credenza with a built-in minifridge and a coffee machine on top. There was a seating area with a sofa and two armchairs upholstered in burgundy leather. Expensive, refined but unpretentious, she concluded.

Then she saw it.

Jason's painting of the tiger. It hung to the

right of Daniel's desk, where he couldn't help seeing it.

"Oh, you framed it," she exclaimed.

Daniel raised his head. "What? Oh, hi." He smiled and rose immediately. "It's good to see you, but sorry—what did you say?"

Paige moved closer to the desk and pointed at Jason's painting of the tiger. Daniel had selected a reddish-brown frame, the finish resembling a tigereye gemstone. Paige thought it couldn't have been inexpensive, but it worked beautifully with Jason's painting.

"I didn't mean to interrupt. It's just that I saw the painting…"

"Yeah! It looks great, doesn't it?"

Paige studied the depiction of the tiger. Daniel's eyes were on her when she turned back to him. He gestured to the sofa in the corner of his office. "Would you like something before we go? A coffee? Some water?"

"I'd love a coffee, thanks."

He made her a cup of coffee, then sat in the armchair kitty-corner to hers. Leaning toward her, he wiped a teardrop from her cheek with a forefinger. He rested his forearms on his knees and linked his hands. "Do you want to tell me about the painting?" he asked gently.

Paige inhaled deeply. Daniel had a right to know, to understand the significance of what

Jason had done. She took another bracing sip of coffee before placing the mug on the coffee table. "You remember me saying Jason painted it for someone else?"

Daniel nodded.

"He painted it for his father."

Daniel unlinked his hands and leaned back. "I thought you said neither of you has had contact with him in years?"

"No. I mean, yes." She chuckled. "That is, no, we haven't had any contact with him and, yes, that's what I told you." She reached for her mug again. She needed something to do with her hands. "I only found out this Christmas, but every year since his father left us, Jason's been making him a Christmas gift. He's been storing them in a box in his closet with the hope of being able to give them to him one day." She shook her head and stared into her mug. "This year, he painted the tiger for him."

Daniel glanced over at the painting. "Jason said he based it on a tiger he saw at the zoo."

"He told you that?"

Daniel nodded again. "I assumed you'd taken him to the zoo during the summer."

Her laugh held no humor. "His father took him the last summer we were together. Jason was three. I had no idea he'd remember that. It's like his fascination with circuses. I told you the last gift his father gave him was a toy circus set. Jason's never actually seen a circus but he's crazy about them because of it."

Daniel rose and came over to sit beside Paige, then draped one arm over her shoulder, drawing her against him. "I'm sorry. I didn't realize. He didn't say anything about it to me." He brushed his lips across her temple. "Would you like the painting back?"

"No." She swept the back of her hand across her cheek. "No. I just wanted you to know."

Daniel tucked a loose strand of her hair behind her ear, cupped her chin in one hand and turned her face up to his. "I'll treasure it that much more. As far as Jason's father goes, I'm sorry I jumped to conclusions. I'll try not to repeat that mistake."

AT LUNCH THEY discussed Paige's meeting that morning. After they returned and Daniel had said good-bye to her, he stood in front of the painting. Jason had painted the tiger for his father and yet had given it to *Daniel*, despite having just met him.

He exhaled loudly.

Either the kid was bighearted or... He wasn't sure how to finish that thought. He didn't want Jason to start thinking of him as a father figure. He'd be no good at that. He already had a soft spot for Jason, and he had no intention of hurting the kid…or his mother.

They needed someone steady, someone who could give them the white picket fence they both longed for, and that wasn't him. He was glad he and Paige had resolved the issue concerning her ex-husband, but where did that leave them? History often repeated itself, and they wouldn't be comfortable in the type of relationship his parents had. Paige and Jason deserved someone with an open, loving heart. That wasn't him. It just wasn't in his makeup.

Things were getting serious between him and Paige, and he wasn't sure what to do about it.

With another lengthy exhalation, he sat down at his desk and tried to focus on a settlement brief he was drafting.

His concentration didn't last long. He heard a soft tap on the doorframe. He glanced up from his computer as Selena came into his office. She sat on one of the chairs in front of his desk and dropped the sheet of paper she was carrying on her lap. "It's getting serious between you and Paige, huh?"

He felt his brows draw together. He wasn't pleased about Selena's words echoing his own thoughts. "Why do you say that?"

"For one thing, in all the years I've worked

for you, I don't think you've ever invited another woman you were dating to the office. Other than for a company function, of course."

Daniel continued to scowl at her.

Selena straightened his inbox, aligning the short side with the edge of his desk. "I like her. She has a good handshake." The right side of her mouth tilted up, and a dimple winked in her cheek. "She seems to bring out your sensitive side."

"My *sensitive* side?"

The other half of Selena's mouth curved up. "Yeah."

Daniel felt an itch at the back of his neck but resisted scratching it. "How did you come to that conclusion?"

Selena gestured toward the framed painting of the tiger. "That, for one thing." She lifted the sheet of paper off her lap and slid it toward him. "This, for another."

He glanced down at the paper. His eyes darted back up. "How did you get this?"

"Okay, before you shoot the messenger, it wasn't my doing. It was included with the florist's statement. You've never placed an order for flowers yourself."

Yeah, he had for Paige, a couple of times, but he wasn't about to confess to Selena.

"Or more to the point, you've never composed your own message before. Certainly not one like this." She reached out with a finger and spun the paper around. In an exaggerated, sultry voice, she started to read: "Beautiful flowers for a beautiful—"

Daniel held up his hands. "Okay, okay, I'm not a poet, and you don't have to read it to me. I know what I wrote." He grabbed the paper. "Why was it sent to you with the statement? I used my personal credit card."

She shrugged. "Maybe they recognized your name and accidentally charged it to our corporate account, but there it is." Before she walked out the door, she turned back and gave him a huge grin. "Just saying!"

It was on the tip of his tongue to tell her to stay out of his personal affairs, but he refrained. She didn't deserve that. They'd known each other far too long and always had each other's back. Instead he raised his voice so she could hear him in the corridor. "Call the florist and have them credit the firm and charge it to me."

Her laughing voice drifted back to him. "Sure thing!"

"And tell them if they make that mistake again, we'll be looking for a new florist."

He could still hear her laughing as she walked back to her desk.

CHAPTER SIXTEEN

PAIGE CLEARED UP after dinner, while Jason sat at the dining room table reading. The phone rang and she reached for a dish towel to wipe her hands before lifting the receiver.

There was an odd tone in her mother's voice as they exchanged greetings.

"I'm not sure how to ask you this, honey," Charlotte began.

"What is it, Mom?" Panic coursed along Paige's spine. She cast a glance toward Jason; his head was still bent over his book. She moved to the far end of the kitchen to be out of earshot.

"Your dad's nurse, Ruth, had a family emergency today so she couldn't come in."

"Is everything okay with Dad?"

"Yes. Yes, it is. The Oakridge Seniors' Center sent another nurse to fill in until Ruth can resume her duties. This nurse has done assignments for Oakridge before, so she knows some of the management team. She said something…strange that I wanted to discuss with you."

Paige's palms were getting clammy, and she wiped her free hand on her jeans. "Okay. What is it?"

"She said that your *husband* made the arrangements for Stephen's care. That the reason it was so affordable was that he made a very large donation to Oakridge. He set up a trust fund to cover the subsidy, with money left over for the Center to use for other purposes. Do you know anything about Mark having done that?"

Paige was speechless. Not only was she certain that Mark wouldn't have done anything of the sort, how on earth would he have known about her father's condition and the care he needed? Her uneasy feeling persisted, and then realization dawned. Her words were calm when she finally responded. "Mom, Mark and I haven't been in contact for years. No, I don't think he had anything to do with it."

"Then who? Oh…" Paige knew her mother had reached the same conclusion.

"Leave it with me, Mom. I'll get back to you. Love you. Give my love to Dad."

"I will, and I love you, too, honey."

Paige finished up in the kitchen. When she was certain that her emotions were under control, she joined Jason at the dining room table. "How's it going, sweetie? It's almost time for bed."

"I'm just about finished, Mom. I was doing some reading ahead of the other kids."

"You were?"

Jason avoided eye contact and started to doodle on the pad next to his book. "I thought I'd do some extra reading now. In case I don't feel so well next week, or some other time."

"Oh, Jason." Paige wrapped an arm around his thin shoulders and kissed the top of his head. Why hadn't she considered the added complexity of Jason's being in school and how much he enjoyed it?

Jason's bright blue eyes were intense when they finally met hers. "I don't want to miss a year because I'm sick."

"Why would you think that?

"'Cause of the surgery. If I've gotta have it. Anyway, I asked my teacher what we'd be working on next, and she told me all the stuff she's going to ask us to do at home for the rest of the school year. I want to do well so I can be an architect…or a lawyer, like Mr. Kinsley."

"You'd make a wonderful architect or lawyer." Paige knew that her little boy's strong will to live was as essential to beating this disease as the miracles of advanced medicine. She was thankful for it. She folded her arms on the table and offered, "Would you like some help?"

AFTER JASON WENT to bed, Paige made herself a cup of tea.

If her assumption was correct, that Daniel was behind the arrangements for her father's care, she was enormously grateful to him. It had allowed her mother to avoid a painful decision. She pulled out the file folder containing the research she'd done for her mother some time ago and ran some numbers. The cost to Daniel to make this happen must have been significant.

Her problem with the situation was two-fold. How could he have not discussed it with her? Okay, it was a wonderful thing he did and extraordinarily generous, but to do it without any input from her at all? Taking away her family's role in deciding on something so fundamental? That might have been moot in this case as, of course, they wanted to keep her father at home. But Daniel had denied her the chance to have her say. What about next time, if the decision wasn't so evident? Wasn't this what Mark used to do? Throw his money around and expect everyone to fall into line?

And what about the money? The cost of subsidizing home care for her father, for however long he'd need it, was huge. Mark had never spent that much on her or Jason. Yet with Mark there was always the underlying expectation that they'd be beholden to him and that whatever was at stake was entirely under his control. They had no say. This had been the driving force behind her trading off any financial support for Jason in favor of having sole legal custody.

How on earth could she make her concerns clear to Daniel without seeming to be a complete ingrate? It certainly wasn't a subject to be discussed over the phone. And it wasn't a discussion she wanted to have when Jason was around. She'd just have to bide her time, but it kept nagging at her.

SUNDAY MORNING, MR. WEATHERLY was taking Jason to an art exhibit on indigenous plants. Mr. Weatherly was interested from a botanical perspective, and Jason loved to see paintings whenever he got a chance.

Paige wondered whether there were other seven-year-olds who preferred art exhibits to video games, but this outing gave her the chance to talk to Daniel about her father's care.

She made him brunch, because it was what

she liked to do. It was also a small way to repay him for his generosity.

They were well into the meal, and she still hadn't found the opportunity to raise the subject with him. She wanted to strike the right balance between ensuring that he knew how much she appreciated what he'd done, and making him understand her concerns as to how he'd gone about it.

Paige toyed with her scrambled eggs. Although she'd rehearsed what she wanted to say a hundred times, all her well-crafted words deserted her. But she had to set the ground rules.

Daniel raised an eyebrow. "Is something wrong?"

She lifted her head and met his eyes. "Why do you ask?"

"For starters, you're playing with your food rather than eating it."

She wished fervently that she didn't need to have this discussion with him. She wished she could remember how she'd decided to say it.

"Tell me what's wrong, and maybe I can help."

"That might be the problem," she murmured.

A confused expression flitted across his face. "Sorry. What?"

"It has to do with your helping. It's about

the incredible deal Mom's getting from the Oakridge Seniors' Center for Dad's care." Paige kept her eyes on Daniel, steady and unblinking. She saw the sudden understanding in his. "You're responsible for it, aren't you?"

Daniel put down his utensils and pushed his plate away. "Yes, I am. How did you find out?"

She had a huge concern, and he was worried about how she'd found out? "How did I find out?" she echoed. A shrill note crept into her voice, and she struggled to control her temper. This was *not* how she wanted the conversation to go. She wanted to be calm and reasonable.

It wasn't working.

"Not the way I should have. How could you do this and not discuss it with me?"

"For this very reason—the way you're reacting right now," he said matter-of-factly.

"That's not fair. Discussing something with me *before* you do it is entirely different from me finding out *after* the fact."

Daniel's patience was obviously nearing its limit. "Look, I was only trying to help. Can't you just say 'thank you'?"

Paige couldn't stop herself. Her utensils clanged as she tossed them on her plate. "*Thank you?* Is that what you want? Is that what this is all about? You want me to be grateful to you? *Indebted* to you?"

"Whoa." Daniel held up his hands, palms out. He hadn't expected Paige to be pleased if she knew what he'd done, but her reaction seemed entirely out of proportion. "Can you calm down? Let's discuss this like adults." He saw the anger flare in her eyes. Okay, maybe he should have left out that last part.

When in doubt, he always fell back on logic. "Like I said, I just wanted to help. To start with, I like your parents. You and your mother were concerned about having to place your father in a home. Neither of you could afford the cost of home care. I can afford it, and I wanted to do this. The net effect is that your father's at home with your mother, which all three of you want, and he's getting the best possible care. Where's the harm in that?"

He could almost see her anger deflate, replaced by—what? Frustration?

"You want to talk about it?" he asked. He was about to add "calmly," but wisely refrained.

Paige took a deep breath. "I'm…I'm sorry. I know I should be thanking you. Instead, I nearly took your head off."

Relieved that the worst seemed to have

passed, Daniel rolled his shoulders to release some of the tension and leaned back in his chair. "I would like to understand why."

Paige shrugged. "First of all, I'm just wound up about everything. I suppose it also has to do with my ex. Again, I'm sorry for that. Mark used his money to—I don't know—buy acceptance. Buy control. The things he thought he didn't have as a kid. Mostly, I think he felt that through money, he could control everyone. Nobody would ignore him. No one would leave him out. There was never any consultation or discussion. No opposing views. When Jason became ill, he tried to apply the same logic. His money, his choices." She shrugged again. "The fact is you made this decision without talking to me about it or even letting me know, and using your money to fix things felt like what Mark used to do."

Daniel wanted to ask whether she saw the difference now that they'd discussed it, but decided to leave things as they were. He didn't want to set off another argument. When he was in a court of law, the argument between two lawyers was intellectual, logical. He enjoyed the challenge of that. But this was emotional. Frankly, emotional outbursts made him uncomfortable.

Maybe he should consider himself lucky to

have lived without them his whole life. "I'm sorry I didn't tell you what I was doing, but I didn't want it to become an issue. I understand that you don't like accepting financial aid. I figured you'd feel the same way about this, and I didn't want your father ending up in a home. No," he broke in when she started to speak. "Let me finish, please. What's done is done. I don't have any ulterior motives. I don't expect anything in return. If it's all the same to you, can we just let it go?"

Daniel reached for her hand, took it into his and stroked his thumb over her knuckles. Raising her hand, he brushed his lips where his thumb had been. "I'm sorry I didn't tell you. I did what I thought was best."

PAIGE EXPLAINED THE situation to her mother. Her mother went on at great length about how kind and generous Daniel was. What an angel he was. How much she appreciated what he'd done for her and Stephen. For *all* of them. Paige held her tongue and—thank goodness her mother couldn't see—rolled her eyes. "We should do something special for him to thank him."

"Mom, I don't think that's a good idea."

"Why ever not? It's the least we can do." Charlotte sounded shocked.

"Uh...Daniel and I had an argument about it. We reached a truce, but I'd rather not open it up again."

"Oh, dear. But, Paige, I *have* to thank him for what he did. It would be rude and ungrateful not to. How about if I send him a thank-you note instead?"

Paige sighed heavily. It would be futile to try to explain her view of it to her mother, and Charlotte did have a point. She knew she sounded ungrateful. But she couldn't help it. She was struggling, still not sure she could trust Daniel if he didn't discuss something this important with her before he acted on it. "Okay, Mom. Go ahead. I need to leave for work."

NOT BEING VERY good at hiding her emotions, especially lately, Paige knew she was visibly upset when she said good-bye to Jason and Mrs. Bennett, and her bad mood lingered when she returned home from work late that evening. Mrs. Bennett insisted they have a cup of tea before she went back to her apartment. Once they were settled on the sofa, Mrs. Bennett asked, "What's worrying you, dear?"

Paige thought about denying there was anything wrong, but maybe she just needed to get it all out, because it was clearly festering inside her. She shook her head. "It shouldn't bother me. He's been absolutely wonderful. But I can't help making comparisons."

"Slow down, dear. I presume we're talking about Daniel, but otherwise I have no idea what you mean."

Paige pushed her hair back from her face with her fingers and took three deep breaths. "Sorry. Yes." She explained to Mrs. Bennett what had happened.

"And you're comparing him to Mark?"

"Yes." The word came out on another loud breath. "I know I shouldn't. But I'm reminded of the way Mark was. And Daniel doesn't see it."

"I've never met your ex-husband, but I find it hard to believe that those similarities exist, based on what you've told me about him and what I've seen of Daniel."

"It's just…"

"Just what?"

"I feel terrible even thinking this. Daniel has been so good to us, and he never asks for anything in return. I know that's not how it was with Mark. Mark was always thinking about how his money and spending it would benefit him." Paige looked at Mrs. Bennett.

"Go on, dear."

Her voice dropped to a whisper. "It *always* had to be about Mark."

"And you think Daniel is like that?" Mrs. Bennett sounded truly shocked.

"No!" If Paige thought about it logically, she knew this wasn't the case. But still… "Daniel *does* have strong opinions. And he's decisive. He makes up his mind, and that's it, while I'm still working things out."

Mrs. Bennett opened her mouth, but Paige rushed on before she could protest. "Again, I know it's not the same as it was with Mark. I know Daniel has Jason's—*our*—best interests at heart. But they're still not his decisions to make. Even if he's helping us out."

"You think he doesn't know that? Doesn't respect it?"

"I think he does. But look at what he did for Dad. He didn't even tell Mom or me about it, let alone discuss it with us. He just went ahead and used his money to get the home care for Dad."

Mrs. Bennett had worn a neutral, even sympathetic, expression on her face the whole time Paige had been speaking, but now her expression showed dismay. "But this wasn't a decision *Daniel* made on your behalf. Both you and your mother made it clear that you wished you had a way to keep your father at home. Daniel *knew* what you both wanted."

"Okay. Yes, but—"

"I've listened to you, dear. Now you listen to *me*. Think it through. What would you or your mother have done if Daniel had come to you and offered to pay for your father's care? For the reasons we've been discussing, you would've said no, wouldn't you?"

Paige thought about it, and it was hard to argue.

"Even without that, it would've been difficult for you to accept that sort of money, especially on an ongoing basis." Mrs. Bennett's voice softened again. "Paige, look at me, dear. He *knew* what you wanted, and he made it happen. He tried to do it in a way that wouldn't upset you or your mother, wouldn't make you feel obligated to him. Where's the harm in that? If you ask me, what he did is extremely kind and generous."

Where's the harm in that? Weren't those the same words Daniel had used? When Paige remained silent, digesting everything that had been said, Mrs. Bennett continued. "If not for that silly goose of a nurse, you would never have known what he'd done. And isn't that the furthest thing from what your ex-husband used to do? Didn't he always want to be recognized and appreciated for everything? It seems to me Daniel wanted exactly the opposite. Do a good deed, and not have anyone know he'd done it. He's certainly not using his money as leverage, not if he didn't want you to know about it. It isn't similar in the least to what your ex used to do. Do you see that?"

Paige sighed again. She seemed to be doing that a lot lately. "Yes. Yes, I suppose I do."

Mrs. Bennett smiled. "There you go. Give him a chance then, dear. You don't want to miss out on something very special, do you?"

CHAPTER SEVENTEEN

DANIEL STARED AT Jason's painting of the tiger. He liked it on his office wall. He liked looking at it. This wasn't some sentimental thing, when a parent was delusional about his kid's talent or lack thereof. This kid really *was* that good.

Daniel preferred to keep it there rather than at home, since that way he could see it more often.

Okay. Maybe there *was* sentiment involved.

He opened a desk drawer and pulled out a file folder. In it was the painting Jason had made of the three of them on Christmas Day. They seemed so happy, so right together.

There was an odd feeling inside him and it seemed to be spreading. He was really starting to care about the kid. He'd never seriously considered having kids. If he couldn't see himself married, there certainly wouldn't be any kids as far as he was concerned. Daniel was old-fashioned in some ways. But getting to know Jason? He couldn't help thinking what a hoot it would be to have a kid just like him. He was smart, polite, well mannered. And talk about strength! Considering what he'd had to deal with all in his short life, he was a pretty courageous kid. And his mother was special, too. He was completely enthralled. Heck, he was more than halfway in love with her.

Back to the kid. What did he want for Christmas? Next to nothing when you thought about the circumstances he was in. No trip to Walt Disney World. No celebrity visits or concerts.

And now his birthday was approaching. There was only one unfulfilled wish on Jason's Christmas list from the Wish I May Foundation.

The kid just wants to be normal. And how could he do that for him?

Part of it was wanting to have a father. Daniel couldn't blame him. Didn't every kid? But that wasn't something Daniel could help with.

He looked back at the painting of the tiger, and it jogged his memory. Hadn't Paige said Jason had never been to a circus, despite his fascination with them? Sure, he'd requested a book on circuses for Christmas and Daniel had obliged, but that gave him an idea. He'd take Jason to a circus for his birthday.

But where on earth was he going to find a

circus, especially at this time of year? They were a rare occurrence these days.

His mind was made up. He knew exactly what he wanted to give Jason for his birthday. He'd just have to figure out how to go about it.

Daniel checked his schedule and decided he had time to take a short drive.

DANIEL DROPPED DOWN in the chair facing Laura Andrews's desk. "Thanks for seeing me without an appointment."

"For you, my door is always open. Besides, business is relatively slow for us right now. What's up?"

"I need your help."

"Not again!" She smiled. "Am I going to have to break the rules this time?"

"I don't think so."

"Okay. Shoot."

"It's about Jason."

"I surmised that much."

"Here's the thing. He loves circuses—it's a long story—but he's never been to one. His birthday's coming up, and I want him to be able to experience a circus. The problem is that there just aren't any around here, and Jason can't travel."

Laura nodded sympathetically, but uncertainty showed on her face.

Daniel leaned forward. "I'm going to give him a circus for his birthday."

Uncertainty turned to skepticism. "You're going to bring a circus to Camden Falls?"

"No. To Hartford. And it's not so much *bringing* a circus here as *creating* one."

"Sorry. You've lost me."

"This is where I need your assistance. Here's what I'm thinking."

Daniel outlined his idea of creating a circus, and his need for a suitable venue and volunteers. Having seen the Foundation's warehouse in Hartford, he thought it would be an ideal location, and with Laura's network of kind-hearted volunteers, he knew she could rally the troops. He showed her a book on magic tricks that he'd purchased on the way to her office. He'd decided he would be a magician for Jason's extravaganza. "Well? What do you think?"

"It sounds ambitious, especially in the time frame you're suggesting. You're welcome to use the warehouse. It's virtually empty, and we can spare it for a few days. As far as our staff and volunteers go, I can send out an email and see who's willing to get involved."

"That's wonderful!" Daniel got up and held out a hand to Laura. "Always a pleasure doing business with you, Ms. Andrews."

When she placed her hand in his, Daniel thought *the heck with it* and pulled her into a hug, not realizing until he'd released her that he felt no discomfort over it.

The wheels were in motion. Now he'd have to rope in Paige's neighbors to help organize the circus, and get Paige and Jason to Hartford without letting them find out why. He'd also have to learn some magic tricks.

MAY FIRST, THE DAY before Jason's birthday, everyone involved in the circus gathered at the Foundation's warehouse. Six of the staff and volunteers were there, as was Chelsea. Mrs. Bennett had assisted by sewing some of the costumes, but they thought it would be better for her not to wear herself out, especially since she was charged with the important task of coaxing Paige and Jason to Hartford the next day. Mr. Weatherly was there, too. He and Laura were in a private huddle in one corner of the large space.

Although some finishing touches were still needed, the warehouse had been transformed. They were there for a rehearsal, costumes and all. The only thing missing was the animals. There was no place to accommodate them overnight, so they were coming in the next day, early in the morning.

A sense of anticipation pervaded the room, and everyone was eager to get going. They were waiting for Laura and Mr. Weatherly. Daniel strode over to get them.

He was surprised to see them jump apart like guilty kids when they heard him approach. "I didn't mean to startle you. We're ready to begin the rehearsal."

"Oh, no problem. Harrison was just telling me a funny story from when he was in the merchant marine."

Harrison? Daniel had been acquainted with Mr. Weatherly for months now. He'd never known his first name. In fact, it had never even occurred to him to ask what it was. He stuffed his hands in his pants pockets and chuckled softly as he followed the other two back to the group.

Once they were gathered together, Daniel clapped his hands to get everyone's attention. "All right, team. Let's get this show on the road."

SATURDAY MORNING, THE DAY of his birthday, Jason was eating his favorite breakfast—chocolate pancakes with raspberries. He'd already opened his cards and gifts. They were just finishing breakfast when Mrs. Bennett arrived at their door.

Paige didn't expect to see Mrs. Bennett so early in the morning, dressed to go out. "Is everything okay?"

"Yes. Yes. Please don't worry. But I do need to ask you a favor."

"Of course." She took Mrs. Bennett's elbow and guided her into the apartment.

Mrs. Bennett waved at Jason. "Happy birthday, dear!"

"What is it you need?" Paige inquired.

"I have a doctor's appointment in Hartford today."

"On a Saturday?"

"Well, yes. It's a clinic. Mr. Weatherly agreed to drive me, but he had an unexpected matter come up. I know it's Jason's birthday, and I'm sorry to impose."

"But I don't have a car."

"That's no problem. Mr. Weatherly left me his." Mrs. Bennett took the keys out of her pocket and handed them to Paige.

It might have been Jason's birthday, but Mrs. Bennett did so much for them and she hardly ever asked for anything in return. Paige couldn't refuse. "Of course. I don't think Jason'll mind staying with Chelsea for a while. I'll check with her to see if it's okay."

"I'm sorry, but that won't work. Chelsea's not available. I tried her, too. She's not home.

Jason will have to come with us. We won't be long."

"All right. When do we have to leave?"

"As soon as you and Jason are ready."

Paige checked her watch. "We should be ready in half an hour."

"I appreciate this. I'll wait for you across the hall."

AN HOUR AND a half later, Paige was following Mrs. Bennett's directions.

"Are you sure this is right?" Paige asked.

"Yes. I have it written down here." She tapped the piece of paper resting on her lap.

In the back, Jason scooted up between the two front seats as far as his seat belt would allow. "I've been to lots of hospitals and clinics. If you ask me, we're lost."

"It's okay, dear." Then Mrs. Bennett pointed. "There. You turn left, up ahead, on that road."

"This can't be right," Paige said. "This looks like an industrial area. There's no clinic here."

"Trust me. Turn here. Now pull into that drive."

Paige slowed the Mustang but didn't take the turn. "There's got to be a mistake. The sign says this is the Wish I May Foundation warehouse." She narrowed her eyes and looked at Mrs. Bennett. "Is there something I should know?"

Mrs. Bennett patted her arm. "Trust me," she said again.

Paige backed the Mustang very carefully into a parking spot. Oddly, there were quite a few cars in the lot. While she waited for Mrs. Bennett and Jason to climb out, she noticed a Mercedes that resembled Daniel's, parked half a dozen cars farther down the row. Frowning, she narrowed her eyes again. What was going on?

Jason slid his hand into hers as they followed Mrs. Bennett to the side door of the building.

With an alacrity that astonished Paige, Mrs. Bennett pounded on the metal door with her fist. Not waiting, she opened the door herself and stood aside to let Paige and Jason enter first.

They took one step over the threshold and came to a halt.

There was a loud chorus of, "Happy birthday!" Then silence.

Jason's whispered, "Mom, look," echoed through the cavernous space, before carnival music blasted, and lights, motion and the scent of buttered popcorn filled the air. Jason tightened his grip on Paige's hand and pulled her forward.

In addition to some of their neighbors, a

number of Jason's friends from school rushed over to greet him and wish him a happy birthday. There were people Paige didn't recognize and others in colorful costumes that concealed their identities.

A multihued tent had been erected inside the warehouse, creating the feel of being under the big top. Hay was scattered across the concrete floors.

Further inside, the aroma of the popcorn mingled with the sweet scent of candied apples and the ripe smell of live animals.

Jason let go of Paige's hand and turned in a slow circle, trying to take it all in. Something caught his attention, and he gave a little whoop, then raced over to a fenced enclosure, followed by his friends. Four piglets were foraging inside. A tall clown, sporting a bushy red wig and a large round plastic nose gamboled over, dressed in baggy polka-dotted pants. He made all the kids giggle. Sounding oddly like their neighbor Mr. Weatherly, the clown peered down at Jason with his blackened eyes and exaggerated red lips on a white-powdered face and asked, "Would you like to come and play with the piggies?"

He didn't have to ask Jason twice. In seconds, Jason was inside the enclosure, stroking and feeding the piglets, laughing at their squealing.

"Young master," the clown announced a while later. "Your presence is requested at the center ring. Our entertainment is about to start."

Jason, his friends, Paige and Mrs. Bennett sat on wooden benches beside a makeshift ring with a sand floor. They all had bags of popcorn and paper cups of soda, and watched acrobats, a juggler and—to Jason's great delight—a masked magician who spoke with an odd accent and even pulled a pink-eyed, snow-white rabbit out of a hat.

After the magician's act, the clown reappeared and escorted them to a group of tables, where they were joined by all the performers for a lunch of French fries and hot dogs cooked on an electric grill.

Jason had confetti in his hair and mustard smeared around his mouth. His face was aglow as he chatted with his classmates and new circus friends.

When all the kids seemed to have had their fill, the clown announced that there was one final attraction. Jason took one look at the center ring, and his mouth fell open. He ran full speed toward the magician, who was holding the reins of a chestnut-brown pony with a pale blond mane and tail. The pony had a blanket and a small saddle on his back, an old straw hat on his head with his ears sticking through, and a garland of flowers around his neck.

Jason came to a skidding halt at the edge of the ring, his friends around him. The excited chatter made Paige smile. She sensed that Jason would be a hero to his school friends for the foreseeable future.

"You'll all get your turn," the magician assured the kids, "but let's start with our birthday boy." He motioned for Jason to hop the low, wooden barrier and join him inside. "Meet Bertie."

The pony's back was slightly higher than the top of Jason's head.

"You can pet Bertie, if you like," the magician said.

Jason stroked the pony's coat, then ran a hand along his silky blond mane. "Wow! I've never touched a horse before!"

"Technically, he's a pony. He's full-grown, so this is as big as he'll get. Would you like to ride him?"

"Yes, please!" Jason bounced up and down with enthusiasm.

The magician showed Jason how to mount the pony and adjusted the stirrups once he was in the saddle. He instructed Jason to hold on tight to the pommel and produced a small cowboy hat, which he plopped on top of Jason's head. "Ready?" At Jason's vigorous nod, the magician proceeded to walk the pony around and around the ring before venturing beyond and ambling through the warehouse.

Paige felt undeniable pleasure and immense gratitude watching her son whoop and holler. As they took one final lap around, Paige knew she'd have to thank the magician for the incredible day. While the clown was the master of ceremonies, there was no doubt in her mind that the magician was the ringmaster.

JASON BARELY TOUCHED his dinner that night, and for once Paige was okay with that. All the excitement and exertion—not to mention popcorn, hot dogs and candied apples—had gotten to him. He was in bed by eight-thirty, and their nightly reading ritual lasted no more than ten minutes before he was sound asleep.

With the rest of the evening to herself, Paige indulged in something she loved but rarely had time for—snuggling up on the sofa with a mug of tea and a good book. She was so engrossed in her book, she jolted when the phone rang. Lunging for it so it wouldn't wake Jason, she curled her legs under her, smiling when she heard Daniel's voice on the other end.

"You sound tired," he commented.

"Tired but happy. Thanks to you."

"Me? What did I do?" he asked innocently.

She tugged at a loose thread in the seam of her sweater. "Well, for one, you pulled a rabbit out of a hat. I mean literally *and* figuratively. Today had to be the best day of Jason's life. I don't know how you did it, but I'm very grateful. It was a wonderful thing to do."

Daniel gave up the charade. "I'm glad he enjoyed himself. I had a lot of fun with it, and a *lot* of help. Are you upset with me for not checking with you first?"

She chuckled. "It would hardly have been a surprise if you had."

"I'm glad—and a little relieved—you see it that way."

"I do have one question. Where did you learn to do those magic tricks?"

"I bought a really good how-to book." After a brief pause, he added, "You might want to keep an eye on Mr. Weatherly."

"What's wrong with him?

Daniel laughed. "Nothing's *wrong* with him. As it turns out, he's quite the charmer. I think he and Laura have a thing going."

"You're joking."

"Mark my words. You'll see."

They hung up shortly after. Rather than returning to her book, Paige leaned back, sipped her tea and thought about Daniel.

She'd been worried about getting involved with him for so many reasons. The timing was wrong. He'd be a distraction when her entire world was focused on Jason. He wouldn't understand her or Jason. She shook her head. How misguided she'd been! He was bringing so much to her life and Jason's, just when they needed it most.

She inserted the bookmark and closed her book, took her mug to the kitchen, and for the first time in a long while, went to bed with a smile on her face and lightness in her heart.

CHAPTER EIGHTEEN

JASON WAS NEARING the end of his treatment regimen. Decision time regarding surgery was fast approaching, and Paige was starting to feel panicked about it.

Jason was having dinner at a friend's house after school. Paige had arranged the playdate so she could meet with Jason's oncologist in the afternoon to discuss the latest MRI. The scans were critical to determine whether the treatments were having the desired effect of shrinking the tumor.

The good news was that the tumor had shrunk again. The bad news was that the doctor still believed Jason's only chance to be cancer-free was to undergo surgery once the tumor was small enough. There was considerable risk, and the surgery didn't come with any guarantees that he'd be free of cancer.

Paige let herself into their apartment and went into the kitchen. She plugged in the kettle, then picked up the phone to call Daniel, planning to cancel their dinner date. She knew she'd be miserable company. She really needed to process what the oncologist had told her and decide what to do.

"How did it go?" Daniel asked.

It always warmed her heart that he thought of Jason first. "Pretty well. The tumor's shrunk another half centimeter."

"That's wonderful news!" He paused. "But you don't sound happy. Why?"

When had he come to know her so well? "Of course, it's great news, but the oncologist still thinks surgery is Jason's only chance."

His voice sobered. "Why don't we talk about it when I get there tonight?"

"Actually, that's why I'm calling. It's probably best if we reschedule. I'm going to be poor company, and I've got a lot to think about."

"Whatever you want to do is fine with me, but I've got a good pair of ears. Is Jason still at his friend's house?"

"Yes. Why?"

"I'd prefer that you weren't alone this evening. Whether you want to talk about it or not, I'd like to see you tonight. Are we still on, then?"

She unplugged the kettle and poured the hot water into her mug. Maybe he was right; maybe it *would* help to talk it through with him. "Yes, we're on. Thanks."

He had a good point about not being alone. She felt relieved when she hung up the phone, knowing she wouldn't have to be. Checking the stove clock, she realized she'd better hustle if she wanted to change and get dinner started before Daniel arrived.

By seven o'clock, she was dressed in her taupe pants and the lilac wool sweater he'd given her for Christmas. Her hair was coiled in a chignon, and she'd taken the time to apply a pale pink lip gloss, one of the few cosmetics she owned.

She had the carbonara sauce for the spaghetti simmering on the stove and a pot of water ready for the pasta. She'd made garlic bread, which was waiting to be put in the oven. And she'd set a couple of wine glasses on the counter, as Daniel had said he'd be bringing a bottle of wine and dessert.

When Daniel arrived, he took her in his arms. "How are you holding up?"

"Better, now that you're here."

He gave her a tender kiss. "I'm glad."

She went back to the kitchen and he followed her, inhaling deeply. "Smells wonderful." He uncorked the bottle of wine and poured while she turned on the burner under the pot of water and slid the garlic bread into the oven.

When she'd finished, Daniel handed her a

glass of wine, and she leaned back against the counter.

She took a sip. "I know with my head that the right thing is to go ahead with the surgery," she began. "But my heart? I keep struggling with the thought of gambling away what little time Jason may have, risking his life for a surgery that could…" As she battled to compose herself, Daniel gathered her in his arms again. "It's just such an enormous decision. It terrifies me that I could make the wrong choice."

She slipped out of his embrace, reached for the wooden spoon and turned to the stove to stir the sauce. "I just don't know what to do."

"I think you do."

She glanced over her shoulder, furrowing her brows. "What do you mean?"

"I think you've made your decision. You're just not ready to admit it yet."

She knew he meant going ahead with the surgery. She thought, again, about the potential consequences. "No, I haven't," she objected, her voice rising.

"Why don't we sit down and talk about it?"

She didn't *want* to sit down. She didn't *want* to talk about it. If they did, it might mean she'd actually have to make the decision. He was right—she wasn't ready for that. Once she decided, the course would be set. Her child's fate sealed. A flood of panic surged through her. "I don't want to sit down. I'm making dinner."

"Paige." Daniel put his glass on the kitchen table and moved behind her. He placed his hands on her shoulders, kneading gently. "You know what you have to do."

"I do *not*." What if she made the wrong decision? Could she live with herself? If Jason had the surgery and something went wrong… But if he didn't, she'd never know.

Daniel dropped a soothing kiss on the nape of her neck. "You have to go through with the surgery. If you need money, I'd like to help." His statement was definitive. His tone calm and matter-of-fact.

Paige wasn't sure which annoyed her more. And he thought he'd just casually toss in that he'd pay for the surgery? Her temper simmered and threatened to turn into a rapid boil. She threw Daniel a smoldering look over her shoulder.

Daniel took a step back. "I'm just trying to be logical here."

Paige whirled around. Carbonara sauce dripped from the wooden spoon and splattered on the floor as she jabbed it toward Daniel. "*Logical?* How am I supposed to be logical about an eight-year-old kid having cancer for the third time?"

Her eyes filled with tears of anger and frustration. As Daniel wiped up the spilled sauce, she turned back to the stove and swallowed a sob.

DANIEL REMEMBERED THE last time he'd seen that look in Paige's eyes, when they'd argued. It had been over his arranging home care for her father. He'd been lucky to get out of that altercation with barely a singe. He didn't want to chance it again. He knew this was a much more important matter and understood why she would be sensitive. But angry? What was it about her that she could be so sweet and gentle but then without warning go off like a rocket? No, he didn't want a repeat performance.

He kept his voice low and what he considered reasonable, a tone he frequently used with agitated clients or moody kids on his softball team. "Can we take this down a notch?"

Paige spun around. "What?"

"Can you not yell, please?"

Her eyebrows shot up. "Why shouldn't I yell? I'm upset!"

He thought about that for a moment. "I don't know. I'm just not comfortable with it."

"Didn't you fight in your family? Raise your voices?"

Her anger seemed to have dissipated, and he was grateful for it. "No, not that I recall. You fought with your parents?" Having witnessed firsthand how close they were, it didn't seem plausible to him.

Paige let out a fleeting laugh. "Ask my mother about my years in high school. She calls them my 'rebellious years.' She'd say there wasn't anything we *didn't* fight about."

"I still can't imagine it. You seem to get along so well. Weren't you close back then?"

"Of course." She angled her head. "Just because we fight doesn't mean we don't love each other. Just the opposite. Mom and Dad have always been my…my safe place. I could tell them anything. They wouldn't judge. They wouldn't placate. They'd tell me exactly what they thought. We didn't always agree, so at times we fought." She chuckled again. "Oh, you should've heard Mom and me go at it sometimes! I think the neighbors could hear us."

Daniel remembered his own quiet, polite upbringing. As far back as he could recall, he'd considered his parents' possible reaction before he said anything. Even as a kid, if he didn't think they'd approve, he'd hold back whatever he'd intended to say. "And it didn't bother you? Or them?"

"I suppose it did at the time. But I knew they loved me. Deep down, even when I argued with them, I knew they had my best interests at heart." She sipped her wine, the confrontation evidently behind them. "You didn't argue with your parents? Not even as a teenager?"

He thought about never having seen his parents show any signs of outward affection. At the other extreme, he truly couldn't remember having seen them angry. Certainly they'd never yelled, at him or at each other. "No," he said slowly. "I don't think I've heard them raise their voices, ever." He took a drink of his wine. "You know, I heard somewhere that the opposite of love isn't hate. It's indifference. Not caring one way or another." He leaned back against the counter, crossed his legs at the ankles and stuck his free hand in his pocket. "I don't think they cared enough to yell." That was disconcerting. Feeling restless, he put his glass down and started to gather what he needed to set the table.

Paige shut off the burners and turned to Daniel, resting a hand on his arm. "I'm sorry I lost my temper. There's so much going on in my mind, and like I said, I'm terrified of making the wrong decision for Jason."

"Apology accepted." He drew her into his arms. "You know, you don't have to do this all on your own."

He could tell she was conflicted. She needed his help, and he was sure she realized it. But it also meant sharing the burden. Letting go a little—letting him in.

Over dinner they discussed the surgery for Jason again. Daniel listened as Paige weighed the pros and cons, at the end coming back to where they'd started—knowing that, under the circumstances, the surgery was the only thing that made sense.

"You're making the right decision," Daniel assured her. "It's his best chance."

Paige had hardly touched her spaghetti. She pushed her plate away, folded her napkin and placed it on the table. "I know," she said with a slight trembling in her voice. "Now I need to figure out how I can pay for it."

"I'll—"

She stopped him before he could finish. "I appreciate what you're going to say. Please let me deal with one major decision at a time, okay? Let me think about it first."

Daniel nodded slowly. "Just know that the money doesn't mean that much to me. Jason does."

PAIGE TALKED THE whole thing over with her mother on Friday. Charlotte had left Stephen with his home care nurse and taken the train to see Paige. The subject wasn't one they wanted to discuss over the phone.

Although Charlotte shared the same doubts and fears, it was a huge relief for Paige to know her mother came to the same conclusion she had. "It's his best chance."

"Thanks, Mom. That's what Daniel said, too."

"Smart man. Speaking of Daniel, how is he, honey?"

"Mom, I…" Paige pressed a hand to her belly.

Charlotte reached forward, stroked her hand along Paige's arm. "What, honey?"

"Oh, Mom." She rubbed her stomach to calm the million butterflies fluttering around, then slid her hand up to cover her heart, to still the pounding. "I think I'm in love with him."

Charlotte smiled, her eyes bright. "That's wonderful! Daniel seems to be a delightful, strong, principled man." The sparkle in her eyes dimmed. "But you don't look happy. Why?"

Paige took her mother's hand and they linked fingers. "Oh, he *is* all that and more." She cast her eyes down. "I don't know what's wrong with me. I'm so unsure about so many things these days. I've never been like this before."

Charlotte gave her hand a squeeze. "You're carrying a huge burden, and you've been through a great deal." Her eyes were warm and brimming with concern. "You and Mark split years ago, but this is the first true relationship you've had in all that time. You're a strong, positive person, but you're not without your limits. Mark left you with a lot of scars and some understandable insecurities. Just remember that Daniel is *not* Mark, and you're a wonderful person, well worth loving."

"Oh, Mom." Paige rested her head on her mother's shoulder. "I'm also worried about what's going to happen with Jason and Daniel."

"I thought he was crazy about Daniel?"

"Yes, he is. That's the trouble. How will he feel if Daniel stops being part of our lives?"

Charlotte nudged Paige's knee. "See? There you go again. You're worrying that Daniel will leave you like Mark did. Think, Paige. You're smarter than that."

This was where Paige's head and her heart parted company. She chewed on her lower lip.

"Give him a chance, honey. Judge him on his own merits."

And wasn't that almost the same thing Mrs. Bennett had told her?

"WHAT'S BOTHERING YOU?" Selena had worked as Daniel's executive assistant for a decade now. He shouldn't have been surprised that she'd know something was troubling him.

"Did you see who just left my office?"

She smiled. "Not only did I see, I made the appointment for him, remember? Aaron Hudson, entrepreneur extraordinaire, pillar of our society, devout family man, yada yada…"

"Right. Well, do you know what he wanted?"

Selena slid into the chair opposite his desk and crossed her legs. Her smile widened. "If you're going to play Twenty Questions, I might as well make myself comfortable." When he stared at her with a raised brow, she added, "Fine. I'll play. Seeing as how you're a divorce lawyer, I expect it's going to be another messy divorce. Now do you want to tell me what's *really* on your mind?"

Daniel spun his chair around and gazed out his window. The picture-perfect family from Christmas had long been replaced by an ad for a Caribbean resort. He gestured toward it. "See that?"

She leaned forward. "What are we looking at?"

He gestured again. "The billboard. See that couple walking arm in arm along the shoreline? Or the inset. The couple holding wineglasses and laughing as if they don't have a care in the world? Who lives like that?"

Selena leaned back again. "Ah, I see. The Hudson divorce is going to be a particularly unpleasant one, huh?"

Daniel turned to face her again and dragged his fingers through his hair. Her eyes followed his hand. "Am I that transparent?"

"Sometimes. Why don't you take off now and go get your hair cut?"

"What?"

"Go get your hair cut," she repeated. "It's a little long. Have a massage. Go smoke a cigar."

"You know I don't smoke."

"Don't be so literal. *Do* something that'll get you out of the office and put you in a better mood."

He tapped his fingers on the desk. "Not a bad idea. I don't think it'll help, though."

Selena tilted her head. "Why?"

"Because it won't change anything. Every day is the same. Just once, I wish I could see a happily married couple."

"Well, you can. Five o'clock today."

He reached for his iPhone. "I have a five o'clock appointment?"

Selena laughed. "Oh, yeah. You're having a bad day, all right. *You* don't have an appointment. *I* do. Tony's picking me up after work. And—back to your question." She waved a hand toward the billboard. "Tony and I live like that."

"It's early yet," he mumbled, and was immediately apologetic. "Sorry. I really am out of it today, huh?"

Selena leaned forward and patted Daniel on the cheek. "Yes, you are," she said fondly.

He dragged his fingers through his hair again, testing the length. "Since I don't smoke and I'm not too keen on massages, maybe I will go get my hair cut."

Selena pushed out of her chair. "Good. I might leave a little early, too."

As Daniel was packing up his briefcase, Selena called him. "I'm sorry to mess up your plans, but you have someone here. No appointment, but I thought you might want to see her."

"Who is it?"

"Laura Andrews from the Wish I May Foundation."

"Okay, please send her in."

CHAPTER NINETEEN

"WHAT CAN I do for you, Laura?" Daniel asked after she was seated in his office.

"I'm sorry to stop by unannounced, but the most impressive family came to see me today. They have two kids, Henry and Lexa. The little boy, Henry, is just six years old, and has muscular dystrophy. He already needs a wheelchair to get around. Lexa is only two. Although she's not showing any symptoms yet, MD is hereditary, and there's a chance she may develop it, as well.

"Dad is working two jobs to make ends meet. He's an engineer, but he works at a factory at night. Mom, who used to be the manager of a clothing store, can no longer work. She needs to be with the kids 24/7. But their spirit, Daniel! You wouldn't believe how positive they are, and how committed to their family. They've been getting by, but they've run into a problem and need help."

"You're looking for sponsorship?" It occurred to him that maybe he should get together with his partners, make a lump sum annual contribution to the Foundation and let Laura decide how to disburse it to the families who needed it the most. Hearing these stories broke his heart but also reinforced his belief in the human spirit.

"No," Laura said.

"Sorry?" He must've been wrapped up in his own thoughts. He could've sworn he just heard Laura say no.

"No, I'm not looking for money today, Daniel. I'm looking for your time. The family is struggling, of course, but they're getting by. I already have a sponsor for them to help with extras. What they need—and can't afford—is some legal advice."

"What kind of advice?"

"They purchased a higher level of insurance to supplement the father's employer's plan, but the company has denied their claim. From what I understand, the family is legally entitled, but the insurance company is refusing to pay Henry's medical expenses. Based on something an adjuster inadvertently let slip during a conversation with the father, it's because they recognize that Henry will never be cured. Just the opposite, in that the disease is progressing and will cause further deterioration in his mobility. His illness can lead to other chronic conditions, too, such as lung failure, scoliosis and cardiac fibrosis. And, as I said, there's a chance that Lexa will develop MD, as well. So, the insurance company obviously sees a high level of ongoing expenditures for the rest of Henry's life, and possibly Lexa's." She took a deep breath.

"So here is the favor I need," she went on. "Could you look at the insurance policy? It would really help them out."

"It's not my area of law, but sure, I can have a look."

Laura pulled a file folder out of her briefcase and handed it to Daniel. He promised her he'd review the policy as soon as possible.

When he did, he was outraged. The family had been paying substantial premiums for the higher level of coverage well before Henry was diagnosed with MD. Under the terms of the policy, they were clearly entitled to the benefits, and they needed them badly. As Laura had surmised, the insurance company had apparently balked once they realized Henry would need medical care for life, and there was a chance his sister would, too. The costs would be enormous.

But there was no question the policy applied. Daniel understood what the company was doing. They thought if they made it challenging—and costly—enough for the family to pursue the matter, they might just give up.

But the company hadn't bargained on Daniel representing them. He got the ball rolling immediately.

It was almost disappointing how quickly the insurance company capitulated once a lawyer was involved. They knew they had no legal basis for denying the claim, but Daniel wished there'd have been a bit more of a fight, since he was raring to go.

When he shared the outcome with the father, the man broke down in tears of gratitude and relief on the phone.

Daniel couldn't remember feeling more satisfied with the outcome of one of his cases in…well, ever.

And that was a sobering realization, one that got him thinking.

Over the next few days, an idea formed in his mind.

By the end of the week, it had gelled sufficiently that he decided to get Paige's perspective on it.

As Paige preferred to cook for them rather than go out to dinner, since it was easier on Jason, Daniel was equally adamant that he'd supply the groceries. He had never dated anyone who actually liked cooking for him, and he enjoyed the simple but delicious comfort foods she prepared. They were having an exceptional meatloaf with mashed potatoes, gravy and mixed vegetables.

Daniel wiped his mouth with his napkin. "I've been thinking about making a change in my career."

Jason was still spooning mashed potatoes soaked in gravy into his mouth, but Paige's fork halted in midair. "I had a case earlier this week." He outlined the situation with the family and their insurance company. "It was one of the most straightforward cases I've ever handled, but being able to tell this family that they would get the payments they were entitled to gave me more satisfaction than I can remember experiencing in my career.

"I think about how much the two of you have brought to my life, and then I go to work each day and deal with nastiness. I'm tired of it."

Jason stared at Daniel. "You're going to quit being a lawyer?"

Daniel chuckled. "Nope. Just practice a different type of law. I wanted your opinion."

Still wide-eyed, Jason pointed at his chest. "Mine?"

Daniel nodded. "Yours. And your mom's. I'm thinking of starting my own practice. I'll continue working with families, but instead of doing divorce and custody cases, I'd help families in need of assistance with hospitals or insurance companies. A kind of legal aid for families with sick children." He looked expectantly from Paige to Daniel. "So, what do you think?"

"That would be a wonderful thing to do…" Paige began.

"I hear a 'but' coming. Go ahead," he told Paige. "I want your opinion."

"I don't mean to sound mercenary, but could you make money at it? I mean, wouldn't these families be much like Jason and me? Their finances would be pretty tight?"

"Yes. But there are options. Government agencies that provide funding, for example. The services could also be funded through charitable organizations, such as the Wish I May Foundation. I discussed it with Laura, and she thought it was a great idea. And in the most dire cases, I can work pro bono."

Paige nodded, but uncertainty showed in her eyes.

"Sure, my billable rates will be lower, and I won't make the same amount of money I do now, but so what? I had a bit of an inheritance from my grandfather. I've invested wisely. I'll still make a good income, and I'll see if I can maintain an interest in my current firm and do some work for them when I have the time. Just not divorce or custody cases. Maybe contract law."

Jason had been following the discussion between his mother and Daniel, and chimed in. "So, you'll be working for kids like me, and helping them?"

Daniel nodded.

"And you'll take away some of the worry from their moms?"

"I hope so."

"That's so cool!"

Jason's simple statements tipped the scales for Daniel.

DANIEL WAS EXCITED about his new business and dove into the preparatory work immediately. He signed an agreement with his partners that allowed him to branch off and start his own practice. To Daniel's delight, they didn't want to lose him; they valued his business acumen and marketing savvy as much as his legal expertise. They drew up a contract that would let Daniel keep his shares in the firm in exchange for ongoing managerial responsibilities. In reciprocity, his partners— believing in what Daniel wanted to do and, admittedly, seeing a tax benefit—took a part interest in his new firm.

The agreement was much more favorable for Daniel than he would have dreamed. Although he'd been prepared to take a significant cut in pay, the fact that he wouldn't have to be too concerned about a big impact to his finances was a huge burden lifted. He was grateful to his partners. As a bonus, Selena would continue to support him both at Lindstrom, Kinsley and McGuire, and his new company, which he decided to call Heartfelt Legal Services. He chose to work out of his home initially, until he had a few relationships established, such as with the Wish I May Foundation. Then he'd be able to better assess where his office should be located. In the interim, if he needed to meet with clients, he could use the boardrooms of Lindstrom, Kinsley and McGuire.

Now he needed to set up his new office, even if it would just be a virtual office to begin with. He needed basic marketing and business collateral, such as a logo, letterhead, business cards and a website. Because it was a smaller boutique firm, Lindstrom, Kinsley and McGuire didn't have the in-house expertise for this type of work. Daniel had to find another way and absorb the cost in Heartfelt's overhead.

Jason raised an unexpected idea one night. "Why doesn't Mom do it for you?"

Daniel shifted his gaze to meet Paige's.

"She used to do stuff like that all the time when she worked for the other company," Jason explained. "I know, 'cause she used to do it at home, too. She was really good at it." There was pride in his voice.

"I bet she was."

"There wasn't much to it," Paige said. "I worked with a company on the visual brand, then used it to create all the templates for business cards and stationery. Since it wasn't a very big enterprise and they didn't need a complicated website, I used an online service provider and set it up for them."

"Really?"

"Mom, give him the website address so he can see!"

Daniel looked up Paige's former company on her computer. He was impressed. The site was clean, appealing, professional and easy to navigate.

They discussed the matter long after Jason went to bed. Finally, Paige agreed that she'd help Daniel set up his virtual office, and she'd work on it from home when she wasn't at the call center. Paige initially resisted accepting payment from Daniel, but he ultimately convinced her that she should treat this as a business venture. After all, if she didn't do it, he'd have to hire someone else. It wasn't as if it was all coming out of his own pocket—which was the biggest stumbling block for her. His agreement with Lindstrom, Kinsley and McGuire had them picking up part of the overhead. This definitely qualified.

Paige was shocked at the hourly rate he offered her. It was nearly twice what she was making at the call center. She loved the idea of helping him and doing something creative for a change. By accepting payment from him, she could scale back her hours at the call center, as long as she worked the minimum necessary to keep her benefits. Best of all, she'd be more available for Jason.

Daniel wasted no time getting her started. He bought her a new laptop, which thrilled Jason, especially when Daniel showed him some of the most popular online games for kids.

PAIGE WAS WORKING on the Heartfelt website at the dining room table, and Jason was sketching.

"Look at this, Mom." Jason spun his sketch pad around so his drawing was facing Paige.

She pulled the pad closer, examined the

drawing and looked up at Jason thoughtfully. "Is this what I think it is?"

Jason made a funny face, grinned but said nothing.

"I assume that means yes. So, tell me about it."

He cleared his throat, sounding very mature and businesslike. "Mr. Kinsley said his company would work for families with sick kids. And you said he needed a...a logo? Is that what it's called?"

"Yes, that's correct."

"Something that *symbolizes* the firm. Something that stands for what it is, right?"

"That's right."

Jason pointed to his drawing. "This is a family. See here? The tall person is the father. This is the mother. And this is their daughter. Oh, and their dog." He turned to Paige and looked at her mischievously. "You know, every family should have a dog."

She kept her eyes on his but didn't say a word.

"Aaanywaaay," he continued, drawing out the word. "This kid here? See how they're all huddled around him, sort of protective and all?"

"Uh-huh."

"It's because he's sick. He's sick…like me. Except he's got a dog…and a dad."

"Oh, sweetie," she murmured.

"They're all there to help the kid," he continued. "And Mr. Kinsley will help him, too. That's what his firm will do. And see this?" He pointed to the heart-shaped outline of the family unit, broader at the shoulders, narrow at their feet and dipping down between the mom and dad. "This shows the name of the company—you know, *Heart*felt—but it also shows that someone cares. That Mr. Kinsley cares, so they know they're not alone." Jason traced the heart-shaped outline of the logo with his finger.

Paige continued to examine the drawing, nodding her head slowly. The drawing was well done. Jason hadn't gone into fine detail, as he was prone to do with his sketches. He seemed to understand that a logo should be simple, representing what a company stood for but easy to reproduce. Easy to identify with. Jason had nailed it. This was an outline— a schematic, really—of a small family with an ill child. The parents and sister clustered around him represented a single family unit. How smart was that of Jason? And the heart shape was somehow buoyant and positive and, as Jason said, showed someone cared.

Paige's laughter was light. "How did you come up with this?"

Jason looked sheepish. "I listened to you and Mr. Kinsley talk about what he wants to do. And I know he cares. A lot." He shrugged. "I just put it on paper."

Paige leaned forward, grasped Jason's face between her hands, and gave him a kiss on the nose. "You, my beloved son, are extraordinary!"

Color rose in his face. "You like it, Mom? Really?"

She gave him another smacking kiss. "Like it? I love it!"

"Do you think Mr. Kinsley will like it? That he'll use it?"

"I can't speak for him, sweetie, but let's show him and see what he thinks. Okay?"

DANIEL WAS EVEN more enthusiastic about the logo than Paige had been.

"Like it? I love it!" he exclaimed.

"Did Mom ask you to say that?"

"No. She didn't. Why would you think so?"

Jason giggled. "Because that's what *she* said!"

"She did, did she?" Daniel picked up the sketch pad and scrutinized the drawing. "Well, she's a smart lady."

Jason bounced in his seat, barely able to contain his excitement. "So? Will you use it?"

Daniel's face turned serious. He put down the sketch pad. "The logo's perfect. I didn't know what I wanted, but you got it right."

Jason looked at Daniel with such hope that Paige thought she'd have to hurt Daniel if he let her little boy down.

"So, you want to use it, right?"

"I do. No question about it. But here's the thing." Daniel turned a shrewd eye on Jason. "How much do you want for it?"

Jason's face revealed a range of emotions until he finally settled on a hesitant smile. "You want to pay me for it?"

"You did the job. You should get paid." After some negotiation with Paige, Daniel gave Jason twenty dollars to buy his design. He'd offered to give him a hundred, but Paige thought that was too much for an eight-year-old. The deal done, Daniel winked at Jason, and with mock seriousness said to Paige, "We need to teach you about the art of negotiation. If you're on the receiving end, the trick is to negotiate the amount *up*, not *down*!"

With the matter of the logo settled, Jason presented another idea. "Mom, why don't you do this stuff for Mr. Kinsley full-time?"

She glanced at Daniel and smiled. "It's a

nice idea, but there's not enough work to keep me busy full-time."

"Then why don't you do it for other people, too? You know, help them set up their offices and websites?"

Paige laughed, but Daniel looked pensive. "The kid's got an idea! Why not, Paige?"

She was at a loss for words. If Daniel was giving it some credence, it might not be as crazy an idea as she'd first thought. She'd loved doing the work for her old company and loved doing it for Daniel even more. She'd toyed with the possibility of returning to the business world, but the hours were always a deterrent. She'd never thought of setting up her own consulting practice. Working from home would be wonderful, but could she make a living at it? And if she left the call center, she'd have to factor in the cost of a private health care plan.

"Think of the advantages, Paige," Daniel continued. "You could set your own hours, be more available for Jason and do something you enjoy and that seems to make you happy. You already have a computer. Why not start your own home-based web design and maintenance company?"

"Oh, no. The computer isn't mine. It's yours. When I'm done with the work for you, you should take it back. And web maintenance is only part of what I did for my old company. I don't know if I'm good enough to do it for others."

"Actually, I wanted to talk to you about that. I'd like to put you on retainer to keep my website up to date, handle social media for the company and deal with any other office-related matters that come up. That means the computer stays with you, and you can use it for other clients, too. If you want my opinion, you can do it."

She felt a bubble of excitement forming in her belly. Oh, to not have to go to the call center anymore! To be able to work from home and do something she enjoyed, something that gave her a sense of accomplishment. "You really think I can do this?"

"Absolutely. You've got your first contract. With me. I'll check with the powers that be at Lindstrom, Kinsley and McGuire, too. See if they need any work done."

She shook her head. "I can't have you giving me all the work!"

He smoothed her hair back and tucked it behind her ear. "I won't have to. I'm just giving you a start. I know your work will sell itself."

"You'll do it?" Jason asked excitedly.

Paige pressed a hand to her belly, where the

bubble had clearly burst and excitement was rioting. "I think so."

Jason did a fist pump in the air, the way he'd seen Chelsea do. "Yay, Mom!"

LINDSTROM, KINSLEY AND McGuire signed a contract with Paige, as did Laura Andrews on behalf of the Wish I May Foundation. Paige was guardedly optimistic about her new business venture. Although she had three contracts, they were all Daniel's doing. It wasn't enough work for her to resign from the call center altogether, but she was thankful for the reduced hours. Her new schedule gave her far more time to be with Jason.

To succeed with her business venture, she knew her focus had to be on getting other contracts on her own merits. That would take time and energy, two things she had in short supply.

CHAPTER TWENTY

AFTER JASON'S LAST MRI, his oncologist delivered very encouraging news. Jason's tumor had shrunk to a size that made surgery viable. They had one more treatment scheduled, but the time had come to set the date for his surgery if they were going to proceed. Paige continued to struggle with the possible consequences, but she knew it was the right—the necessary—thing to do.

Friday night, Daniel arrived shortly before seven. "What's that?" Paige asked, pointing to the yellow folder in his hand.

"Let's discuss it later." He gave her the brown paper bag in his other hand. "This is for now, for dinner." When she accepted the bag and pulled out a bottle of merlot, he tucked the folder inside the sleeve of his jacket and hung it up.

As they ate dinner, Daniel updated them on the clients his new firm was already representing. "The work's highly gratifying," he concluded. "I'm enthusiastic about making a difference for families who really need it."

Jason squirmed in his chair. "Mom, tell Mr. Kinsley *your* good news!"

He turned to her expectantly.

She grinned. "I signed my first new client. It's a local pet store that wants to expand its reach by offering their products online."

"Tell him *how* you got your new client, Mom!"

Paige chuckled. "Jason sold them."

"Can I tell it, Mom?"

"*May.* Yes, you *may.*"

"We were walking home from school and Mom let me go inside to see if they had any puppies. They didn't. The lady said it's cruel to have them in stores. But we were just talking to her, and she was saying how she wanted to sell some of the stuff she has in the store online. I told her what Mom did. The lady checked the Wish I May Foundation website right then. She called Ms. Andrews to see how she liked working with Mom. Sort of a report card. Then she asked Mom to give her a price."

Daniel smiled broadly. "Congratulations!"

Paige shrugged but couldn't hide the fact that she was thrilled. "I should put Jason on payroll."

"She really liked the work Mom did for the Wish I May Foundation."

"See?" Paige said to Daniel. "My top salesman."

Later that night, with Jason tucked into bed, Daniel retrieved the folder he'd brought with him. Paige had nearly forgotten about it. Seeing it aroused her curiosity, but she also felt an odd sense of trepidation.

He must have read her expression since he was quick to reassure her. "It's nothing bad. I promise." He took it to the dining table with him and put it down there.

He tapped a finger on the file folder. "I've been doing some research."

Paige's eyes went to the folder, then up to his in question. "On?"

"Cancer treatment facilities."

Paige felt her doubts resurface. She responded with a noncommittal, "Okay." "Here's what I came up with, *for your consideration*." He emphasized those words, making it clear to Paige that he realized it was her decision and respected that. He flipped open the folder. "Perhaps no surprise, the Karlsen Center for Cancer Care is the best in the country."

"They're located in Pennsylvania? No, wait. Maryland, right?"

He nodded. "East Baltimore. And they can

do the surgery and follow it up with the treatment that's been prescribed for Jason. They've had very good results. Significantly better than other hospitals. Here, have a look." He withdrew a single sheet from the folder and slid it toward Paige. "They're willing to consider Jason's case."

Paige perused the statistics. She had to be grateful, even if Daniel had, once again, acted unilaterally. This was too important. Only one thing mattered—that Jason's chances would clearly be better at the Karlsen Center. "What about timing? When could they do the surgery?"

"Under the circumstances, they'd accommodate Jason. They have many operating rooms, and they can reassign as needed. The Karlsen Center also has reciprocal agreements with a number of area hospitals for use of their operating rooms, if necessary. They committed to hold a date for Jason based on his oncologist's recommended timing, subject to your choosing their facility."

He slid two more pages toward Paige. "This one." He tapped a finger on the first page. "It gives you an overview of their programs." He moved his finger to the other sheet. "This one provides brief bios of their oncologists and surgical staff."

Paige scanned the pages. When she was finished, he handed her a multipage, stapled document. He didn't need to explain what it was. She could read for herself. It was an application form. The proposed date of surgery was marked at the top.

"This all sounds too good to be true. But the expense," Paige objected. "I could never afford it."

"You don't have to. I'll take care of it. Please don't argue. Forget the money, Paige. Think of what's best for Jason."

Of course that was where she would've ended up anyway. When it came right down to it, nothing else was important. Although she'd already decided what had to be done, there were still times she vacillated. The money issue aside, and even with the increased rate of success at the Karlsen Center, it was an agonizing decision.

But Jason had a chance for a life free of cancer. She thought of the woman she'd met whose daughter had been through the same surgery. How happy and vibrant the little girl was. Then she thought of a discussion she and Jason had earlier that week. There'd been an article on the front page of the local paper about third-world conditions that had sparked his interest. She remembered his words distinctly. *I'm going to beat this thing, Mom. I want to grow up and be an architect, and help people in places like that where there aren't any schools or hospitals. I want to help people, kinda like Mr. Kinsley, only different.*

If Jason was that determined, if he had such a strong resolve to live, how could she not give him the best chance he had?

"All right," she whispered.

"Paige…"

"Yes. I want to go ahead with the Karlsen Center." Her voice gained strength and determination as she spoke. "Jason deserves the greatest chance he has to beat his disease, and this is it." Her strength drained, tears of gratitude, hope and fear coursed down her cheeks. "Thank you," she breathed.

DANIEL GATHERED PAIGE in his arms, stroked her hair and held her tightly as she cried. He could feel tears in his own eyes.

As he held her, a decision became crystal clear to him. Acknowledging his deep love for Paige and Jason, Daniel knew unquestionably what he wanted.

Daniel drew back, his eyes meeting hers. "Paige, I don't know what the future will hold, but whatever it is, I want to spend it with you and Jason."

He took her face in both of his hands. "I love you, Paige. Will you marry me?"

PAIGE STARED AT Daniel in disbelief. She knew she loved Daniel—more than she would ever have imagined—but how could she consider marriage now? "But Jason…"

He placed a fingertip on her lips to silence her protest. "Paige, I love you. I love you beyond reason. I want to marry you, and I want us to spend our lives together. But I also want Jason to be part of my life and I want to be part of his. I'd like to be there for Jason—to be his father in every way I can. Now that you've made your decision and we're doing this, I want to be his father *before* we go to the Karlsen Center."

If she thought she couldn't have loved Daniel more, at that moment her love for him nearly overwhelmed her. He wanted her *and* he wanted Jason. As his son.

"Don't answer me right now," he said. "As much as I want to hear it, I want Jason to be part of this, too. It's hard for me to wait, but please think about it. Don't say anything just yet."

They spent long hours that night talking about the challenges and opportunities that lay ahead of them. It was well after midnight when Daniel left, but they'd agreed that he'd come back Saturday morning so they could talk to Jason about getting married. Paige had made it clear that as much as they loved each other, if Jason wasn't entirely comfortable with it, she couldn't marry Daniel. It was equally important to Daniel that Jason approve.

SATURDAY MORNING WAS nearly over, and there was still no sign of Daniel. Although he'd called to tell Paige he'd be later than planned, Paige couldn't help being afraid that he'd had a change of heart. Her insecurities were taking hold. She knew it was illogical. Daniel had never let her down. He was a man of his word, and yet…

When he finally showed up, she searched his face for any indication that he'd changed his mind. She was quickly reassured.

He enveloped her in a big hug, his eyes glowing, his face ecstatic. He greeted Jason just as warmly.

He winked at Paige and then turned to Jason. "I'd like to have a little man-to-man discussion with you, if that's okay."

Jason stuck out his chest, as Daniel had seen him do before. "Sure."

"Can we use your room?"

"Uh-huh."

In his room, Jason sat on the edge of his bed and looked at Daniel expectantly.

Daniel pulled the desk chair over. He rested his forearms on his knees, bringing his eyes level with Jason's. "You know I love your mother, right?"

Jason blushed a little. "I guess."

"And I'm a very lucky guy because she loves me, too. Are you okay with that?"

Jason's color rose. "Yeah. You make her happy, and I like that."

"Good. So do I. Now, I'd like to marry your mom, and I believe I can make her happy. I want to know how you feel about that, but before you tell me, I'd like to say a couple more things."

Jason looked uncertain. "'Kay."

Daniel rested his hand on Jason's shoulder. "It's not just about your mom, Jason. It's about you, too. I hope you're good with this. With all of it..." Daniel paused. There was a huge lump in his throat, and he was having difficulty getting words past it. He hadn't realized it would be as emotional for him to ask Jason as it had been asking Paige. He turned his head and coughed. When he looked back at Jason, the boy's face shone, his freckles more pronounced, and his lips slightly parted. "Jason, what I'm trying to say is that I love you, too.

I'd like to be your father. What do you think about that?"

The words weren't fully out of Daniel's mouth when Jason launched himself into his arms. Daniel gathered him close and held tight. He rested his chin on Jason's mop of blond hair and closed his eyes. He really loved this little kid who'd entrenched himself so firmly in his heart. Jason's acceptance meant the world to him. "So, is that a yes?"

Jason just nodded his head exuberantly.

When Daniel let him go, Jason swiped the back of his hand across his eyes, and they grinned foolishly at each other. Finally, Jason asked shyly, "Will I be able to call you Dad?"

Daniel nearly choked up again but nodded with a smile. "I was hoping you would."

"That is *so* great! You're gonna ask Mom now, right?"

"That's the plan."

"Okay. I'll wait here."

Daniel shook his head. "No. If you don't mind, I'd like you to be with me."

Daniel had always thought the saying "grinning from ear to ear" was an odd one, but the kid's smile practically did extend from one ear to the other. "Okay, then. Ready?"

Jason hopped off the bed and reached for Daniel's hand. "Yup!"

"Now, this is serious stuff. Can you look serious when we walk out of here? Like this?" Daniel made a face.

Jason nodded and mimicked Daniel.

Daniel burst out laughing. "That'll do it."

PAIGE DIDN'T KNOW what to think when she saw the matching looks on Daniel's and Jason's faces as they emerged from the bedroom. She played along when Daniel asked her to sit on the sofa with Jason.

When they were settled, Daniel lowered himself to one knee in front of Paige. Jason tried to suppress a giggle by covering his mouth with both hands, but he failed miserably. Daniel gave him his mock-stern look, which only made Jason giggle harder. Paige didn't hear that sound from her little boy often enough. If her heart wasn't already overflowing, that would have done it.

"So." Daniel turned his attention back to Paige and ceremoniously took her left hand in his. "Paige Summerville, would you do me the great honor of becoming my wife?" He glanced over at Jason. "And granting me the equally great honor of being Jason's father? Before you answer..." He reached into his pocket and pulled out a small box covered in gold velvet. He flipped the lid open to reveal a spectacular antique ring. It had a large central diamond with a couple of smaller diamond baguettes on either side, all set in white gold.

Paige's mouth dropped open as she stared at the ring. Daniel tilted the box slightly so Jason could see it, too.

"It was my grandmother's. She gave it to me shortly before she passed away, saying she hoped I'd use it when I got married. She said she also hoped it would bring me and the lady who'd wear it as much love and joy as it had brought her and my grandfather."

Speechless, Paige nodded, still gazing down at the ring.

"Unlike my parents', theirs was a marriage of unquestionable love. I'd forgotten that over the years. I became focused on the negatives. In retrospect, that was wrong. I also had positive role models in my life for a happy and fulfilling marriage. My grandparents had been married for nearly fifty-five years when my grandfather passed away.

"I'd nearly forgotten about this ring, too. I'd just put it, along with any idea of marriage, out of my mind. But when I decided I wanted us to be married, I thought of my grandparents, and I couldn't think of a more appropriate symbol of my love and commitment to you.

"The reason I was late is because I had to

wait for the bank to open to get the ring from my safety deposit box." He paused. "If you don't like it, I can get you another one."

He looked from Paige to Jason and back again. "So, what do you say? Will you both make me the happiest man on the planet?"

Paige had a huge grin on her face but her lips were trembling. She turned to Jason, who was grinning broadly, too. He nodded before she could ask the question. She definitely had Jason's support. "Yes. Oh, yes." She threw one arm around Daniel's neck and the other around her son.

DANIEL STILL COULDN'T believe he was engaged, but he knew down to his bones that it was the absolute right thing. To be a family with Paige and Jason. He had to admit the thought of having more kids with Paige made him feel warm inside. He'd shared the news with his parents and was pleasantly surprised by how happy they seemed. Maybe he'd judged them too harshly. They were anxious to meet their future daughter-in-law. His mother was downright joyous. Go figure.

After some debate, he and Paige set their wedding date for the Saturday before Jason's surgery. That might have been cutting it close, but despite the fact that their wedding would be small and intimate, there were still arrangements to be made, and they needed to get a marriage license. They also agreed to file papers for Daniel to legally adopt Jason. His firm pulled out all the stops and called in favors to make it possible by the wedding.

He and Paige had discussed where they'd like to live. They considered Hartford, Camden Falls, Great Barrington and a number of other locations within a reasonable driving distance.

They finally decided on Camden Falls. First, because Jason's needs took priority. His school and his friends were there, and many of his doctors were local, too. Jason, being the remarkable kid he was, had offered no resistance to relocation, but they thought he had enough upheaval and uncertainty in his life. On top of that, Paige had all her friends—a solid support system for her and Jason—right there. Daniel and Paige didn't want her to lose contact with her friends again, as she had when she'd moved to Camden Falls. These people— Chelsea, the Bennetts, Mr. Weatherly—were too important to all three of them.

Finally, for Jason and for any other kids they'd be fortunate enough to have, Camden Falls was a wonderful place to grow up. It was a reasonable commute to Paige's parents

and to Daniel's Lindstrom, Kinsley and Mc-
Guire offices.

For all these reasons, they decided to make
their home in Camden Falls.

Home.

What a concept. Not just a house but a
home. Daniel had a house, but had he ever
called it a home? He thought again of the billboard he'd seen outside his office at Christmas—the idyllic family scene—and now he
was setting up a home with Paige and Jason.

He could hardly wait until they were officially a family.

They decided to delay the honeymoon until
after Jason's surgery, whenever he was feeling
well enough to join them. Daniel marveled at
how easily he and Paige made decisions together. These days, they were almost always
like-minded. Including the decision about
wanting Jason along on their honeymoon.

Sooner or later, they'd take a romantic trip,
just the two of them, maybe to Bali or Phuket
in Thailand. But for now, they wanted to build
their little family. Daniel had retained a real
estate agent to find them a house. Either the
agent was unusually good or they were exceptionally lucky. They found a house all three of
them loved in no time at all.

It had a large yard backing onto a forested

ravine, with a swimming pool and a kids' wooden jungle gym, perfect for Jason. Daniel laughed when they first pulled up outside the house, since it had an actual white picket fence.

Paige loved the kitchen. For Daniel, it had a three-car garage, a small workshop, and an office big enough to accommodate the needs of his new business, at least for the short term. The office had an exterior door, too, so he could see clients at home, if he chose to, without having them traipsing through the rest of the house. There was a small fourth bedroom on the main floor that they decided would make an excellent office for Paige.

With this completely unplanned turn of events, Daniel was glad he hadn't moved too quickly to set up a physical office for Heartfelt Legal Services. He loved the thought that both he and Paige could work from home. That way, they didn't have to spend eight to ten hours a day apart from each other and from Jason.

By next Christmas, they'd be like that family on the billboard outside his office—only better. *Real*. They'd be just as Jason had depicted them in his painting, the portrait of them at Christmas, because their feelings for each other were genuine.

As they walked through one last time, the real estate agent overheard them talking about converting the fourth bedroom into an office for Paige's business. Coincidentally, she needed someone to help her refresh her website. Before they'd closed the transaction on the house, Paige had another client.

As the house was already vacant, they were able to negotiate a closing date that would allow them to take possession, if not fully move in, prior to Jason's surgery.

Jason was very excited about the prospect of living in a house. He'd been too young when his parents split to remember much about the house they'd lived in.

In a moment of weakness, Jason got them to agree that once he'd recovered from the surgery, he could get a puppy.

A wife, a child, a home, a dog and a new job—all in the span of a few months—should have rattled Daniel. It didn't. It felt good. Daniel had never been more enthusiastic about the future.

They just had to get through Jason's surgery first.

CHAPTER TWENTY-ONE

NOW THAT THE surgery was scheduled, Paige knew she had to inform Jason's father, irrespective of not having a relationship with him. She and Daniel had discussed it, and they agreed she owed it to him. Paige believed he had a right to know what his son was facing and the possible consequences. Although Mark had surrendered all parental rights, she also needed to tell him about Daniel's plan to adopt Jason.

Daniel offered to have someone in his office locate Mark, but Paige declined. She felt it was her responsibility. Doing a basic web search, she found him without too much trouble, and obtained his home phone number.

Mark Summerville was living in Vermont. From what she could glean from the internet, Mark was running a mobile devices business. He had a new family, a wife and two young daughters.

Paige wasn't sure how she felt about that. She didn't care for herself. She had no residual feelings for Mark. All the love she'd once felt for him had withered away long ago. She had Daniel now. But her heart ached for Jason. How would he feel, knowing his biological father wouldn't have anything to do with him, and yet he had two other children not that much younger than he was?

Then again, maybe it was a good thing. If Mark had other children he was raising, he might be more sympathetic to Jason's medical plight.

Daniel encouraged her to get it over with and call Mark right after Jason went to bed. For privacy, she went into her bedroom and, using her long-distance calling card, placed the call.

"Hello?" A female voice answered the phone.

"Could I speak to Mark Summerville, please."

"May I ask who's calling?" The voice cooled by several degrees.

"It's Paige…Summerville."

"Oh. I see." Now there was frost in the voice. "Hold on a minute and I'll see if he's available."

Paige tapped the top of her night table.

"Paige?"

"Hello, Mark." She couldn't force herself to

engage in the niceties of asking how he was or how he'd been.

"What do you want?"

Clearly he wasn't interested in niceties, either. "To talk to you about Jason."

"Jason?"

Her nerves were taut, stretched to the limit and ready to snap. "Yes. Jason, your *son*."

"What about him?" He sounded defensive. "If this is about money…"

"No," she retorted. "Money is the least of it, Mark." Her voice became subdued. "Jason's cancer is back."

She heard him inhale swiftly and heave the breath out, then nothing. She wasn't sure he was still on the line. "Mark?"

Another deep, heavy breath. "Yeah. I'm here."

"I'm not asking for anything, Mark. I just thought you should know."

"Okay. How…how is he?"

There seemed to be genuine concern in his tone. Was it possible that after all these years of having no contact with his son, Mark still had feelings for him? Paige sighed. "He's a wonderful boy, Mark. He's trying so hard and keeping such a positive attitude." She wanted to say that he should be proud of his son but held her tongue. "It's bad this time."

"You mean to suggest it wasn't before?"

"No. But it's worse."

"What do you want from me?"

Disappointment cut her like the sharp edge of a blade. He hadn't even asked about Jason's condition. The glimmer of hope that had sparked to life—the hope that he still felt something for his son—was extinguished. "I told you I don't want anything. I thought you might want to...to maybe see him."

She heard some muffled sounds, as if he was moving around or covering the mouthpiece. "Paige, I have a family now."

And what had she and Jason been? she wondered sadly.

"Two little girls," he added.

"I don't understand why that should stop you. He's your child, too. But it's up to you." She just wanted to end the call. She felt soiled, unclean somehow, talking to Mark. "If you change your mind, call me." She gave him her phone number at the call center. She didn't want to take the risk that Jason might answer the phone at home if Mark did call. It would be too painful and confusing for him. Only after she hung up did she realize that she hadn't mentioned that Daniel was adopting Jason.

Paige was thankful that Daniel was in the other room. The brief call had brought back too many difficult memories, and she was re-lieved that she wouldn't have the opportunity to wallow in them on her own.

Daniel didn't ask how it had gone when she came out of her bedroom. He simply rose, walked over to her and encircled her in his arms.

THERE WAS A message from Mark waiting for Paige when she arrived at work the next day. She stared at the notice on her computer screen, not quite believing it, expecting the type to waver in front of her eyes and disap-pear. But it didn't. Her shift was due to start in a few minutes, and she didn't want to rush the call, so she decided to return it during her first break.

When the time came, she left her worksta-tion and went to one of the break rooms to en-sure privacy. She closed the door behind her, then dropped down in a chair at the table. She pulled the telephone that sat in the middle to-ward her and dialed the number she'd jotted down on a slip of paper.

"Mark, it's Paige," she announced when the phone was answered.

"I'll keep this short," he said. "Jason is my son and I…I care about him. I don't know if I want to see him, though. I don't know if I *can*." She detected a trace of the old terror that used to claim him back when they were married and discussing Jason's care.

"I have a wife and two young daughters now—they're two and three—and you have to realize I can't help you financially this time. Our agreement aside, I don't have the money. I made some investments that didn't turn out well, so I'm working to support Becky, the girls and me. Are we clear on that?"

"Yes," Paige acknowledged. Money hadn't been the motivation for her call. Mark should have known that, but she supposed some things never changed.

"So, as I said, I doubt I'll see him, but I'd like you to tell me about the situation."

"The *situation, as I already told you,* is that Jason has cancer again. He's doing as well as can be expected under the circumstances. He's a great kid." Paige understood it wasn't what he'd wanted to hear, but *she* wanted him to know. Then she told him all the details. "We decided to go ahead with the surgery," she concluded, and held her breath, not knowing what kind of response to expect.

There was a long pause. "Why wouldn't they keep him on the drug until the tumor's gone and avoid surgery altogether?"

She explained to Mark that attempting it

would require too many treatments and at significantly higher dosages, which would be dangerous for Jason.

"I see." The two words were quiet and controlled, giving Paige no indication of what her ex-husband was thinking. "And when is the surgery scheduled?"

Paige gave him that information, too.

"Okay. Thank you."

The words were still said in a controlled manner, but she heard the fury in them. And that concluded their conversation. He abruptly said good-bye and left Paige holding the receiver until the loud off-hook tone prompted her to hang up.

She wasn't sure what the significance of their conversation had been, other than letting Mark know about the condition of their son.

LESS THAN A week later, Paige learned the significance. A patient care representative from the Karlsen Center for Cancer Care called her late Tuesday afternoon.

"I'm afraid we have a problem with respect to Jason's surgery," she advised Paige.

Her heart was ready to burst out of her chest, and she found it nearly impossible to breathe. "A problem? What kind of a problem?"

"I'm sorry to tell you we won't be able to proceed with the surgery."

"*What*...what did you say?"

"We cannot proceed with Jason's surgery."

Paige felt the room spin and steadied herself against the kitchen counter before taking a peek into the living room to make sure Jason was still in his room. "I...I don't understand."

"We received a letter from a lawyer acting on behalf of Jason's father. The letter instructs us *not* to proceed with the surgery."

Paige took a step back, bumped into the wall and slid bonelessly to the floor. "What?" She couldn't have been hearing the woman correctly.

"I thought you'd know, but Jason's father doesn't want Jason to have the surgery. We have to respect his wishes."

Grasping the significance of what Mark had done, she found anger replacing the shock. Her fight instinct had definitely kicked in. "Jason's father has *no right* to block the surgery. I have sole legal custody of Jason. Our agreement makes it very clear that I have full decision-making authority with regard to my son's welfare. I've signed all the necessary papers, and I can provide a copy of the agreement."

"Please try to stay calm, Ms. Summerville. Mr. Summerville's lawyer made all of that plain in his letter. Still, his lawyer makes a very strong case—he is Jason's father, after all—and our attorneys have advised us not to proceed. Mr. Summerville indicated that he would take legal action if we did."

Paige pushed herself up off the floor. "Don't ask me to stay calm! It isn't your child's life we're talking about. This is crazy. Jason *needs* the surgery! You're worried about legal action when my son's life is at stake?" Remembering that Jason was just a couple of rooms away, she lowered her voice to an insistent whisper. "Without the surgery, he doesn't have a chance. You have to reconsider. Get your lawyers to reconsider."

"I'm sorry, Ms. Summerville, but there's nothing we can do."

"Yes, there is." Paige needed to call Daniel, but first she had to ensure that she wouldn't lose the scheduled date. "I intend to pursue this matter. I have to do what's best for my son. Can you at least hold his surgery date? And I need a copy of that letter. You have to give me a chance to respond." She pulled her phone book from a kitchen drawer and searched for Daniel's business card. "Please send it to this number, attention Daniel Kinsley," and she read out Daniel's fax number.

As soon as Paige had hung up, she called

Daniel's cell phone. There was no answer. She called his number at Lindstrom, Kinsley and McGuire. Her agitation must have been obvious; Selena said she'd get him immediately, although he was with a client for Heartfelt.

A few minutes later, Daniel was on the line. Paige's words tumbled over each other as she tried to explain what had happened.

"Hold on a second, Paige. I'm having trouble following you, but Selena just brought in a fax that she seems to think might have something to do with what you're talking about." Paige tried to compose herself while she waited for Daniel to read the fax.

"Where are you?" he asked.

"I'm at home."

"I'm on my way. I want you to stay right where you are. What's Chelsea's number?"

It didn't occur to Paige to ask why he wanted it. She gave it to him, and they hung up. She was sitting on the sofa, elbows resting on her knees, her head in her hands when her apartment door flew open. Startled, Paige looked up. Chelsea was rushing toward her.

"How did you—?

"Your spare key, remember?" Chelsea cut her off. "I'm not supposed to talk to you about whatever's going on, but Daniel made me promise to come down and stay with you until he gets here. Just tell me this. Is Jason okay?"

"Yes, he is." Paige massaged her forehead with her thumb and forefinger. "Oh, Chels. What am I going to do?"

Daniel got to the apartment an hour later. Jason had finished his homework; he and Chelsea were playing Scrabble. Jason was in good spirits, but he kept casting worried glances at his mother, obviously aware of the tension tightly coiled inside her.

Daniel immediately took charge. "Thanks for coming down, Chelsea." He gave her arm a little squeeze. "I really appreciate it. Now, would you do me another favor? Would you take Jason up to your place for a while? Play a computer game with him?"

Jason's face lit up and he grinned eagerly at Chelsea.

"No problem." She dropped her hand onto Jason's shoulder. "Okay, Squirt. Let's see if I can kick *your* butt for a change."

As soon as the door closed behind them, Daniel stepped forward and opened his arms. "Come here," he urged Paige.

She welcomed the warmth and support of his embrace. "How could Mark *do* this? What am I going to do?"

"It's not what you're going to do, but what

we're going to do. Technically, it's what I'm going to do on our behalf, and no objections, please. I'm a lawyer, remember? This is exactly the type of thing my new firm does." When she drew a deep breath and her eyelids fluttered closed, he brushed his lips lightly across them.

After Jason had gone to bed, Daniel laid out a plan of action, and he promised to get the best lawyers at Lindstrom, Kinsley and McGuire to help him work on it first thing in the morning.

TRUE TO HIS word, Daniel cleared his schedule and worked with one of his partners to get a letter off to the hospital's legal team by the end of the day. Mission accomplished, he made a copy to take to Paige that evening.

He arrived at her apartment to pandemonium. The building's entry doors were propped open. There were service trucks parked in the drive and workmen scurrying around.

He stepped over a thick black hose and headed toward Paige's apartment. "What's going on?" he asked the first worker who wasn't rushing by.

"There's been a flood. A burst pipe on the second floor. A ground-floor apartment got the worst of it. We're trying to clean it up."

Daniel glanced toward Paige's apartment and with a sinking heart saw that her door was also propped open. He absently thanked the man and hurried down the hall, following the black hose that snaked into her apartment. He nearly bumped into the back of the man who was wielding what appeared to be a vacuum at the end of the hose. He was using it to suck up water that had pooled on the floor. Looking around, he saw Paige in the kitchen. She was drying things and placing them on all available surfaces above floor level.

"Paige!" he called out. He splashed over to her, heedless of his shoes and trousers. "Where's Jason?"

"He's next door with Mr. Weatherly. He's fine. There are people working in Chelsea's apartment, too, but Mr. Weatherly's wasn't damaged, so he offered to watch Jason."

Daniel pulled her into a hug. "You should have called me. I would've come right away."

"I know, but you were working on the letter for Jason, and it all happened so fast, I didn't get a chance."

"I'm so sorry about this."

"It's not your fault."

"No. But that doesn't mean I can't feel bad for you. Anyway, the legal letter was sent to the Karlsen Center early this afternoon. I've got a copy for you, but that can wait." He took off his jacket, draped it over a chair and rolled up his shirt sleeves. "How can I help?"

It was nearly midnight when the work crews finally left. Paige and Daniel sat on her sofa, holding hands, heads resting against the cushions.

They'd preserved as many of Paige and Jason's belongings as they could. The apartment looked as if a hurricane had hit it, with items stacked haphazardly on any and all surfaces. The carpets had been removed to be steam-cleaned, although it was questionable whether they could be saved.

Paige had checked on Jason earlier in the evening. Since the teams were still working diligently to get things cleaned up, she tucked him in on Mr. Weatherly's sofa for the night. There was no point waking him or bringing him back to their musty apartment.

Finally Daniel rose. "I'd better go and let you get some sleep. Do you want me to take you to a hotel for the night?"

"Thanks, but no. I want to stay close to Jason."

"You can't sleep here until the place is aired out."

She rubbed her right temple. "No. I'll stay with Chelsea tonight. Her apartment's fine now." Paige rose, too, and walked Daniel to her front door. He remembered the legal letter as he was shrugging into his jacket. He took it out of his pocket and handed it to her.

"The guy I worked with on this is the best in his field. This letter should do the trick." He kissed her good-night. "Please don't worry about this. We'll get it sorted out. I promise."

CHAPTER TWENTY-TWO

As neither Paige nor Jason was staying in the apartment overnight, Paige left all the windows ajar to air the place out. One of the workmen had cut pieces of wood for her to put in the window tracks so she could leave them unlatched and slightly open, but they couldn't be forced open any further, ensuring that the apartment remained secure.

It had done the trick. By morning, the musty smell was mostly gone. Paige closed the windows and went to Mr. Weatherly's to fetch Jason.

They had breakfast in their own apartment, and then they walked to school.

Fortunately, it was Paige's day off from the call center. She planned to use the time to restore order to their apartment. Her day was interrupted at about two o'clock when the nurse from Jason's school called. Jason had the sniffles, was running a fever and seemed to be feeling lethargic. She suggested Paige come and pick him up.

If Jason was feeling under the weather, she didn't want him walking home. She decided to see if Mr. Weatherly was home, since today was normally one of his days off. If he was there, she'd ask to borrow his car.

Paige was beginning to wonder if he was out when he finally opened the door partway. Paige explained the situation. He agreed to lend her his car without hesitation.

As he hurried to get the keys, the door swung open a bit more. Paige couldn't believe her eyes. Laura Andrews from the Wish I May Foundation was sitting, prim and proper, in Mr. Weatherly's living room, sipping tea.

Equally astonishing, Laura was wearing a pretty flower-patterned dress rather than the usual neutral-toned suits Paige was accustomed to seeing her in.

When they made eye contact, Laura blushed slightly. Daniel's words the day of the circus came to mind, and Paige had to smother a grin. She said hello, but refrained from further conversation, not wanting to add to Laura's obvious discomfiture. Realizing that Paige had seen Laura, Mr. Weatherly stammered something about both of them having the day off as he handed her the keys. She thanked him, but neither of them made any other reference to his guest.

Paige was worried about Jason when she got him home. His fever had risen to over a hundred and one, yet he looked pale rather than flushed, and he was listless. She called his doctor, who advised that if Jason's temperature climbed any higher, she should take him to a nearby health clinic, because the fever likely wasn't related to his treatment. She'd tried to reach Daniel, but Selena explained that he was in court.

Paige asked Mr. Weatherly if she could hold on to his car keys, just in case.

Daniel called her as soon as he got her message. He offered to come over, but by then Jason was resting and she wanted to keep things quiet for him. Relieved that Daniel was available if they needed him, she returned Mr. Weatherly's keys.

Paige checked on Jason a number of times during the night. Although the fever hadn't broken by morning, it hadn't risen, either. When Jason woke up, he was clammy and a bit queasy. Consequently, he ate very little for breakfast and went back to bed right after.

Daniel called Paige early in the morning to check on Jason's condition and then again shortly before noon. He had excellent news. The Karlsen Center's legal team had reassessed the situation and must have realized their liability exposure was far greater if they didn't allow the surgery to proceed. They concluded, as Daniel and his colleague had categorically pointed out in their letter, that Mark's assertions and threats were without legal merit.

The hospital confirmed that Jason's surgery could go ahead as planned.

With that obstacle behind them and with the scheduled date of the surgery only days away, Jason's health became the determining factor. He had to be as strong as possible and in good health for his surgery. If he had a cold or flu, the hospital would have to cancel. Paige knew they were racing against time, since even without the virus Jason had picked up, his energy was declining. If his resistance and resilience were compromised much further, the risks that came with surgery would increase dramatically, to the point that the surgeon might decide it was too dangerous to proceed.

By late afternoon, there was still no appreciable improvement in Jason's condition, and he'd been unable to keep any food down.

Paige was frantic. After speaking with Jason's oncologist, she asked Daniel to come over, and they took Jason back to the clinic. She bundled Jason in his warmest clothes to ward off his chills, and wrapped a blanket around him. Daniel carried him to the car and then into the clinic.

Based on Jason's overall medical condition, they triaged him quickly, and a doctor saw him in under fifteen minutes. Daniel was prepared to stay in the waiting area, but both Paige and Jason insisted he come with them.

The doctor assured them that it was definitely nothing more than a virus. He said Jason might have picked it up from one of the many workers who were in and out of their apartment because he was more susceptible due to his compromised immune system.

Paige explained to the doctor her concern about Jason's upcoming surgery. Like Jason's oncologist, he cautioned that the surgery shouldn't take place if Jason was unwell. He went through the reasons, but it was all lost on Paige; she heard only a buzzing in her ear from that point onward.

The doctor prescribed some antihistamines to make Jason more comfortable, but there wasn't much more that could be done other than letting the cold run its course over the next few days. As they were leaving, he advised them again that they should contact Jason's surgeon, either directly or through their oncologist, to make him aware of Jason's illness.

Daniel carried Jason from his car into the apartment, the boy's head on his chest. One thin arm was nestled between them, while the other hung limply at Jason's side. Holding his son-to-be in his arms, a feeling so powerful and all-consuming coursed through Daniel that he knew he'd do anything in his power to protect and shelter this little boy. Anyone who tried to harm Jason would have to answer to him.

The feeling was unlike anything he'd ever experienced in his life. It staggered him. When Paige reached for Jason, Daniel shook his head and carried him into the bedroom himself. He pulled back the covers, snuggled his teddy in the crook of his arm and tucked the covers around him. Jason didn't stir once.

Daniel rejoined Paige in the living room. She was curled up in the corner of the sofa, arms wrapped around her torso. There was a deep furrow in her forehead and a distinct slouch to her shoulders. "I just don't understand it. What more can go wrong?" She raised her eyes toward the ceiling. "What could I have done that was so bad it brought this upon us?"

Daniel's heart was breaking. He sat down beside her and drew her against him. "Paige, this isn't anything you did. Yes, these are ob-

stacles. We *will* overcome them. Together."
He opened his mouth, then closed it again. He
was about to say "I promise," but this time he
wasn't so sure he could unconditionally make
that pledge.

Daniel left a voice mail for Selena and told
her he'd be unavailable for meetings for a couple of days. He made it plain to Paige that he
was going to stay with them for the next little while. He'd make himself comfortable on
her sofa, but he wanted to be close by in case
Jason needed to be taken to the hospital. He
also planned to be the liaison with the Karlsen
Center about Jason's condition.

Paige didn't argue. Truth be told, she was
relieved. Having Daniel there was a comfort.
She didn't want to think about how much she
was coming to rely on him. Her fierce need
for independence after she was free of Mark's
controlling ways seemed to have diminished
in the last few months. All that mattered was
Jason and doing everything she could—*they
could*—for him.

The go or no-go deadline for surgery was
Thursday, just three days away. If Jason didn't
get an all-clear by noon on Thursday, the hospital would cancel his surgery and reallo-
cate the slot to another patient. It might have
sounded callous, but operating-room time was

at a premium, and there were other patients who could be scheduled for life-saving surgery.

Mrs. Bennett dropped by with homemade chicken soup. Chelsea brought down her laptop and played a couple of games with Jason. When he got tired, she simply left the computer with him to use when he was up to it. She even loaded a couple of movies for him to watch.

Mr. Weatherly stopped in and asked if he could have a friend join him. "I imagine everyone knows by now anyway," he said awkwardly. He and Laura brought Jason a miniature replica of his buttercup-yellow 1965 Mustang. In addition, he gave Jason one of his prized bonsai trees, which Jason had always been fascinated by. He explained that the little tree, no taller than five inches, was actually about the same age as Jason.

Daniel brought sketch pads, pastels and paints, and a small easel specifically designed to be used in a bed.

Through it all, Paige made Jason some of his favorite meals, the ones that would be easiest on his tummy, and did all she could to keep his spirits up.

Wednesday evening, he still wasn't feeling appreciably better. All their neighbors visited at some point during the evening. As upbeat as everyone tried to be, there was a general sense of gloom that was hard to mask.

Long after Jason fell asleep, Paige sat on the sofa, leaning against Daniel, his arm protectively around her shoulder. They were on their second movie, both black-and-white classics from the fifties, but neither of them was paying much attention. Paige dozed periodically. When she could no longer keep her eyes open, Daniel insisted she to go to bed. It was past two in the morning, and she'd need her strength later, regardless of what the day would bring.

"I can't. I just can't sleep. There's so much that keeps circling around in my mind."

Daniel kissed her forehead. "I can imagine. But you need sleep. Now go."

She finally obliged, falling into a fitful sleep around three o'clock.

In the middle of a troubling nightmare, she felt something brush her face and swatted at it. When she felt it again, it roused her. Utterly exhausted, she slowly opened her eyes.

Jason stood beside her bed, one arm cuddling his teddy, the other resting beside her face on her pillow.

She bolted upright and reached for Jason. "Baby, what's wrong?"

"Nothing, Mom. I was thirsty. I wanted to tell you, I think I'm feeling better. I'm hungry, too."

That was the best sign of all. Paige drew Jason into her arms. "Oh, sweetie. I'm so glad." She swung her legs over the edge of the bed, glanced at her bedside clock. It was well past her customary wake-up time of six in the morning. "Let's go take your temperature, okay? Then I'll make you some breakfast."

He nodded. She put on her bathrobe and they went to the kitchen.

Daniel had again slept on the sofa. He was already up and in the bathroom, and she couldn't wait to share the great news with him.

Jason's fever had, indeed, broken. His eyes were clear, his color good and his throat no longer irritated. Just to be certain, they drove Jason to the clinic, and the doctor they'd seen on their previous visit gave them the all-clear.

Daniel not only called the hospital but, to ensure there was no mix-up, he also had Selena prepare a letter and fax it to the Karlsen Center's administrator. The confirmation came back almost immediately. Jason's surgery would proceed as scheduled.

JASON'S SURGERY WAS four days away. With the passing of each day, Paige became more and more jittery. She tried to put on a brave face for Jason, but there was no denying that she was progressively more anxious about what would come.

Was she doing the right thing? Had she made the right decision and picked the right hospital? There were so many variables. So many things that could go wrong.

Just thinking about them all was driving her to the verge of panic.

Jason had to be okay. He just *had* to be.

How could she *live* without him? How could she go on?

Jason had to make it through the surgery, and he had to make it through whole and free of cancer. Life couldn't be so cruel as to take her son away from her.

Restlessly pacing her bedroom, she stopped in front of her dresser mirror and stared at her own reflection. Her eyes looked huge in her pale face. They were red rimmed from lack of sleep. She could see the frown lines between her eyebrows and at the sides of her mouth. When had those appeared? Her hair was without its characteristic luster and in need of a wash.

What was happening to her? She couldn't fall apart. She had to keep it together for Jason's sake.

She pushed her hair away from her face. A brilliant flash drew her eye to her left hand. Her engagement ring had caught and refracted the light.

She lowered her hand and stared at the ring. She backed up slowly until she bumped into her mattress and lowered herself onto the bed.

The ring was beautiful—stunning, really. She'd never asked, because it wasn't important to her, but it had to be at least a carat. She adjusted it with the thumb and forefinger of her other hand to center it on her ring finger. They were getting married the day after tomorrow.

The panic rose again, threatening to choke her.

What was she thinking? Daniel would make a wonderful husband and father. She knew that without a doubt. She loved him and so did Jason. But how could she marry him? And *now*?

Her priority was Jason. No question. Daniel understood that.

But what if the unthinkable happened? What if the surgery wasn't successful? If she lost Jason? She knew she'd die inside. She wouldn't be a fit wife for Daniel. And if Jason survived the surgery but there were consequences—those horrible, unimaginable risks the doctors kept reminding her about? She'd spend the rest of her life taking care of Jason. Again, what kind of wife would she be then?

She twisted the ring again and watched the diamonds sparkle. "Oh, no. Oh, no, what am I doing?"

She felt a stab of pain in her chest. It built and built until it brought tears to her eyes. She drew up her knees, hugged them to her, rested her forehead against them.

She couldn't go through with the wedding. She shouldn't be preoccupied with it when her entire focus had to be Jason right now. And it wasn't fair to Daniel. She had no idea what the future held, and she could offer him no guarantees of happily ever after.

Throwing her head back, she stared up at the ceiling.

And what about her? Hadn't she once thought she'd have a happily-ever-after with Mark? She wouldn't have married him otherwise. Mark had left her and left Jason because he couldn't deal with Jason's illness.

Her eyes darted around the room, and her breath came fast and shallow.

What about Daniel? He'd already proven he didn't deal with personal conflict all that well, hadn't he? What would happen when they argued? What if it was about something really important? Something to do with Jason?

Would he just shut down? Or would he, like Mark—and the guy she'd dated briefly—walk out on her? She didn't want to think about a third strike.

That insistent little voice in her head said she shouldn't compare Daniel with Mark, but she couldn't help it. She hadn't realized that the fear was still lurking in the dark corners of her mind, along with all her other worries. It wasn't the primary consideration behind her decision, but it was a factor.

Tears flowed down her face, and her chest was so tight she could barely breathe, but she pulled the ring off her finger.

She rose on unsteady legs and walked back to her dresser. Opening the top drawer, she took out the little gold velvet box and nestled the ring back in its slot. She bit her lip as she closed the lid and replaced the box.

She nearly went back to bed but she couldn't. She had to think of Jason, and be strong.

She also had to figure out how to break the news to Daniel…and to Jason.

She didn't want to hurt Daniel, especially after everything he'd done for her and Jason. She'd understand if he didn't want to have any-thing to do with her once she told him, but she'd be so grateful if they could at least re-main friends. Just the thought of not seeing him again caused the pain in her chest to sear through the rest of her body, bringing more tears to her eyes.

No longer having him in her life, just when she'd come to rely on him so much, was unimaginable. No, she wouldn't consider that a possibility. She'd find a way to tell him, a way that didn't upset him, and they'd be able to remain friends.

"Yeah, right," she murmured. Who was she kidding? Daniel had been very understanding, but she knew this would test him. She knew he'd be upset, but she couldn't imagine going through with the wedding at a time like this, with Jason's future—and hers—so uncertain. Not to mention the persistent fear that he, too, would leave her.

Daniel would understand. He had to. And if he didn't...there was nothing she could do about that. Jason was her priority.

It would be just as hard telling Jason. Daniel meant so much to him.

Paige's resolve wavered. The last thing she wanted to do was distress Jason, especially so close to his surgery. But she had to think long-term, not just about tomorrow or the day after.

Jason would be disappointed, but he'd have to understand her decision, too.

DANIEL TOOK PAIGE in his arms and dropped a light kiss on her lips when he arrived that evening. "How was your day?"

"Hard."

He glanced around the apartment. "Where's Jason?"

"With Mrs. Bennett."

He drew back and searched her face, looked deep into her eyes. He was about to ask her if she was all ready for their wedding, but her expression caused him to hold back. He felt a wave of apprehension. He knew that now was not the time to get into any sort of confrontation with her. Whatever she needed, he loved her, and he was here to provide it.

Paige led Daniel into the living room, sat next to him on the sofa and lifted her face to his. Her eyes were clouded but earnest. "There's something I need to say, and I don't think you're going to like it." She continued to meet his eyes. "I...I love you, Daniel. Please know that."

"I do. I love you, too. You're my world. You and Jason." As calm as he sounded, the wave turned into a torrent. "Can't we just leave it at that?" he asked, hoping to forestall the "but" he knew was coming.

Her eyes were huge, her face chalk white. "I...I can't go through with the wedding. Not right now." She was shaking visibly as she reached for his hand and placed the velvet box in his palm, curling his fingers over it.

It was impossible. She was backing out of their wedding? He wanted to disagree, to argue, to yell. But looking at her, seeing how completely broken and defeated she was, he didn't have the heart. Regardless of the hurt and disappointment he was feeling, he didn't have it in him to add to her pain, sorrow and worry.

"Okay." He could hardly believe that he'd managed to get a word past the constriction in his throat. "If that's what you want. I can't force you to marry me. But I think you're making a big mistake. Whatever happens won't change that I love you and want you." He realized he must appear remarkably calm, but she couldn't know that his heart was shattered and an intense anger was brewing—not at her but at fate—threating to overtake the hurt and anxiety.

"You can't say that," she cried out. "Things change. People change. I've already experienced it."

His eyes were hard, his lips compressed into a straight line before he spoke, softly, emphatically. "So, that's what this is about? You still think I'll desert you like your ex did?"

Paige shook her head. "No! That's not it."
She wanted to take his hands in hers, slip into
his arms and have him hold her until the hurt
subsided. But she knew she had no right. Not
any longer. She didn't sound convincing to
her own ears, and with everything else to consider, she couldn't lie to him. "At least not all
of it," and she tried to explain her reasons. She
couldn't read his face, his body language, but
a little twitch in his left eye made her realize
how tense he must be. She raised her hands,
let them fall back on her lap. "I'm sorry, Daniel. I don't know what else to say."

He rose and fiddled with the small velvet box
before shoving it in his pocket. "I'm sorry, too.
No, you don't need to see me out," he added
when she moved to rise as well. "I can find
the way."

Paige was relieved to stay where she was.
She was terrified her legs would buckle if she
tried to stand.

Daniel retrieved his jacket from the closet.
His hand on the doorknob, he turned back to
Paige. "I understand what you've said, but *I*
want to be there for Jason's surgery. I still want
to take you, and I want to be there."

Her mouth opened, but before she could say
anything, he continued.

"I'll let you do what you want, but don't

argue with me on this. I need to be there. You know I love Jason, too. I will pick you up Monday as planned and take you to the Karlsen Center." He opened the door and pulled it shut behind him. She'd expected him to slam it, but somehow that unflappable control of his as he walked out the door just added to the intensity of her pain.

CHAPTER TWENTY-THREE

Paige and Daniel had very little contact over the following days. Just enough to confirm that Daniel was taking them to the Karlsen Center and would be picking them up at home.

She had to inform her parents and friends that the wedding had been called off. Hardest of all was explaining it to Jason. As she'd expected, he was distraught. Paige knew how important it was to keep up his spirits for surgery, and she did everything she could to lift his mood, without success.

The day of the surgery, Paige opened the door to Daniel. "You're early," she said. "Hours early." She'd just awakened, and she was dressed in black yoga pants and a blue T-shirt. Paige ran her hand self-consciously through her sleep-tousled hair. She knew she was a mess.

"I am. Yes." In contrast, Daniel was impeccably dressed, as always. He wore a gray sweater over a white button-down shirt and indigo jeans. Just looking at him made her heart ache. "May I come in?"

"Sure." Paige stepped aside so he could enter. "Would you like some coffee?" She was astonished by how calm she was being, when her heart had broken into a million small fragments.

"No, thanks. I'm okay for now." He glanced toward the bedroom where Jason was still sleeping. "Why don't you get yourself a cup of coffee and sit down with me? I have something I'd like to discuss with you."

Not knowing what else to do, she did as he asked.

Soon they were both seated on the sofa. Paige had her hands wrapped around her coffee mug.

"Remember our first dinner, at Pietro's?"

Paige drew her brows together, not because she didn't remember—how could she forget that magical evening?—but because she had no idea where the conversation would lead. Hesitantly, she nodded.

"Okay." A small smile played across Daniel's lips. "That's good. Then you might remember that one of the things I said I admired about you was your positive attitude. Your unwavering optimism."

She recalled that she'd laughed it off at the

time. Her brows knit more tightly together. "Uh-huh."

"I'm counting on that optimism right now. Jason's going to have the surgery, and he is going to be perfectly fine and free of cancer. Do you believe that like I do?"

She was squeezing her mug so tightly, her knuckles were turning white. "Daniel, where are you going with this?"

He waved her objection away with one hand. "Just humor me. Yes or no?"

"Of course. I *have* to believe that."

"Fine. Next, consider your parents. How long have they been married?"

"What?" She wasn't following him. What did her parents' marriage have to do with Jason's cancer?

"Just humor me," he repeated. "How long?"

"Nearly fifty years now."

"And they've had some notable hardships, but they're still together and still in love."

"Yes, but—"

"No buts. Not yet, at least. Being the eternal optimist and knowing, *knowing*—" he emphasized the word "—that Jason will be fine, and that everlasting love is possible…" Daniel paused, she presumed to give her a chance to object. She remained silent.

"Believing those two things, what possible reason could you have for not marrying me?"

Paige covered her forehead with the palm of one hand and exhaled. "You don't want to discuss this today of all days, do you?"

"Yes. Today *is* the day to discuss this."

Paige smacked her mug down on the table. "You can't be serious!"

Daniel reached for her hands and folded them in his own. He only held them more tightly when she tried to pull free. "Just hear me out. No," he said when she started to speak. "Listen for a minute longer, please. When you told me you wouldn't marry me, you gave me two reasons. First, the risk of Jason's surgery and how it might impact us. Second, you admitted that you couldn't help being concerned about what happened with your ex and how it could happen again. Correct?"

Paige looked at him suspiciously, but she nodded.

"You answered those two questions yourself a moment ago," he continued. "Jason *will* be fine and there *is such a thing as* everlasting love." This time he placed a finger over her lips when she was about to speak. "So what's left? What other reason do you have for not marrying me?"

Paige shot a nervous glance over her shoulder at Jason's bedroom. "Do we really have to go into this now?"

"Don't answer a question with a question. You answer mine first, and I'll answer yours."

"Daniel…"

"Okay, I'll finish, then. I've thought about this long and hard since you gave me back the ring. What I said then still holds. I love you and I love Jason. I want to be there for both of you, and I want to be there as your husband." He paused. "I want to be there as Jason's father."

"But—"

"No buts. You refuted your own two objections. Is there anything else?"

Paige felt her eyes glistening with unshed tears. She chewed on her lower lip as she struggled with what to say.

Daniel reached into his pocket and pulled out the lovely velvet box. Flipping open the lid, he removed the ring and held it in his right hand. He took Paige's left hand in his. "Paige, will you marry me?"

"Can't we talk about this after Jason's surgery?"

"No, because I want to marry you today."

"What?" The word exploded from her lips, and she quickly looked back at Jason's door. "Are you *crazy*? We have to leave for

the Karlsen Center in—" She glanced at the clock on the wall unit. "Just over two hours."

"I know."

Her confusion was back. "I don't understand. How...?"

Daniel grinned. "The paperwork we completed for the marriage license is still valid, and I brought a justice of the peace with me. That's one of the advantages of being a lawyer. I have friends in high places. So, we have a small civil ceremony right now. You, Jason and me, with a couple of your neighbors as witnesses. Because of all the strings one of my partners and I pulled, the adoption can be made official as soon as we're married."

"But—"

"After Jason's back home and recovered, we'll have the ceremony, as we'd planned, with our family and friends. What do you say?"

Paige started hiccupping and tears flowed down her cheeks as she threw herself into Daniel's arms.

"Can I safely assume that's a yes?"

Her head was burrowed against his neck, but she nodded and managed a muffled, "Yes."

PAIGE AND DANIEL were married by the justice of the peace in her apartment. Mr. and Mrs. Bennett were witnesses, and Chelsea and

Mr. Weatherly served as maid of honor and groomsman. Mr. Weatherly brought Laura, too. They arranged for Paige's parents to be part of the proceedings via speakerphone.

Jason was elated by this turn of events. He did double duty, giving his mother away and acting as Daniel's best man.

Mr. Weatherly supplied a bouquet that Laura happened to catch when Paige tossed it. Thanks to Chelsea's quick thinking, they even had a first dance, to Tracy Byrd's "The Keeper of the Stars."

Come what may, Jason now had a dad. And Paige had a husband, a partner and an unquestionable source of strength and comfort. Jason was so excited, so happy, he didn't have a chance to worry about his upcoming ordeal later that day.

Daniel had arranged for a minivan to transport them to East Baltimore. They arrived well in advance of the appointed time and walked into the hospital holding hands, Jason between his parents. Jason was beaming. Looking at him, no one would have guessed he was on his way to have major surgery.

They went through the patient registration procedure and were escorted to Jason's room. Daniel had booked a semiprivate room. He and Paige had discussed it, and although they planned to be there the entire time Jason was in the hospital, they felt it might be better for him to have company near his own age, as well.

Shane, his roommate, was nine years old and in for a bone marrow transplant for myeloma. The boy was outgoing and upbeat despite his illness, and he and Jason bonded immediately.

It was almost time for Jason to be taken to pre-op when the hospital room door creaked open.

A man of average height and build, with a thick crop of longish blond hair, stood in the doorway. Daniel and Jason looked at the man with no recognition, but Paige felt herself grow faint. She fumbled around in an effort to grasp Daniel's hand.

"May I come in?" the man asked, directing the question to Paige.

Paige glanced at her son. Satisfied that there was no obvious reaction, she got up and came forward. "Let's step outside," she suggested. Her voice quavered, but her delivery was resolute. Hearing it, Daniel followed his wife.

In the corridor, Paige closed the door behind them and spun around to face the visitor. "You're not going to stop the surgery, Mark.

You don't want to know what I'm capable of if you so much as try."

The exchange obviously clarified for Daniel who the man was, and he stepped up behind Paige and rested his hands on her shoulders. "I second that."

"Who are you?" Mark shot back.

Daniel straightened even further, and it gave Paige some small satisfaction that he now had a good four inches on Mark Summerville. "I'm Paige's husband."

He paused to let the words sink in. Paige watched as Mark's mouth opened and closed without any words coming out.

"I'm also Jason's father. I've legally adopted him."

Paige silently thanked the powers that be that Daniel had been able to call in all sorts of favors to push the adoption through so quickly.

Finally, his tone menacing, Daniel added, "I am also her lawyer."

Mark's mouth worked, but he was evidently at a loss for words. He turned his attention to Paige. He held out a hand, almost as if he was reaching for hers.

"Paige, I'm not here to cause trouble or to try to stop the surgery." He shifted his gaze briefly to Daniel. "You won that battle."

His voice dropped to a whisper. "I'm here to see my little boy."

Paige searched her ex-husband's face, looking for any indication that might belie his words. Mark seemed humbled, genuine and... distressed. She saw a maturity in him that had been lacking when they were married, a seriousness that had never existed before. And, yes, even a sincerity that he would've been incapable of when they were together.

Paige placed her hand on Daniel's, which still rested on her shoulder, and glanced back at him. "Would you give us a moment, please?"

"Sure." He cast a warning glance at Mark and slipped back into the hospital room.

"What's this all about, Mark?"

Mark rubbed his forehead. "You have every right to turn me away, Paige. I know that." He seemed to reach for her again, but lowered his hand. "I've been doing a lot of thinking since you called me. I've also talked it over with Becky, my wife. I wasn't fair to you, or to Jason. Not all those years ago, and not when you called me." He rubbed his temple again.

"I never should've tried to stop the surgery. *Sorry* isn't enough. Not for that, and not for what I did before. Becky wasn't happy when you called at first. We've had our challenges, money being one of them. But she came around, and she helped me see that you've only ever wanted what's best for Jason. Deep down, I knew that, too. I was just messed up— still am in some ways—but I've been getting help. Becky gave me an ultimatum a couple of years ago, and she was right. If I'd done that when you and I were together… Well, that's water under the bridge.

"But the more I thought about it, the more I realized I want Jason in my life—if he can forgive me. I want him to know me, and I want him to know his half sisters."

Paige was about to respond, but Mark interjected. "We can talk about it later. At the moment I just want to see my little boy, okay?"

Paige stared at Mark for long moments. Finally, she nodded. "Okay." With her hand already on the door handle, she paused and turned. "Mark, I'm trusting you, but if you do anything—I mean *anything*—to hurt Jason or make this harder for him than it already is, I promise you will be sorrier than you can imagine."

His Adam's apple bobbed once, then again. He nodded in acknowledgment.

Jason was speaking animatedly with Shane,

while Daniel was standing back in a corner, when they reentered the room.

Jason's eyes were wary and focused on the man to his mother's left. He took a good look, and a deep line appeared between his brows. His eyes narrowed in speculation. "Do I know you?"

Mark stepped forward and slid into the chair next to the bed. "I hope you will, Jason. I really hope you will."

Jason seemed confused and shifted his gaze from the man to his mother and back again. "Who are you?"

"I'm your father, Jason." Glancing at Daniel, he amended, "Your birth father. I'm Mark Summerville."

Satisfied that Mark meant no harm to Jason, and wanting to be respectful to allow him some time alone with his son, Paige and Daniel took Shane to the playroom, knowing his parent's wouldn't mind. By the time they returned, Mark and Jason both had tear tracks on their faces, but they were laughing and holding hands.

KISSING HER SON good-bye before the surgery was the hardest thing Paige had ever done.

All three of them remained in the surgical waiting room. Daniel and Paige sat huddled together, almost always touching. Mark alternatively sat or paced. Very few words were exchanged among the three of them.

Try as she might, Paige couldn't find any resentment toward her ex-husband for the years he'd spent away from his son. All that mattered to her was the delight on Jason's face when he'd chatted with his father. Whatever might have happened before, his father had come to see Jason at this crucial time. She believed Mark was truly remorseful and committed to rebuilding his relationship with his son. She was glad of it. Jason had said—just before he was taken to be prepped for surgery—that he couldn't believe his good fortune at having two dads, after having spent most of his life without one. He'd gone on to say that with his newfound good luck, he knew the surgery would go well.

The wait was excruciating. Nearly four hours later, the surgeon finally walked into the room, wiping perspiration from his forehead. Paige rose immediately, with Daniel by her side. Mark, too, hurried over to the man in scrubs.

Noting the surgeon's drawn features, fatigue clearly evident on his face, Paige was filled with terror. Then she saw the corners of his mouth turn upward. She clutched Daniel's hand more firmly and stepped forward, still afraid to ask.

"We removed the tumor, Mrs. Kinsley. There's no evidence the cancer has metastasized, and there were no complications."

Paige sagged against Daniel and started to weep. Daniel held her tightly as the doctor continued. "While there's always risk of infection, we'll be watching for it. Jason should make a full recovery."

PAIGE, DANIEL AND JASON were holding hands again the day they left the hospital. It was a clear evening with bright pinpricks of stars overhead. Paige was stunned by the changes in her life in a few short months. A husband she loved and cherished. A future full of hope and promise. And—most important—her little boy would be looking forward to many more Christmases.

The surgeon had explained that if Jason's tests were clear over the next six months, he would be deemed cancer-free. Yes, there'd be retests, but that six-month period would be crucial. By Christmas, they could have the most precious gift of all: Jason's clean bill of health.

With Jason's hand warm in hers, Paige gazed up at the night sky and silently said thanks for all the incredible blessings in her life.

EPILOGUE

"OUCH!" PAIGE EXCLAIMED. She yanked her hand back from the pot on the stove and stuck her burned thumb in her mouth

Daniel put aside the Christmas cake he'd just set on a plate and was immediately behind her, reaching around. "Are you okay? Did you hurt yourself?"

"I did," she mumbled, her thumb still in her mouth. "But I'm okay."

He turned her to face him, his hands resting on her waist. "Let me have a look anyway." He pulled her thumb out of her mouth, examined it and placed a kiss on the tip. "I think you'll live, but do that to the rest of your fingers and you could have a promising career in crime." When she stared at him blankly, he elaborated. "No fingerprints! You used to find me funnier before the hormones got the better of you."

She put her hands on his shoulders, rose up on her toes and kissed him. "I still find you sweet and incredibly sexy. Doesn't that count for something?"

"Well..." Daniel was just drawing her toward him when the kitchen's door flew open, and eight-year-old Jason came tearing in with a gangling black puppy on his heels. Jason screeched to a halt, but the puppy wasn't so quick and skidded into the back of Jason's legs.

Jason pretended to cover his eyes with his hands. "Yeesh! You guys at it again?" The look on his face told a different story. He was obviously delighted to see his parents so happy and close.

"Aaanywaaay." Jason stretched out the syllables. "Everyone wants to know when dinner will be ready."

Paige slipped out of Daniel's embrace and stroked Jason's back. "You can tell them it'll be soon. Why don't the two of you go out there and entertain everyone while I finish up in here?"

Daniel rested a hand on Jason's shoulder. "We've been given our marching orders. Let's get to it." Jason scooped up the puppy and trailed Daniel out of the kitchen.

Paige watched her son and her husband walk out together, and wiped her eyes with one hand while sliding the other across her stomach. The hormones really *were* affecting her.

Fifteen minutes later, she pushed the door ajar, poked her head out and called for Daniel. Everything was prepared and laid out on serving platters. Paige clasped her hands together. "What do you think?"

He swept a loose strand of hair away from her face and trailed his lips over the spot where his finger had been. "It's perfect. Just like you."

She drew in a deep breath. "All right. Let's get this show on the road, then."

"Paige, there's no need to be nervous."

"Are you kidding? Our first Christmas together with your family and mine, *and* with our news?"

"It's all good." He lifted the turkey platter. "As I said, nothing to be nervous about." He balanced the bowl of mashed sweet potatoes on the same arm and turned to Paige. "Ready."

AFTER THE TURKEY and accompaniments had been cleared, dessert and coffee consumed, Daniel and Paige excused themselves. They returned with Daniel carrying an ice bucket holding a bottle of Dom Pérignon and Paige a tray with twelve champagne flutes. A hush fell over the room.

"What's all this?" It was Paige's father asking. "Looks like a celebration."

Paige placed the tray on the table and gave her father a hug and a kiss. "It is, Dad. One we wanted to share with all of you."

As Daniel popped the cork, there were cheers and excited murmurs. Laughter followed when the puppy, startled by the noise, let out a volley of high-pitched barks. "Shh. Quiet, Scout," Jason struggled to get him settled and finally lifted him onto his lap, to be rewarded with lavish doggie kisses.

Flutes were filled and passed around. Two flutes were reserved for apple juice and placed at the head of the table, where Paige now stood.

Daniel moved beside her and slid his arm around her waist. "Jason, would you come join us, please? Why don't you let Chelsea hold Scout for now?"

Jason obliged and went to stand with his parents.

"It was a year ago tomorrow that I met this remarkable woman," Daniel began and turned to Paige, giving her a wide smile. "It all started that Christmas Day, when I had the pleasure of delivering a Christmas gift to Jason." He smiled down at the boy, who was grinning up at him in return.

"And that act gave me the most unexpected

and wonderful Christmas gifts imaginable—
my wife and my son."

"Hear, hear!" Mr. Weatherly, having had
a touch more to drink that evening than was
customary for him—after all, he and Laura
had their own recent engagement to celebrate—raised his glass in a toast.

"Okay, let's toast to that, but please save
some champagne." Daniel handed one of the
flutes filled with apple juice to Jason, and
Paige reached for the other.

"But that gift, the gift I received last Christmas, as unbelievable and miraculous as it was,
is actually surpassed this year," Daniel continued. "Although tomorrow's the day we'll be
opening most of our gifts, there are a couple
we'd like to share with you tonight. Paige..."

Paige briefly turned into her husband's arm
for a quick hug. She then faced their guests—
her mom and dad, Daniel's parents, Mr. and
Mrs. Bennett, Chelsea, Mr. Weatherly and
Laura. "You are such wonderful family and
friends and have been so unfailingly supportive as we faced our challenges. Each one of
you is very special to us, and you are unconditionally in our hearts. It's for this reason that
we'd like to share these gifts.

"First, you all know that Jason had his final
MRI last week—six months after his sur-

gery. I think you also know how important this test was. If there was no recurrence, then the chances are very good that he's clear of cancer." She squeezed her eyes shut, but then opened them and smiled through her tears. Daniel snuggled her closer against his side, and Jason reached up to take her other hand. "So…the test…it came back clear!"

"That is the most precious Christmas gift of all!" Daniel added. There were loud cheers, plenty of hugs, gasps of joy and warm, heartfelt exclamations. A toast was called and they again sipped their champagne.

"Save some of your champagne, please!" Daniel advised again. He waited until their guests were quiet once more. "Now, if we thought our life couldn't be more perfect, we have one more gift to share with you this evening." With an arm around Paige and the other around Jason, he looked at their family and friends. He glanced at Paige, winked at Jason, and the three of them in unison exclaimed, "We're having a baby!"

Paige stood in the circle of their arms. Everything had seemed so bleak and hopeless just a year ago, and here she was today, with her son and her husband in their new home. Jason's birth father had made good on his promise to be a part of his son's life. He and his family had stopped by for a visit a few days earlier. Jason was finally able to give his father the shoe box full of Christmas gifts he'd made for him. He'd replaced last year's tiger painting with a new one—and he had created a very special gift for Mark's entire family. There'd been tears all around.

Now, here were all the people most important to Paige—her parents, Daniel's parents, her former neighbors and, of course, Laura. Of all their blessings that Christmas, the most precious were a sibling on the way for Jason and Jason himself being healthy and whole.

With the sound of whoops and hollers and more cheers, Paige accepted Daniel's kiss and thought about the miracle of Christmas, reflecting that the most wonderful gifts of all were the ones that couldn't be wrapped, but resided in the heart.

* * * * *

LARGER-PRINT BOOKS!
GET 2 FREE LARGER-PRINT NOVELS PLUS
2 FREE GIFTS!

HARLEQUIN®

Romance

From the Heart, For the Heart

LARGER-PRINT BOOKS!
GET 2 FREE LARGER-PRINT NOVELS PLUS
2 FREE GIFTS!

◊ HARLEQUIN®

super romance®

More Story...More Romance

LARGER-PRINT BOOKS!

GET 2 FREE
LARGER-PRINT NOVELS
PLUS 2 FREE
MYSTERY GIFTS

Love Inspired

Larger-print novels are now available...

LILPDIR13R

ReaderService.com

Manage your account online!

- Review your order history
- Manage your payments
- Update your address

*We've designed
the Harlequin® Reader Service
website just for you.*

Enjoy all the features!

- Reader excerpts from any series
- Respond to mailings and
  special monthly offers
- Discover new series available to you
- Browse the Bonus Bucks catalog
- Share your feedback

Visit us at:

ReaderService.com